L. A.
Burning

Also available by D. C. Taylor

Michael Cassidy Series
(Writing as David C. Taylor)
Night Watch
Night Work
Night Life

L. A.
Burning

A Novel

~

D. C. TAYLOR

CROOKED
LANE

NEW YORK

Published in the United States by Crooked Lane Books, an imprint of The Quick Brown Fox & Company LLC.

Crooked Lane Books and its logo are trademarks of The Quick Brown Fox & Company LLC.

Library of Congress Catalog-in-Publication data available upon request.

ISBN (hardcover): 978-1-64385-778-7
ISBN (ebook): 978-1-64385-779-4

Cover design by Patrick Sullivan

Printed in the United States.

www.crookedlanebooks.com

Crooked Lane Books
34 West 27th St., 10th Floor
New York, NY 10001

First Edition: February 2022

10 9 8 7 6 5 4 3 2 1

For Priscilla, Susannah, Jennifer,
Jacob, and Felix, with love.
And in memory of my friend Carlos Davis.

Perhaps all the dragons in our lives are princesses who are only waiting to see us act, just once, with beauty and courage.

—*Rainer Maria Rilke*

Chapter One

✍

No one oversleeps the day they come to release you from prison.

I was awake at four thirty.

Five years in cement teaches you how to wait. Time in prison is a routine of gray monotony sometimes made bright by anger, violence, or fear. I watched the light change in the cell as the sun rose and tried to keep my mind blank. Don't think of what might go wrong, what order might be changed, what new charges they might decide to bring.

At seven the corrections officer we called Pinky opened my cell door.

"What the hell, Bonner? You ain't even packed. Can't stand to leave us, huh?"

"I'm packed." I stood up. Nothing in the cell was coming with me. I was done with it. This part of my life was over. All I was taking with me was what I had learned.

Pinky was a tall man with a soft body, thinning pale hair, and red-rimmed eyes. "Let's go, then." As usual, he stood in the doorway so I would have to squeeze by him, and as I did, he pushed his groin against me and ran his hand over my ass. "Going to miss that."

I said nothing.

"Hands back."

I put my hands behind me, and he put the cuffs on. He took a moment to grope my breast while he grinned at me with yellow teeth. I stood like stone and told myself it was the last time, the last time, the last time.

"Let's go. Let's go." Our footsteps echoed on the concrete floor as we walked the cellblock tier. Some of the other women came to their cell doors as we passed. Some called my name and said good-bye. Some called me a lucky bitch. Some just watched me go, headed out to the world they couldn't have.

Pinky took the cuffs off in Receiving & Release and nodded toward a cardboard box on a metal table against a dull-green wall. It had my name on it, Cody Bonner, along with DRESS OUT CLOTHING in big black letters in handwriting I didn't recognize, not my mother's anyway, an assistant's, someone at the studio. Someone had slit the tape on the box to search the contents. "Get to it," Pinky said.

A woman CO was supposed be on duty for dress-out and release, but she wasn't there. Prison worked on the barter system both for inmates and for guards. Whoever was supposed to be here wanted something Pinky could give, and Pinky was willing to trade it for her not showing up.

I could feel his eyes as I carried the box to the dressing cubicle and pulled the curtain shut. The box held a pair of blue jeans, a plain white shirt, a belt, a pair of socks, a pair of running shoes, a fleece jacket, just what I had asked my mother to send. And black lacy underwear. That wasn't on the list, but my mother believed sexy underwear was a basic foundation for any woman's day.

I laid the clothes on a wooden bench and stripped off the blue polyester prison shirt and pants, the cotton underwear and socks. I reached for the new clothes. The curtain rattled back as Pinky pushed it aside with his baton. I didn't look at him as I stepped into the panties and picked up the bra and put it on.

"A waste of time," he said. "You're just going to have to take it off again."

I said nothing and reached for the blue jeans, but he pinned them to the bench with the tip of his baton. "Uh-uh."

I waited.

"We've been a long time coming to this," he said.

"You've been a long time, not me, not any of us."

"Well, we're here now."

"How do you think this is going to work, Pinky?"

"Don't you be calling me that. I could violate you back up to that cell. You ain't out of here yet, you stuck-up bitch."

"What would you tell them? That I was trying to escape the day they were letting me go?"

He stepped toward me and poked me in the stomach with the baton. When I didn't step back, he poked me again. I slapped the baton aside and went by him before he could react. I heard his startled, "Hey," as I went out the door from R & R. I was already halfway to where I wanted to go when I heard him come into the corridor behind me. "You hold up there, Bonner, goddamn it. Hold up."

I banged through the door of the corrections officers' break room. There were four COs drinking morning coffee, three men and Sara Brodsky, not a bad hack but a low-grade grafter, twenty dollars for a pack of cigarettes or tampons, that kind of thing. They all looked up, startled. The men fixed on my underwear. Brodsky watched my face. "There's supposed to be a woman CO on R & R," I said. "All I've got is Sergeant Loomis, and he wants to help me get dressed."

"Paula Sanchez has the duty today," Brodsky said. "I guess she called in sick."

"I see your name on the roster over there." Everyone looked at the erase board on the wall near the coffeemaker like they'd never noticed it before.

Pinky came in behind me.

"No one told me there was a release today," Brodsky said.

"I see my name. It says release at eight o'clock."

A hack we called Gomer said, "Hell, Brodsky, you don't want to do it, I'll take the duty."

She glanced at him for a moment and then looked past me to where Pinky was standing near the door. She shrugged and stood up. "Okay. Let's go."

"I got it, Brodsky," Pinky said.

"Yeah, yeah," she said, and pushed me toward the door.

Pinky poked me in the side when I went by him. "You'll be back."

"I won't."

"Yeah, you will. Stupid bitches like you always come back. And I'll be here." He hit me hard on the shoulder once to regain some sense of dominance. Nobody said anything. As I went out the door, one of the assholes wolf whistled.

* * *

They check you at two posts before they let you out the gate to make sure you're the one who's supposed to be going. Name: Cody Bonner. Age: twenty-six. Check the file photo against the person. Length of sentence: five years. Time served: five years, two days, eighteen hours. Do it all again at the next post. "Okay, you can go. Have a nice day."

* * *

When the prison van drove out through the gate and the walls were behind me, I began to breathe. An hour's drive to the city across a brown late-winter landscape. The driver checked me out in the mirror a few times, but he said nothing. He wore earbuds and bopped in his seat to the beat of whatever was feeding his head. The van dropped me at the Greyhound bus terminal in a downtown neighborhood of brick tenements, boarded-up storefronts, and uncollected trash. I had a state-issued ID, $200 in gate money, $85 in earnings from my work in the prison library, and a ticket to the county where I'd been arrested. I wasn't going back there. I was going home.

The next bus for LA left in an hour and a half and arrived the next morning, nineteen hours riding the dog. I turned in my local ticket, which brought the bankroll up to $320. I asked the woman at the ticket window where I could find a pay phone. She gave me a puzzled look and asked, "Don't you have a cell phone?"

"No."

"There used to be one downstairs near the ladies'." She pointed across the waiting room to stairs under a restrooms sign. "I think it's still there. Don't know if it works."

"Thanks. Can I buy some change?" I pushed three dollars across to her, took the change she gave me, and turned away from the window.

Someone was watching me. In prison you learn to feel when eyes are on you. You learn to be aware of who's in a room when you enter it, who's behind you, who might be dangerous.

There, the janitor over near the newsstand. He stopped sweeping to watch me cross. Okay. So what? You're out. You're free. No one knows you. No one holds a grudge for words passed in the yard. No one here wants anything from you. No one owes you, and you owe no one. A man checks out a young woman walking across a room. Normal. Get used to it.

I found an old-fashioned phone booth downstairs near the doors to the restrooms. The phone book had been ripped from its chain, and the bottom of the door glass had been kicked out by someone listening to someone tell him something he didn't want to hear, but the receiver hummed with a dial tone, and 411 gave me the numbers of three airlines. Flights to LA left almost every hour on the hour, and the cheapest one cost $365, $45 more than I had. I guessed I'd be taking the bus after all. Hey, it could be worse. I could be waiting to go to the mess hall to eat macaroni and cheese.

As I pushed open the door of the booth, the janitor came down the stairs and opened a metal door with a key chained to his belt. The room he opened held mops and buckets and other cleaning gear. There was an iron cot covered by a sleeping bag against the back wall. The janitor leaned his broom in with the others and came out. He left the door open. "How're you doing?"

"Fine." I started toward the stairs.

He was in his midthirties. He had a pointed, bony face just the wrong side of looking like a rat's. His hair was dirty blond, but his beard came in darker. His sleeves were rolled high to expose his tattoos and his weight lifter's biceps. His teeth were very white when he grinned. "Just out?" he asked.

Fuck. What was this about?

"I can tell. A lot of you come through here. This is where they drop you if you don't have someone picking you up. Wearing them—what do they call them?—dress-out clothes. The shoes are the thing. The shoes are new. No dirt on the soles yet or anything."

"Is that right?"

"So, you want to get high? A little celebration for getting out?"

"No thanks."

Another man came down the stairs and stopped near the janitor. They knew each other. The second man was older, bigger. His thinning black hair was gelled to his scalp. His jeans rode low enough for his belly to hang over his belt. He wore a faded Red Hot Chili Peppers T-shirt and cowboy boots and had the lumpy broken-nosed face of a man who'd been hit more than a few times.

"I've got weed. I've got blow. You name it." The janitor waved a hand at the room with the cot. "I know you've got that gate money."

"No thanks."

"Looks like she doesn't want to party, Frank," the second man said.

"Sure she does, Willie. She's just playing hard to get."

"Christ, look at her. No wonder Pinky's got a bone for her."

"Shut up, Willie."

So it wasn't just about the money. My heart surged. "You don't want to do this."

"Do what? What are we going to do?" Frank grinned. "We're just going to have some fun, the three of us. Everybody likes a little fun, don't they, Willie?"

"Shit yeah. Everybody likes a little fun."

There was nowhere to run. They were between the stairs and me. A look passed between them, and Frank, the janitor, nodded. He was the leader, but Willie worried me more. He outweighed me by a hundred pounds, and if he got his hands on me, his bulk would be too much to handle. They moved, and I took a step back. They were herding me toward the open door to the room with the cot. In the room they could crowd me back, trap me, and once they had me on the ground, I was done. I couldn't let them get me in the room.

I slid a couple of steps to the side. The men mirrored the move. The big one, Willie, made sure I had no angle to the stairs. Willie's smile had nothing to do with humor. "Jesus, I like it when they fight. Honey, I've got a bone for you you'll never forget."

"You want to go to prison for rape?"

"No one's going nowhere for nothing, honey, except you're going in that room for a good time."

The problem with stupid people is they have no thought for what their actions might bring down on them. The mantra *Live for the moment* can get you in a world of trouble. I was an expert on that.

"Let's do it," Frank said, "Before some asshole comes down to the can."

Now I would find out how much I had learned. Ginger had always warned me that practice, half-speed strikes, sparring, even the gladiator fights in the yard were one thing, but you never knew what you had until someone went after you for real.

They came at me, grinning, two big men on one woman. Nothing to worry about there. Willie in first to grab me and hold me. I made a move toward the stairs, and Willie took the feint. I came back the other way, and while he was wrong-footed, I hit him with a jab that broke his mouth. His hands went up to the pain. I stabbed a straight kick to his belly, and when he bent over, I kept turning and drove my elbow into the side of his jaw with all my weight behind it. He went down hard. Frank hesitated. I hit him with a kick to the chest. It drove him into the wall near the open door, and when he bounced off, I smashed his mouth with my elbow. The blow banged him back against the wall again. I stepped forward and kicked him in the balls, and he slid to the floor with a moan.

The whole thing had taken seconds. Willie was still down and not moving. I went through his pockets and found $140 in tens and twenties. I pulled Frank away from the wall and searched him. He had a plastic baggie of white powder in a buttoned breast pocket and $340 in his jeans back pocket. I took the money, left the dope on his chest, and went upstairs.

No one paid attention to me as I crossed through the crowded waiting room. My left hand was bleeding from Willie's teeth, and my elbow hurt. My heart still zoomed with the adrenaline rush. As I went out into the cold morning, I couldn't stop smiling. I found a cab at the curb and took it to the airport.

I fell asleep on the plane and woke when it dropped down over the San Gabriel Mountains toward the Los Angeles basin. I could see the small blue rectangles of swimming pools in the backyards in Anaheim and Lakewood as we swung out over the coast. A Santa Ana wind off the desert was blowing the air clear, and a brownish bank of smog lay a few miles offshore, waiting for the wind to change and blow it back. It was the wrong time of year for the Santa Ana. They usually blew in the fall, but things were changing, and maybe the Santa Ana had decided to be part of that.

The glass towers of downtown rose in the distance. New ones had sprouted in the years I'd been gone. The sprawl of the rest of the city spread from Pasadena to the sea, home to thirteen million people, dream chasers, working stiffs, lovers, haters, madmen, strivers, bums, poets, artists, saints, and monsters, every weird, wonderful, and awful animal in the human zoo. Los Angeles. I never could figure out whether I loved it or hated it.

Somewhere down there was my sister's murderer. Who was he? Where was he? Could I find him? What if I did? What would I do then?

Chapter Two

～

The taxi from the airport took me north on the 405 Freeway to the 10 and then out through the McClure Tunnel to the Pacific Coast Highway. I opened the window to catch the salt smell of the sea. There were few people on the wide beach. Waves ran up onto the sand and retreated with a hiss. Looking over my shoulder through the back window, I could see the Ferris wheel on the Santa Monica pier turning lazily against the blue sky.

This was a route from the map of my childhood and my life until I got busted. I'd been sure that prison had changed me profoundly, that it had scrubbed out the molecules of my past self, but the stir of memories mocked that certainty. I closed my eyes, but the past can't be shut out that easily.

There was a red light at Entrada. A young woman came out from the curb to panhandle the northbound lanes. She carried a sign, red marker letters printed on box cardboard: HOMELESS—NEED MONEY FOR FOOD AND SHELTER. She had made an effort to draw the letters evenly, but she had run out of space and the last ones dribbled away. I recognized myself in her tired shuffle along the line of cars. I understood the hopeful hesitation when she held up the sign to the driver, the disappointment, and then the shuffle to the next car. Jesus, that's close to the bone. Maybe I'm not ready for this.

It was hard to tell how old she was, late teens or early twenties. Life on the street ages you fast. She wore battered running shoes, jeans ripped at the knee and cut off raggedly above the shoes, a Modelo beer T-shirt, and a jeans jacket a couple of sizes too big. Her hair had been chopped short and dyed green in streaks. Most drivers looked straight ahead and refused to see her. A woman in a Mercedes cracked her window enough to slip a bill through the gap and then closed it quickly to avoid the contagion of poverty and bad luck. The young woman took the money, thanked the closed window, and moved on. I rolled down my window and waved her over. "How are you doing?" I held out four twenties from my dwindled stash.

Her eyes widened at the amount. "I'm okay." But clearly she wasn't. She was pale and underweight. Her hair under the bright dye was lifeless. Her eyes were dull.

"Get something to eat," I said.

"Sure." When she reached for the money, her sleeve pulled up enough to show track marks on her forearm.

The light changed. The young woman went back to the sidewalk. The traffic moved on. My cab turned right and climbed Chautauqua toward the top of the bluff.

"You should not give them money," the cab driver said. He had an accent I couldn't identify. He looked at me in the rearview mirror to emphasize his point.

"Why not?"

"They must work. This is not work to stand and ask for money. When I came to this country, I did not ask for money. I found a job. They must get a job."

Get a job. How many times had I been told that while I was standing on a street corner holding a cardboard sign?

Half a mile later the cab turned left and started out toward the edge of the palisade. "You can drop me here," I said.

"Is still more blocks."

"I want to walk."

When I got out of the car, the hot, dry wind lifted my hair and fluttered my jacket. It filled my nose with the smell of the distant desert and rattled the fronds of the palm trees that lined the street. I took off my jacket and carried it as I walked.

This was the neighborhood I grew up in. The street was lined with big houses shaded by mature trees. Many of the older houses were

Spanish-style white stucco with red-tiled roofs. A house where my friend Aurora had lived had been torn down and replaced by a huge cube of aluminum and glass that filled the lot. Shiny columns flanked the tall hammered-copper door. A man came out of the house and opened the door to a Porsche parked in the drive. Instead of getting in, he watched me suspiciously as I passed. People who lived around here jogged these blocks or walked their dogs. Housekeepers walked to Sunset to catch the bus. I didn't look like any of those. After a moment he dismissed me and got in the car. How dangerous could a lone young woman be?

I stopped when I could see my mother's house. Our house? The house I grew up in? Fuck it. Stop making things complicated. It was home. Sometimes I had run away from it, and sometimes I had run toward it, and I still didn't know exactly what drove me in either direction.

Mom said the house had been built by some producer from the silent-movie days. When he owned it, it was the only one on the street, and photographs of the time showed that its front lawn ran out to the very edge of the bluff. One of the later owners had sold off pieces of land, and while the house still sat on a double lot, now there were houses around it behind privacy walls. At some point the city put in a new street that ran through what had been the wide front lawn, and the view of the Pacific had been partially blocked by a house that an idiot had built on the strip at the bluff's edge. The house was condemned and abandoned the year I blew town when its swimming pool, undercut by erosion, broke off and tumbled a hundred feet down the cliff and blocked three lanes of the Pacific Coast Highway until work crews could clear the wreckage. The house remained empty at the edge of the drop, waiting, like the rest of California, for the day it would fall into the sea.

Our house was three stories high. It was made of wood with a low-pitched roof line and broad overhanging eaves. Banana plants and birds of paradise shaded the porch that ran along the front. My mother, Karen Bonner, had grown up there. Her father was a successful TV producer, and her mother was a famous costume designer. My sister Julie and I never knew them. They had been killed by a drunk driver in the wrong lane on the Pacific Coast Highway while they were driving home from a party after the Academy Awards. My grandmother had just won her third Oscar for costume design. The cops found the Oscar in the wreck and returned it to my mother, scraped and slightly bent. My mother kept it on the living room mantel next to her own. We moved into the house after the funeral, and Mom had lived there ever since.

We grew up in a special neighborhood of LA called The Movie Business, or The Industry, as if no one else in the city really made anything. There was a wider world out there, full of people doing all the things people do, but we didn't know them unless something sucked them into the orbit of the Industry and they landed on our planet for a while. It was a strange planet built on the certainty that any dream could come true. You could be living in your car one day and six months later put down money on a $5 million house. You could go from waiting on tables to starring in a movie that grossed $400 million and put you on the cover of *People*. You could write a screenplay between dog-walking assignments and sell it for more money than your father made in a lifetime. We lived in a place where fantasy and reality ran hand in hand and often blurred one into the other, a place where people living in a desert imported snow for a child's birthday party, where movie stars insisted *I do my own stunts*, where a girl who "had everything" could wake up one morning and decide that robbing a bank was a good idea.

A polished limousine was parked in the side driveway. The uniformed driver was concentrating on his phone's screen, but my movement past the car caught his eye. He started to put the phone down, then realized I wasn't who he was waiting for.

The house key was still hidden under a planter on the front porch. When I stepped into the front hall, my mother was coming down the stairs. I was struck, as I had been so many times, by what a beautiful woman she was. She was dressed in tailored oatmeal-colored linen pants, a green silk shirt, and half boots with spike heels. Her red-blonde hair was pulled back and tied with a ribbon that matched the shirt. Age had not touched her face in the years I'd been gone. Or maybe she'd had work done. It was hard to tell in that light. When she saw me, she stopped and put her hand to her throat in a familiar gesture of surprise and said, "Julie?" in a strangled voice.

"No, Mom. Cody."

"Cody? Cody." She came down the stairs in a rush and threw her arms around me. "You're here. You're here. Let me look at you." She pushed me back to arm's length. "Look at you. You look wonderful. Oh my god, I'm so happy you're here." She pulled me back for another hug, and when she'd had enough, she stepped away and dabbed at her eyes. "I'm going to cry. Oh, my poor baby. Are you all right? Look at you. Look at you. Oh, I'm not ready. I shouldn't be crying." She dabbed her eyes again. "I didn't expect you today. You said tomorrow."

"I had enough money to take the plane. I thought I'd surprise you." Oh god, she doesn't like surprises. I should have remembered that. Home for a minute and already off-balance.

"I'm so glad." A hesitation. "Oh, darling, I wish you'd phoned. I have a call at Twentieth in forty minutes. I'm going to be late. The traffic is awful these days. I asked them to schedule around me tomorrow, because that's when I thought you were arriving, but it's too late now, and we'll be shooting late." Twentieth was now Twenty-First Century Fox, but my mother stuck with the old ways.

"That's okay. Is it a good part?" It was always safe ground to talk about the movie she was doing.

"Yes, and a good director. Actually, I think you know him. Brandon Tower? He's very hot now. His last film did two hundred fifty million domestic." Mom, Karen Bonner to the world, was a four-time Academy Award nominee, a winner ten years ago, a star.

"Yeah, Brandon. He was a couple of classes above us at school. He lived over on El Medio. Julie went out with him for like fifteen minutes. Voted the most likely to succeed."

"He has. Two hundred fifty million domestic is definitely a success." She looked at her watch.

"You better go, Mom. I'll be fine."

"Are you sure?"

She wanted to go. She was most alive on a movie set. Sometimes I thought she just marked time until someone called *Action*.

"I'm sure."

"We'll have tomorrow. I'm completely free. We'll do something fun."

"Great."

She checked herself in the mirror by the door. "Oh god, my eyes are red. Well, no close-ups scheduled today." She turned at the door and offered me a smile. "I'm so glad you're here." And then she was gone. My mother had always been good at entrances and exits.

Was she glad I was home? I didn't know. She was a really good actress, and I could never tell. Julie had had an easy way with her, but I'd banged up against her from the earliest I could remember. Julie figured it out early and tried to get me to see. "Don't fight her all the time," she said when we were about fourteen. "Let her have her way. She's used to it." I couldn't do it. I don't know why. Maybe I just wanted her to see *me*.

Would she remember that when she stopped on the stairs and looked down, she thought her dead twin daughter was waiting for her, not her live one?

* * *

I went upstairs and down the hall to my room. When was the last time I'd been in it? After the first rehab? After the second bank robbery? That time in my life tended to blur.

My mother redecorated the house from top to bottom every few years, an urge I did not understand. But I understood what she had done in my room. Every trace of me was gone—my pictures, the old furniture, books, gone. It was now a guest room in a house that already had three guest rooms. I had been erased. Wait, not quite. When I lay in bed at night as a child, I looked up at a sprinkle of glowing stars stuck to the ceiling. Whoever had painted the room had painted over them, but they were still there.

I went downstairs and found a screwdriver in a drawer in the kitchen and brought it back up to the room. The closet was empty except for two terry cloth robes my mother always provided for guests. I pushed them aside and knelt to undo the four screws that held down a board in the back corner of the closet floor. I pried the board up with the screwdriver. I reached into the gap and felt around. For a moment I thought it was gone, and then my fingers scraped against cloth, and I stretched, got a grip, and pulled out the vinyl bag I had hidden there in another life. I carried it to the bed, unzipped it, and dumped the money out on the spread.

Four thousand dollars in wrapped stacks with the bank's name still on the bands.

Chapter Three

I left the money and went down the hall to Julie's room. It was as she had left it when she went off to Stanford. There were framed photographs on the top of the shelves that ran under the row of windows that looked out on the swimming pool and tennis court. Most of the photos were of Julie and me. We were identical twins, indistinguishable to almost everybody, sometimes even to our parents. There were times when there were no boundaries between us, when we had the same thoughts simultaneously, shared moods without speaking them, woke in the morning to find we had dreamed the same dream. When I was eleven, I broke my right ankle jumping from a friend's tree house on a dare. At the same moment, Julie, walking through the living room here, collapsed on the rug with a sharp pain in her right ankle.

We were mirror twins. We had identical birthmarks on our arms. Mine was on the left, but Julie's was on the right. I had a mole on my left shoulder. She had one on her right. She was calm, accommodating, generous, patient, an instinctive scholar. I was not.

She was my best friend. We could tell each other anything and everything. I loved her, and she loved me through every storm I brewed, every agony I visited on her. She was my better half. The day of her death, I collapsed in the prison yard knowing that something awful had happened to Julie. Her body wasn't found for three days, but I knew she was gone, knew a part of me had been cut away as surely as I'd have felt the amputation of my leg. When they told me she had been murdered, they had to sedate me in the infirmary.

Julie had left the law firm where she worked at the normal time. Her naked body was found on the beach in Malibu three days later. The police were following leads. An arrest was imminent. That was all they could tell me.

The arrest never happened.

*   *   *

Mom had us when she was seventeen, a child having children. She and our father, Julian Bonner, got married six months before our birth. I was out first by three minutes, showing a lack of patience even then. Dad was a pilot, a sometime stuntman, a sometime actor. I remember him as a smiling man, full of energy. He was always willing to carry us on his shoulders, to play with us in the backyard pool, to help build forts and hideaways. He made my mother laugh. That's what I remember from that time, the sound of laughter in the house. Then it stopped. I still don't really know what broke up their marriage. "He was a restless man" was my mother's explanation, pretty much all she ever gave us, except for "We'll talk about it when you're older and can understand." But we never did.

He married a woman from Thailand whom my mother always referred to as "the Princess," said with just enough edge to make the title a lie. They moved to Bangkok.

The last time we saw him was on our tenth birthday. He was in town to raise money for a hotel on a beach somewhere, the most beautiful beach in the world, he told us, a sure moneymaker. He took us to Disneyland, and at the end of the day, he hugged us and said, "When the hotel's up and running, you can come. I'll teach you how to open a coconut with a machete." Then we heard he'd moved to Singapore. Then we heard nothing.

Our first stepfather, Jerry, was an actor on a TV show about a family with eight kids. It was called *Family Feeling*. Julie and I were on it. We played the youngest sister, Maisie. Both of us. So for a while we truly were one person, just a made-up one. We were eight when we started, so by law each of us could work only four hours a day. TV shows shoot at least eight hours in a day. By casting twins they got an eight-hour shooting day out of us for the character of Maisie. I hated it. Julie loved it. After a couple of years, I did what I always did when I didn't want to do something anymore. I fucked it up, and they fired me. And they fired Julie, because half a twin set didn't work. She never said anything, but I think that was the first time I did something she really didn't like.

Jerry didn't like kids, though he pretended to for a while. He was tall, good looking, athletic, and he wanted to be a movie star, not a TV star. Mom got him parts in movies she was doing, but they never led anywhere. He got tired of being Mr. Karen Bonner. He took a TV show about a detective who lived on a boat in Key West. He went to Florida to shoot the pilot. He never came back. It was an LA story familiar to many of the kids in our school.

Our second stepfather said he was an artist. He took over half the pool house in the backyard for his studio. He painted big paintings full of shards of bright colors that were hard to look at. Mom paid for shows at a gallery in Bergamot Station in Santa Monica. He didn't sell much, except to a few people in the movie business who were trying to suck up to Karen Bonner.

The artist liked kids a little too much. He walked in a few times on Julie and me when we were changing into our bathing suits, and then we discovered he had drilled a hole between his "studio" and the changing room. He was a creep, but we didn't know how to tell Mom. It was too weird for thirteen-year-olds to think their stepfather was trying to get a look at their asses. The problem took care of itself when Mom caught him screwing the housekeeper. Another LA story rerun again and again.

That was the end of husbands. There were men, of course. She couldn't stand being alone. Some of them ignored us. Some of them checked us out when Mom wasn't looking. "As if," we said to each other. "I mean, what is he, thirty-five years old?" They were all attached to the Industry in one way or another, and when we were in our teens, we realized that none of them was as successful as our mother. They were there hoping some of the magic would rub off.

So Dad was gone, and Mom was busy. We were brought up mostly by au pairs, a fancy name for expensive babysitters. Some of them were cool. Some of them liked us and we liked them. Some of them just wanted to work for a movie star. Some of them were dictators who ruled by punishment; some were happy to smoke dope out by the pool and were almost competent enough to keep us from drowning. None of them lasted very long.

*　*　*

In the afternoon, I went down to the garage and found two cars, my mother's Mercedes convertible and an older BMW. It was Julie's car. I found the keys under the mat. The car started after a few minutes of cranking.

I drove down to Santa Monica to the computer store I remembered on Wilshire, but it was gone. I asked around, and a man in a shoe store directed me to the mall at the end of the Third Street Promenade. The Promenade was a three-block pedestrian street lined with shops and restaurants. It was where I first got drunk. Mom was on location shooting some spy thing with George Clooney. Julie was at a friend's house studying. My friend Lori and I bought a pint of rum off a homeless guy and drank it in a restroom stall at Johnny Rockets. When Lori's father picked us up, he knew something was wrong, and when we threw up booze and hamburgers in the car, he could smell the culprit. He took us to the hospital, where they pumped out what was left in our stomachs.

There it is. The shrinks will tell you, as they have told me, that I am the fucked up result of a broken home, an often-absent, self-involved mother, and an early taste for inappropriate stimulants. So what about Julie? The same influences but a very different result. She was the good one, and I was the bad one. Mirror twins. I always wondered if it would have been different if we'd been more alike inside instead of outside, if I'd had more of what made her good. Then she would have had some of my crap, and why would I wish that on her?

I found the computer store on the second floor of the mall building at the end of the Promenade. I automatically stopped in front of its door. A man looked at me strangely and brushed by me to enter. I caught myself and followed him. Doors are locked in prison. You don't open them. You wait for someone else to do it. There was a lot of learned behavior I would have to discard.

I bought a laptop computer and a smartphone for cash. "Do you want the new Apple iPhone?" the sales guy asked.

"I don't know. I haven't had one for almost six years."

"Where've you been, the moon?"

"Kind of."

"I'd get the iPhone. You can sync it to the computer, and it's got the app so they can't track you."

"Who can't?"

"I don't know. Them, they, whoever."

"I'll take it." In prison they always know where you are. I was finished with that.

For another hundred the sales guy took a break and brought me up to speed on how both devices worked. They don't let you play with the internet in the joint. There's too much information that can be used for mischief by people with time on their hands.

I went to the food court and spent a long time trying to figure out what I wanted to eat. Choice, another thing I'd have to get used to. I ate a turkey, avocado, tomato, and lettuce roll-up and drank a fruit smoothie and walked to the Santa Monica library.

*   *   *

A man stood behind the open vertical wing door of a black Lamborghini parked in front of a fire hydrant on Fourth Street near Santa Monica Boulevard. His silk shirt was tailored to his muscular build. He was bald as an egg. There was a spider-shaped reddish birthmark high on his forehead. He tossed his attaché case onto the passenger seat. As he ducked into the car, a young woman in blue jeans and a white shirt angled past the front of the car to cross the street. She carried a laptop case slung from her shoulder. When she turned to check for oncoming traffic, he saw her clearly. Instinctively he ducked his head to hide his face.

She caught a break in traffic, crossed the street quickly, and went into the library.

He punched a number on his phone. It was answered on the second ring. "I'm in a meeting," the man at the other end said.

"I thought I just saw a ghost."

"Who?"

"Julie Bonner. I just saw her."

Silence on the other end, then, "Hold."

The man on the other end went away for a minute and then came back. "The twin. Cody Bonner. She was released from prison yesterday."

"Do you think it's going to be a problem?"

"I don't see how."

"Okay." They broke the connection. The man looked toward the library. Was there anything to do? If there was, he couldn't think of it. He got into the car, fired it up, and drove away.

*　　*　　*

I set up in a quiet part of the library where the only sounds were the clicking of other keyboards, the scrape of a chair, the occasional cough, and the muted hum of street traffic. Google took me quickly to where I did not want to go.

The first headline was from the Local section of the *L.A. Times*: **Body Found on Malibu Beach**. *Maddie Allen decided it was a perfect morning for an early jog before she went into Venice to meet clients. It wasn't. Ms. Allen, a yoga instructor with GloYoga in Venice, found the dead body of a young woman on the beach at the Malibu Colony.*

The story went on to say that the woman was unidentified. She appeared to be in her mid to late twenties. There were signs of violence. Ms. Allen said she had never seen anything like that before and would never forget it.

The next day Julie was identified as the daughter of the movie star Karen Bonner, and suddenly everyone cared. The story became national news on the networks and the internet. Maddie Allen had taken photos with her phone to make sure she could remind herself about what she would never forget. The photos went viral. They showed Julie sprawled slack and naked at the edge of the water. Her face was turned away from the camera. One arm was tucked under her head. The other was flung to the side. There was something tangled in her hair, maybe seaweed. Her right leg was bent. It looked like a piece of rope was tied around the ankle. Maddie Allen did interviews. Maddie Allen went on talk shows. Maddie Allen had her moment in the light. Another LA story.

Later stories ran photos that Mom must have given out. They showed Julie bright and beautiful and very alive. They traced her through

Stanford and Boalt law school. After graduation she went to work for a Century City law firm, Mitchell, Collier, & Brown. The firm put out statements of loss and sorrow.

The police said they were following leads. The stories petered out. Other tragedies commanded attention.

I wrote down all the names in the news reports I thought might be useful—Maddie Allen who'd found Julie, the partners at the law firm, a man named Tony Riordan who had dated her, a neighbor who didn't want her name used, friends from school. It was a start. I wanted to believe it would lead me someplace.

When I drove home from the library, the homeless girl was no longer at Entrada. Maybe she'd made her daily nut. Maybe the cops had rousted her. Street life was without certainty except one: on the street girls were a commodity—money and sex. Money because girls were better earners than the boys, and sex was connection. Everyone was looking for connection, but I'd never known anyone on the street who'd found the connection she needed.

Julie used to come find me when I was out there. I don't know how she did it. She called it twin GPS. At first she tried to persuade me to come home, but after a while she gave that up and just came to be with me until I got weirded by her being there or by what I needed to do that I didn't want her to see. I went out on the street at sixteen. There was no thought about it, no plan. One day I just went. I still don't know whether I was running away or running toward something. The drugs made that kind of abstract thinking too hard. The only time I found something out there worth having was when I robbed a bank.

I had plenty of time to think about that in prison, but I could never get it right. The closest I could come was—control: my choice, my plan, my risk, my gain or my loss. No one else was involved; no one else had requirements, suggestions, rules, opinions, fears, needs, whatever. It terrified me, and there was something in that fear that pulled. Could I overcome it? Would it paralyze me when the time came? It was all on me, succeed or fail.

Robbing a bank was better than any drug I ever took.

Chapter Four

～

The first one I robbed was the Ocean Park branch of the Empire State Bank. A group of us were squatting in an abandoned building off Lincoln that was slated for teardown, and I walked by the bank almost every day on my way to a corner where I panhandled. I don't know where the idea came from. You think of a lot of weird shit when you're on drugs, but once I started thinking about it, I couldn't let it go. How would I go in? How would I leave? What were the escape routes? What would I wear? If I wore a disguise, wouldn't someone notice me as I came in? Were there cameras in the bank? It took over my life like a drug habit. Nothing else mattered, even drugs. I stopped taking them. They interfered with rational thinking.

Rational? That's what it felt like then.

Julie loved school. I hated it. Another day, trapped, listening to the dusty voices of teachers telling me stuff I didn't care about. But now I spent hours on library computers reading about bank robberies. The internet is a criminal's DIY dream. I learned how the dye packs that banks hide in cash packets work, the angles cameras can cover, the amount of safe time you have in a bank before the cops arrive. I read about disguise, about how to change the shape of my face, the use of wigs, how to temporarily change my height, my weight, my walk, the color of my eyes. I read it, learned it, absorbed it.

And no drugs. Bank robbery, the perfect rehab program.

I studied the Empire branch for weeks. I went in and out of it in different clothes and never drew a look. I knew the setup of the cameras, the guards, exits, which tellers were bright and alert and which dragged through their shifts. I knew when the bank was crowded, when it was empty, and the variations between. I wanted enough customers so the tellers were occupied but not enough so I'd have to stand in line too long. I bought a black plastic water pistol that was a replica of a real gun. It had an orange plastic insert in the barrel so if you pointed it at someone he'd know it wasn't real. I dyed it black with a marker pen. I was ready.

I chickened out twice—once when a cop car drove slowly by as I was approaching the door. The second time, something just felt wrong, and I walked away.

More rational thinking.

Then I did it. Early afternoon, after the lunchtime customers had thinned out. A cool, gray day that allowed for a dark raincoat. Padding underneath to make me look twenty pounds heavier. Platform heels to raise my height. A dark wig, glasses with thick black rims, bright-red lipstick to draw the eye away from other features, cotton inserts high up in my cheeks to change the shape of my face.

In through the street door and across the marble floor. My heart pounded and I was breathing too fast, but my mind was clear. My senses were supercharged. I could see everything, hear everything. The guard near the door yawned and hitched his gun belt higher. A desk drawer shut with a bang. A woman laughed, and someone tried to stifle a sneeze. The sound of traffic grew loud for a moment as someone came in through the street door. I headed towards the tellers' windows, and as I did, a customer stepped away from the teller I wanted as if he had been part of the plan. I wanted a woman. Not a man. Men think they have to be heroes. The teller I chose was a slow-moving, placid woman in her thirties. She smiled when I got to the window. I passed her the note and opened my coat enough to let her see the black butt of the water pistol. Her eyes went wide. "It's okay," I said, my voice pitched as deep as I could make it. "It's their money, not yours. I'm not going to hurt you. Put the money in an envelope. Fifties and hundreds. No dye packs, no trackers." I glanced left and right. No one was paying attention to us.

She fumbled at the cash in the drawer and dropped a few bills. She looked up at me, scared I might do something. "Chill," I told her. "It's all okay. Be cool. Nothing's going to happen. Just the big bills." She was breathing hard, and her face turned red. "You're doing great," I said. She pushed the envelope to me and tried to smile. As I turned away, she automatically said, "Have a nice day." I crossed the lobby fast, but not fast enough to draw attention. Just someone a little late for an appointment. I went out the door to the parking lot. They would think I was headed for a getaway car. In LA a car was the default. No one walks.

I went through the lot and into an alley between a sex shop and an auto parts store. As I walked, I took a folded shopping bag from under my coat. I dropped the money envelope into it and then the glasses and the wig. I spat the cotton inserts on top, stopped long enough to take off the coat and shed the padding underneath, and stuffed them down on top. I used wet wipes from a plastic sandwich bag in my pocket to scrub the makeup from my face.

Police sirens wailed closer and closer.

I went out the far end of the alley, turned down the street, and walked two blocks and in through the back entrance of a four-story brick building. Down the hall, into the locker room. The bag into the bottom of my locker. I stripped quickly to the yoga pants and T-shirt under my clothes, locked the locker, and went down the hall to a Gyrotonics class that was just into warm-ups. A dozen young women stretching and talking quietly. Gayle, the instructor, smiled at me. "All right," she said. "Let's get started."

A cop car went by the plate glass window, lights and sirens.

I felt so alive. Does that make any sense? I still don't know.

Chapter Five

~

The house was empty when I got home from the library. My mother had said she would be shooting late. I went up to my old room and left the new computer and phone on the bed. I put what was left of the money in a desk drawer.

My mother had thrown away all my old clothes, so I went down the hall to Julie's room and found a green-and-blue one-piece bathing suit more modest than anything I would have bought. I looked at myself in the full-length mirror on the back of the bathroom door. Julie's room and Julie's bathing suit, but me looking back. Did I expect to see my sister in the mirror? I don't know what I expected, maybe some presence, some sign that she was still with me. I found flip-flops on the floor of her closet and a piece of cotton batik for a wrap hanging on a hook next to a small canvas sack. I grabbed a towel from the bathroom and stuffed it and my state ID in the sack and went back to the car.

I drove Sunset to Temescal Canyon and dropped down to the Coast Highway. When the light changed, I crossed to the Will Rogers Beach parking lot. It was late afternoon now, and the rush hour traffic was a metal river headed north. The sun was low, but the air was still hot with the Santa Ana. It blew on my back and fluttered the batik wrapped around me and blew stinging sand against my legs as I walked to the water. I left my things just above the high-tide line weighted by a rock and walked down across the last hardpack to the water's edge. The waves were short and steep against the offshore breeze. When they broke, they ran up the sand and covered my feet with cold water. I walked out until I was thigh deep and dove forward. The shock of the cold went right through me. I swam out with the ebb, timed the next incoming wave, dove deep, swam through it, and kept going till my arms and legs grew heavy. When I stopped, I was in deep water out beyond the break line.

Julie and I were water kids. There were years when we swam every day when we came home from school, no matter what the weather, a point of pride. We first surfed off Will Rogers where I was now, and then up and down the coast when driver's licenses appeared in our group. We had little fear of the ocean. Our bodies are 60 percent water. Women are tidal creatures. The sea is in us. Did Julie go into the sea alive? If she did, it should have saved her. How could Julie drown?

The current pushed me south. The cold water sucked the heat out of me. When I swam back to the beach, I was all the way down to the volleyball courts near the south end of the parking lot. I walked back on rubbery legs along the packed sand at the water's edge until I found my bag and towel. I was dry by then from the hot wind, and the salt was stiff on my skin. I drove back to the house and took a hot shower and got dressed in clothes from Julie's closet. The big house was empty and quiet. It's never quiet in prison. Even in the middle of the night the cellblock is alive with the shouts of the insomniacs and wackos, the choked cries of sleepers tangled in their dreams. Silence was a luxury.

I looked in the refrigerator for something to eat, but my mother's idea of home cooking ran to yogurt and green leaves. For some reason the quiet in the house put my teeth on edge. It wasn't what I needed right then. I needed protein. I needed people. I needed action.

The internet gave me the name of a dance club in Venice. I drove down to Santa Monica and had a hamburger at Chez Jay's not far from the pier. It was a funky dive bar and restaurant, one of the few places in the area that hadn't changed much since the 1950s. We drank there with our first fake IDs. Chez Jay's is one of those promises you make to yourself when you're locked up. A martini and a hamburger at the bar, free at last.

The martini was cold, crisp, and astringent. The hamburger was as thick and juicy as I remembered it, but being there gave me none of the joy I'd hoped for in my lockup fantasies. It sucks when reality doesn't match the dream.

The dance club was just over the Venice line. It was a big room with a DJ's booth at the far end and a bar area raised a couple of steps above the dance floor so you could sit at the bar and watch the dancers. The crowd was my age, some older, some younger, and they were there to have a good time. The volume was high, the lights were muted, and the floor was crowded but not packed. Women danced with men, danced with other women, or danced by themselves. I watched for a while and then went out on the floor and let the music take me over. I was near a group of women. I knew they were friends from the easy way they had with each other. Guys would sometimes dance in toward them, and they would either turn to hold them off or accept them on the edge of the group, or a woman would take a guy up until she felt it was time to let him go again. They knew some of the men, but some they didn't. I liked how they let some join and rejected others without a sign I could catch.

A guy was circling me, offering without really pushing. I had been holding him off while I thought about it. He was cute and he was a good dancer, and he busted a move that made me laugh, so I let him in, and we danced together until the DJ broke. It was fun. Fun had been in short supply. He asked if he could buy me a drink, and I said yes. We found seats at the end of the bar where we could talk without shouting and ordered some high-end bourbon he proposed that I'd never heard of.

"What's your name?"

"Cody."

"Alex Ames." He reached over and shook my hand. I liked the gesture. For some reason it seemed more intimate than a kiss. "My friends call me Dub, for double A."

"I think I'll call you Alex."

He grinned. "What do you do, Cody?"

"I'm retired."

"Retired what?"

"Dope fiend and bank robber."

"No shit. Is there much money in that?" He thought it was a line.

"Some, but bad hours, lousy working conditions, and no pension, no medical. What do you do?"

"I sell really expensive cars in Beverly Hills to guys with too much money and not enough brains to know that buying a three-hundred-thousand-dollar Ferrari 812 Superfast isn't going to make them who they want to be."

"If I get back into the business, you could be my getaway driver."

"Is that a salaried position or a partnership?"

* * *

The drinks came. We talked about fast cars, about people with too much money, about LA. He was funny and bright and good on his feet. We danced, we drank, we talked, and we laughed. I liked him, and the dance at the bar wasn't a lot different from the one on the floor. We made up the steps, but we knew where we were headed.

We had been together for more than an hour when he said, "My place is a couple of blocks from here. It's got a great view over the beach to the water. The moon's almost full tonight."

I said nothing, but my heart sped up. Was this what I wanted? Now that we were at the moment, I wasn't sure.

He said, "Okay, okay. I get it. We could have dinner. Like on Wednesday or something." He waited.

"I want to see your view."

I didn't get to see it for a while.

Sex in prison is like looking for comfort in broken glass. I had been a long time without affection, without gentleness. I was greedy for everything he offered.

We stood on the balcony and looked out across the beach to the waves breaking in a white line on the sand. The hot air dried our sweat. We didn't need to talk much, and almost anything we said made us laugh. I put my hand on his hip, and he put his arm around my waist, and we went back to bed.

I took a shower while he slept. He woke up while I was getting dressed.

"Where are you going?"

"Home."

"You could stay. We could have breakfast together. Breakfast kind of seals the deal. And then maybe we could have dinner."

I smiled. "I can't."

"How about your phone number? I'll call and remind you how cool I am."

"Wow, something to look forward to." He deserved more. "How about I take yours?"

"And call me?"

"I don't know."

"Something I did?"

"No. You were perfect."

"That's good. Perfect is good. Perfect is hard to find. You want to hold on to that thought. Perfect is much better than sucks."

I laughed. "Give me your number."

"Will you call?"

"I might." I leaned down to kiss him.

"You're a mysterious woman, Cody no-last-name. Call me."

When I got home, my mother's light was still on. She heard me come up the stairs. "Is that you, Cody?"

Mom was propped up in her custom king-size bed reading a script, a yellow marker in her hand. It was a big room with two armchairs and a sofa near the windows that looked out toward the ocean. There was a stone fireplace on the north wall. On colder winter days when we were kids, we would come up here after school and light the fire and do our homework on her bed while she sat on the sofa and went over a script, highlighting her lines with a yellow marker. Tonight her hair was bound in a turban and her face was covered with a green cosmetic mask that was stiff enough to keep her features from moving much when she spoke.

"I wondered where you were."

After all these years I still heard the mother tone saying, *Why didn't you tell me where you were going? Why didn't you leave a note?*

"I took Julie's car. I went down to Chez Jay's and had a martini and a hamburger. I'd been thinking about doing just that for a while. Then I went dancing."

"With friends?"

"Yes. Sure."

"Oh, good. From school? Where'd you go? Not that I know any of the places anymore."

"A club called Onyx down in Venice."

"You and Julie were always such good dancers." She put the script down. "Are you all right? Being out must be such a relief, but it must be difficult. The change and all." The green mask hid her expression.

"Yes. No. I don't know what it's like yet. I slept on the plane, and when I woke up, I didn't know where I was. I had the window seat, and I'd been sleeping tight against the wall, and for a moment I thought I was back in my cell. I wait for other people to open doors, because that's what happens in prison. The doors are locked. Someone else has to open them. I went for a long swim. I thought that would wash away some of the crap, but I guess it's not going to be that easy. I guess it's going to take time."

"Is there anything I can do to help?" Her fingers tapped the script. She wanted to get back to it.

"I don't know, Mom. I don't think so. I'll let you know if I think of something. I'm beat. I think I better go to bed before I fall down. I'll see you tomorrow."

"Oh, darling, they changed the schedule. I've got a forced call at nine. But we're only shooting five-day weeks. We'll have the weekend."

"Okay." I bent to kiss her, and she turned her head enough to offer me the bare skin near her ear rather than the green mask. She was reading the script again before I was out of the room.

I went to my room, threw my clothes in the direction of a chair, crashed into bed, asleep as my head hit the pillow.

Chapter Six

Julie's body was found in Malibu, but Malibu has no police department. The law comes through the LA Sheriff's Department. Google told me the Malibu station was in Calabasas. I took Julie's car, filled it with gas in Pacific Palisades Village, and drove out the Coast Highway. The sun was bright. The air was clear. The Santa Ana still held the dirty fog bank offshore. I turned up Malibu Canyon Road and climbed away from the ocean through dry tan hills. The road was littered with the leathery leaves of eucalyptus trees blown down by the hot wind. The brush on the hillsides was dry. A random spark would light it off.

There are four seasons in LA: earthquake, fire, mudslides, and the Academy Awards. Only the Oscars are on a known schedule. Earthquakes are a disaster waiting to happen. Everyone knows the Big One is coming. We don't know when. We don't know how bad it's going to be, just that it's going to be awful. It's one of the reasons a hum of anxiety runs under LA life like background music.

The fires are yearly. The brush dries out on the hillsides when the rains don't come. Something touches it off: a homeless person's campfire, a cigarette carelessly tossed from a car window, an electric spark, a lightning strike, an asshole with a match and a need to see things burn. Suddenly the hills are in flames. Whole neighborhoods go up in smoke, and days later the owners stand in the blackened rubble and tell the TV cameras they're going to rebuild in the same spot.

The fires burn the vegetation that holds the earth in place, and when the rains come, the hills slough off in mudslides, destroying houses, carrying away cars. Again the cameras show people in their ruined door-yards swearing to rebuild in the same spot. A triumph of hope over reality.

Another LA story.

The LA Sheriff's station in Calabasas was on Agoura Road, a wide street that runs through the Ventura Valley from here to there with little between except strip malls and low-rise housing developments. The station was a one-story white building with a green metal roof set back from the road past a scruffy lawn, a box hedge, and a parking lot. I left the car between a Sheriff's cruiser and a silver Porsche and went up the wide concrete steps and in through the glass doors to the chill of air conditioning.

The cop behind the desk looked at me for a moment and then went back to typing something into his computer. I waited. He looked up over the tops of black-rimmed glasses. "Can I help you?" It was a half-assed offer by a man who didn't mean it.

"My name's Cody Bonner. A couple of years ago my sister was found dead on the beach in Malibu. I wondered if there was someone here at the station who handled the case and could tell me something about it."

"Something like what?"

"Where she was found exactly. What the officers saw when they first got there. I only know what I read online."

"Why do you want to know more?"

Cops are suspicious of civilians the way Amazon tribes are suspicious of explorers. They live in a closed society, and strangers usually bring trouble. "She was my sister. I wasn't here when it happened. I'd like to know more. Is that a problem?"

He thought it over. "Take a seat. I'll call around and see if someone can talk to you. What was the victim's name?"

"Julie Bonner."

"When did it happen?"

"About two years ago, May fifteenth."

"You got ID?"

I handed over the state ID they gave me on release. He looked it over. "You got anything else?"

"No."

"Take a seat." He held on to the ID and picked up a phone. I crossed the room and sat in a plastic chair against the wall. After a while another uniformed officer came into the area behind the desk from a door in the back wall. He and the deskman exchanged a few words in voices too low for me to hear. He picked up my ID and came out through a gate in the counter.

"Cody Bonner?"

I stood up. "Yes."

"I'm Lieutenant Moreno. Follow me, please." He was in his thirties. His uniform was tailored. His dark hair was cut short. He wasn't a big man, but he carried himself straight and tall and walked with crisp, measured steps.

He led me down the corridor. I waited while he punched in a code and opened the door at the end. The door let us into a corridor of offices, and I followed him to his.

"Take a seat." He went behind the desk.

I sat facing him in a visitor's chair close to the desk. The window behind him gave out on a parking lot filled with Sheriff's Department patrol cars and the civilian cars of the officers on duty. A filmy curtain covered the glass to cut the glare. A computer on the side of the desk was turned so only Moreno could read the screen. "Your sister was killed two years ago. How come you're showing up now?"

"I was away."

"Away where?"

I leaned over and took my ID from his desk. "You already know that. Your deskman told you I only had a state ID, so you ran my name through the database."

He was unembarrassed. "Who's your parole officer?"

"I'm not on parole. I served out. That's in the database." Suspicion of a convicted felon comes naturally to a cop. He had answers to the questions he was asking. He thought as a felon I might lie out of habit.

"What do you want to know about your sister?"

"Where exactly was she found? What was the cause of death? I'd like to talk to the responding officers."

He turned to the computer and typed for a while. "She was found just past Malibu Point."

"On the Colony beach."

"Yeah. But that doesn't signify. According to the report she could have gone in the water almost anywhere. Currents move both north and south around there."

"Cause of death?"

"Asphyxiation. And there was evidence that she'd been beaten."

"What evidence?"

He checked the computer. "Bruises on her torso and abdomen. Signs of choking, a broken nose."

"Drugs?"

"That would be in the autopsy report." He looked across the desk at me. "Where are you taking this?"

"I just want to know. I want to talk to the responding officers."

He didn't like it. He went back to the computer. "One's retired. Moved to Idaho. The other switched over to Highway Patrol. He's up north."

"Can I have their names?"

He thought about it for a while. "Okay." He copied them out on a piece of scratch paper and handed it over.

"How about a copy of the preliminary report?"

"Can't do it. Don't have the authority."

"Who does?"

"Captain Yerkes. He's at a conference in Nevada. Back in a couple of days."

"Who was the homicide investigator?"

He drummed his fingers on the desk. "I'll have to get back to you on that." He stood up. We were done here.

I wrote my phone number on his scratch pad and pushed it toward him. "So you can get back to me." We both knew that wasn't going to happen. Cops don't like felons. Cops don't like civilians poking around in their business. I was both.

I walked out into the heat, got in the car, and drove away before someone figured out that if I only had a state ID card, I didn't have a driver's license. That would be just the kind of shitty bust cops like to run on someone like me to keep me clear on my standing in their eyes.

Bruises on her torso, signs of strangulation, a broken nose. My sister. I pulled to the side of the road and sat for a while until I could see well enough to drive.

*   *   *

GloYoga was in a storefront off Main Street in Venice. The big window gave you a view from the sidewalk of people going through the poses on their colored mats under the lead of a young woman in yoga pants and a T-shirt. They moved from pose to pose as limber as cats. The country tilts every once in a while and beautiful young people from every state slide down to California to see what their beauty will win them.

A young woman smiled at me with perfect teeth from behind a desk in the small front lobby. "Hi, welcome to GloYoga. I'm Amanda. Are you interested in joining a class?"

"I'm looking for someone who used to work here. Maybe she still does. Maddie Allen?"

"Maddie Allen? Gee, I don't think so, at least not since I've been here. Hold on. Let me check the records." She typed into a computer on her desk. "Oh, sure. Maddie. She started her own studio. It's called Maddie's and it's up in the Brentwood Country Mart. You know where that is?"

The Brentwood Country Mart is on the corner of Twenty-Sixth Street and San Vicente Boulevard, the border between Santa Monica and Brentwood, neighborhoods awash with money. Most of the buildings that make up the Mart are red-painted wood, and they look like someone dropped farm buildings by mistake on their way someplace else. The Mart would be insulted if you called it a mall, but that's what it is—a mall that sells $60 crystal wineglasses, ham from Spain for $100 a pound, artisanal cheeses, handcrafted cutting boards, and $300 hand-made playsuits for two-year-olds. Nannies pushing baby carriages that cost as much as small used cars gather in the central court to gossip, while the neighborhood women, freed of child duty, spend hours in the beauty salons, spas, and places like Maddie's working hard to stay beautiful in hopes of fending off the would-be trophy wives trolling for their husbands.

A woman behind the desk at Maddie's looked up when I came in. She dropped what she was reading and said, "Oh my god," and clapped a hand to her face in shock. "You're the twin."

"Maddie?"

"Yes. Cody, right? Cody." She came out from behind the desk and hugged me. "I'm so sorry. I'm so sorry."

I wasn't ready for that. I put a hand on her back and patted her. "It's okay."

She stepped back and pulled herself together. "I know you've heard it before, but it's amazing how much you look alike. I never thought I'd actually meet you." She was tall and spare with the long, lean body of an athlete. Her dark hair was streaked with gray and pulled back and tied with a piece of red cloth.

"Here I am." I liked her immediately and resented it. This woman had sold photos of my dead sister to the tabloids.

"You want to talk."

"Yes."

"Let's go someplace. We'll never have any privacy here." She opened a door behind the desk and called in, "Brianna, I'm going to take off for a while. I don't have any singles, and Jen can take my two o'clock class."

"Okay," a woman's voice replied.

She closed the door and turned to study me for a moment. "Do you want to see where I found her, or is that too much?"

"No. I have to see it."

We drove to the Malibu Lagoon Beach, parked, and walked the dirt road to the water's edge and along it to where the Malibu Colony houses began. The first house was a large black building. A wall ran from it to the high-tide line.

"Assholes," Maddie said, and waved a hand at the house. "The law says the beach belongs to everybody from the high-tide mark down, but the richie riches don't want people in their expensive view, so they built the wall to make it hard to get on the beach when the tide's high. Half the reason I come here to run is because I know it pisses them off."

We crossed to the Colony beach on a patch of black-and-gray stones exposed by the low tide. Beyond the wall the beach was wide, but farther north it narrowed to a strip of sand in front of the retaining walls of the house lots. Maddie stopped after we had gone a short distance. She looked up at the houses at the top of the beach to check her bearings. "Here." She pointed to the packed sand near the edge of the water.

There was nothing to see—sand, a gleam of water, a few blowholes from snails burrowed down below the surface. I crouched down and dug my fingers into the sand. I pulled up a handful and let it sift back down. Was I touching anything of Julie, a few molecules, some lingering haunt? Fantasy. I stood and brushed the sand from my hands. "Tell me what you saw."

"It was early, before six, and it was still kind of dark out here. When I came up the beach from the point, I thought at first it was a log, and then when I got close . . ." She shrugged and sighed.

"What did you do?"

"I kind of knelt down beside her, because I thought she might be hurt or, I don't know, asleep. Sounds stupid now, but I wasn't thinking very clearly. I touched her, and she was cold. I mean real cold, not just like she'd been swimming."

"Dead."

"Yes. I touched her throat like for the pulse. But I knew before I did, because she was so cold. There was a piece of rope around her right ankle. It was colored. I remember thinking that it looked like rope we used to use for water-skiing."

"Plastic rope?"

"Yes. It was longer than she was, about six feet, and it was frayed at the end."

"That's all?"

"There was some seaweed in her hair. It looked wrong, and I wanted to take it out, but I thought I better not touch anything until the police got there. I called 911. It was like they took forever. The tide was coming in, and I was afraid it would reach her. I didn't know what to do. But they got here. Two guys from the Sheriff's Department, one old and one young."

"Mercer and Ross?"

"Yeah. That's right. Mercer and Ross. Mercer was the older guy."

"What did they do?"

"They took a lot of pictures with their phones. The tide was starting to get to her, so they moved her up the beach."

There was something in her face. She was holding back. "What, Maddie?"

She hesitated for a moment. "They were making those comments men make. You know, nice tits, what a waste. That kind of shit. I jumped on them. Told them to show a little respect. They didn't like it. They said I was through here, to get lost."

"Thank you for sticking up for her."

"Ah, Jesus, I mean enough is enough."

On the drive back to the Brentwood Country Mart, Maddie spent most of her time looking out the window. She was working through something, and I didn't mind the silence. I kept thinking about my sister, cold and dead on the sand with a piece of plastic rope around one ankle and seaweed in her hair.

I parked on San Vicente, and we sat for a moment. "Thanks. That wasn't easy."

"Easier for me than you. Cody, I owe you something. You and your mother." She stopped. I waited. "I took pictures of your sister while she was lying there. I don't know why, but I did. I sold some of them, and I sold my story, because once she was identified as Karen Bonner's daughter, everyone wanted to know everything. So I was famous for about five minutes, and you know what it's like in this town. If you're even a little famous for a few seconds, people come out of the woodwork to grab on to you. I saw it was my chance, and I took it. I found some investors, I got the place here, and it's been great. Except when I feel like a shit for selling photos of a beautiful dead girl on a beach."

"It's all right. Some good came out of it."

"Oh, wow, okay." She took a deep breath and let it out. "You knew, didn't you? About the photos."

"Yes."

"Thank you for being kind."

Kind? Huh. A weird thing to call me.

Just before she got out of the car, I asked her if she remembered the name of the Sheriff's homicide investigator who interviewed her.

"Sure. Paul Gurwitz. He talked to me a couple of times."

Chapter Seven

～

"Who the fuck are you to come into my house and tell me I haven't done my job?"

"I'm not saying you didn't do your job. I just want to ask you some questions about my sister's case." LA Sheriff's Department homicide investigator Paul Gurwitz glared at me across his desk. He was a thick man in his late forties with thinning black hair and a blurred, loose face. His small, dark eyes were hot with anger.

"I worked my ass off on that case. A beautiful girl. That shouldn't happen. Not to mention that every asshole with the Department's number was calling to say I better get this right. You know who her mother is? A movie star, Karen Bonner."

"She's my mother too."

Deputy Gurwitz ignored that. He had things to say.

"You know how much weight a movie star throws in this town? I had half the command structure up my ass twenty-four/seven. I ran down every lead. I checked every person who knew her. I got nothing. Julie Bonner left her office and showed up dead three days later on a beach in Malibu. I don't need some split tail coming in here raking me over the coals two years later. I did my job."

"Pump your brakes, Paul." The only other officer in the room was a woman at a desk near the window. "She's the sister. Look at her. She's the twin. She just wants to ask some questions."

"Fuck you, Fran, and the sisterhood of the traveling pants, or whatever the fuck it is."

"Me Too."

"Yeah, that too." He stood up hard enough to send his chair back to smack the wall. He pointed a finger at me across the desk. "You want to ask questions, put them in writing, send them in through the proper channels." He bulled his way around the desk and stomped out through the nearest door.

I looked across the room to the woman he called Fran. She gave me a *What can you do?* shrug. "What are the proper channels?" I asked.

"Beats me. We try to cut Paul a little slack these days. His wife just left him." She raised a hand. "Don't say it. He's a good cop, and he can be a good guy most of the time. She left him for another woman, and that's thrown him. He never saw that coming." She got up and came across the room. She was a stocky woman in her midthirties in an unflattering tan uniform. She carried an automatic in a holster high on her right hip. Her black hair was cut short enough to comb with her fingers. She had a broad face, high, prominent cheekbones, and smart dark eyes. She looked competent and tough, with none of the belligerence that marked many of the women corrections officers in prison. She offered me her hand. "Fran Tovar." Her hand was dry and padded with muscle.

She pulled Gurwitz's chair away from the wall and sat down across the desk from me. "What do you want to know? I'll answer what I can. I worked the case with Paul in the beginning when the heat was on."

Sisterhood would go only so far. She was a cop. If I stepped on her toes, she'd back off. Start with something simple, something without threat. "Why do think there was a piece of rope tied around her ankle?"

She took a moment. "I think whoever dumped her tied a weight to her, a cinder block or something. It frayed through the rope and she popped up. We checked every house for a couple of miles in both directions along the beach to see who might have a boat they could have used to get her out into deep water. You'd think there'd be a lot of boats along there, but there aren't. The ones there are checked out okay."

"They didn't need a boat. Every one of those houses has at least one surfboard, or a paddleboard, or an ocean kayak, something you could launch easily from the beach."

Tovar wiped a hand across her face. "Okay. Goddamn it. Surfboards. It never occurred to us. Gurwitz grew up in Kansas. I grew up outside of Modesto. A lot of shotguns and skateboards but very few surfboards. What's a paddleboard?"

"It's bigger than a surfboard. You can stand on it and use a long paddle."

"Oh boy. A lot of houses to go back and check."

"You said *they*, not *he*. You think more than one person was involved."

"Your sister weighed about a hundred twenty. Add the cinder block, it's a load to move. One strong guy could do it. Two would make it easier."

"You said cinder block or something, and then you came back to cinder block. You didn't say weight. You said cinder block again."

Tovar looked at me for a long moment before answering. "You don't let anything slip, do you? There were some bits and pieces of concrete in the rope braid near where it frayed off. They were consistent with the stuff in concrete blocks. Of course, the rope could have been tied to a block weeks before, had nothing to do with your sister. What else?"

"Was she raped?"

"No real call on that. The autopsy shows vaginal bruising, but it could be consistent with rough sex. Was your sister into that?"

"I don't know." You can know who your twin is without knowing what she does. Rough sex? She liked sex, but I had no idea of her details. "Any DNA?"

"No. Some residue of spermicide found on condoms."

"I'd like to see a copy of the autopsy report."

Tovar thought. "Here's what I'll do. I'll make you a copy today, but you go home, go online, and apply for it. It's a public record. You and your mother are next of kin. It shouldn't be a problem. That'll cover my ass if someone comes back at me about how you got it."

"Thanks."

"No problem." She typed into the computer on Gurwitz's desk and hit a button. "It'll take a minute." Across the room a printer on a counter began to whirr. "You were in prison when she was killed."

"Yes."

"What for?"

"You don't know?"

"Yeah, I know. Bank robbery. But why'd you do it?"

"I was doing a lot of dope at the time. I'd given it up for a while, but I was back to it. I was broke. I needed money to score." Not the whole story, just the part that was easy to explain.

"What happened?"

"There was an off-duty deputy sheriff making a mortgage payment. He had a Glock. I had a black plastic water pistol."

"Oops." Tovar laughed. "You're lucky he didn't shoot you."

"I know."

"A lot of guys would've taken the opportunity to pop you just to see how it feels. The board would've called it a righteous shoot." The idea amused her. "You on parole?"

"No. I served out."

"I get it. You didn't want anyone looking over your shoulder when you walked. And now you want to find out what happened to your sister. Dickless Tracy? Going to bring the bad guys in when the cops couldn't do it?"

"Why not?"

"Fat chance, but maybe new eyes will see something we missed. You knew your sister in ways no one else could. But if you get the slightest sniff of something, you bring it to me. You don't go running in someplace with a water pistol in your hand."

"Deal."

"One more thing. I'll be right back." She left the room and came back a few minutes later carrying an evidence bag. She put it on the desk. "Your sister's laptop. We were hoping to get into it, but it's password protected. We were going to ask the geniuses in the lab if they could crack it, but someone had a better idea of calling her law firm to see if they had a way in. They slapped us with an injunction. No entry. Something about proprietary information and client-attorney privilege. Our attorneys say we have to release it. You're kin. You might as well take it home."

She went to the printer and brought back a thick sheaf of papers, the autopsy report and some case notes. I slid them into the evidence bag with the computer. "Did she drown?" I asked.

"No, but there was a little freshwater in her lungs. It had chlorine in it. The coroner believed she was strangled in a swimming pool or hot tub."

Chapter Eight

〜

His name was Paco. He came in fast and tried a roundhouse leg strike. I blocked it wide with a forearm and, while he was off-balance, hit him with two quick fist strikes. Normally you start sparring with someone you don't know at half or three-quarter speed, but Paco had come hard from the beginning to take me out, to show me I didn't belong in the ring with him. I had been holding him off while I looked for his weaknesses. I dodged some of his strikes and absorbed others with my arms. He was in a hurry, and he thought he was better than he was. I feinted a right to bring his hands up and hit him with a leg to the kidneys. That brought his hands down. I continued turning and caught him on the side of his head with an elbow. It was too high, but it drove him back against the ropes, and when he bounced off, I got him with a roundhouse kick that dropped him. He tried to get up but fell back and pawed weakly at the lowest rope to get up. He failed.

"Okay, okay." Sakchai, the Thai owner of the gym, beat on the canvas with the flat of his hand. "Enough." He held the ropes apart while I ducked through. I peeled off the gloves and left them on the canvas. Sakchai glanced once at Paco to make sure he was going to live and then turned to study me. It was hard to tell his age, but I guessed he was in his midforties. He wore black gym pants and a white T-shirt. He was barefoot like a lot of Muay Thai fighters.

I had been looking for a place to spar. The first three gyms that advertised Muay Thai were aerobics spas filled with people in expensive exercise clothes shadowboxing in front of mirrors under the instruction of young men with frosted hair. Sakchai's place was a one-story cinder block cube set back from a street in Ocean Park a few blocks west of the 405 Freeway. There were two rings in the big open room and a couple of big mat-covered areas where people could spar if the rings were busy. Light and heavy bags hung from chains near a free-weight area. The place smelled of sweat and disinfectant.

"We don't take women in here," Sakchai said when I told him I was looking for a place to work out.

"Any women ever asked?"

"No."

"So you don't know if you take them."

"We don't. Never have, never will."

"Why not? You afraid some girl'll come in here, kick someone's ass, and you'll lose all your clients?"

"No, I ain't afraid of that."

"Let me go with someone. See if I measure up to the high standards of the gym."

"You giving me shit?"

"Yes, I am." I smiled at him.

He thought about it for a moment and then called Paco over from where he was pounding a heavy bag with big roundhouse kicks. Paco outweighed me by about thirty pounds. His shoulders and chest were covered with muddy tattoos. His hair was cut to stubble on one side of his head, and the rest was grown long and gelled to hang down the other side almost to his shoulders. He had hooded eyes and a perpetual half sneer. He looked me over like I was something he might want to eat.

"Spar with the lady," Sakchai said.

"A chick? You shitting me?"

"No."

"Okay. Whatever." He pounded his gloves together, looked me over again, and stuck out his tongue. "Let's go, baby."

Sakchai pointed to a door across the room. "You can use the store-room to change."

When I came out, they were leaning on the ring apron, talking. They stopped when they saw me coming. Sakchai picked up a couple of training helmets. "You want one?"

"No."

"Paco?"

"What? Like she's going to hurt me?"

Then we got in the ring.

Sakchai watched Paco weave toward the locker room and then turned to me. "You train with Ginger Kitkam? She liked that combo—fake, then leg strike, then elbow."

"Yes."

"How long?"

"Five years."

"She still running those gladiator fights in the yard?"

"Yes."

"You fight in them?"

"Yes."

"I hear they're rough."

"Angry women with nothing to lose."

"Ginger's the best. They ever going to let her out?"

"No."

"It's a hundred bucks a month. You want lessons, I charge fifty bucks an hour. I see some things we could work on. We'll find more. I'll give you a list of names for sparring partners."

We shook hands, and I gave him $200.

* * *

The first two weeks in prison I was terrified every minute of the day. Nothing in my privileged life had prepared me for this. When I was in the yard, or on the tier, or in the mess hall, I could feel the eyes on me as people weighed me, appraised me, tried to figure out where my place was in the pecking order—toward the bottom where anyone could have me any way they wanted, toward the top where I made the choices, or somewhere in between? I walked with my head down, unwilling to make eye contact. It was just a matter of time before someone made a run at me, and I didn't know what I'd do when it happened.

When I was in the yard, I never stopped moving. Movement was going to save me. I walked circuits, making sure my path took me through the least populated areas of the yard. My circuit always took me past the area where Ginger Kitkam's crew practiced some sort of martial arts. The other prisoners always gave them room, so I used it as a safe passage. "Get your eyes up."

"What?" I looked up.

"Lift your head. Walk like you own the place, or someone's going to own you." Ginger Kitkam stood in front of me with her fists on her hips. She was a black-haired Asian woman of no particular age. She was no more than five feet tall, tight, compact, and muscular. Energy came out of her like there was something burning at her core. "You hear me?"

"Yes."

"Then do it." She waited long enough to be sure the command had penetrated and then turned away. She clapped her hands once, and the five pairs of women waiting on her went back to sparring. She didn't look back at me.

I tried, but I didn't know how to make it work. You can't make people believe you own the place if you know you're a fraud.

Someone bumped me in the food line, bumped me hard, drove her groin into my butt. When I turned, I had to look up to see her eyes. She was about six feet tall and 180 pounds of hard fat. Her name was Jasco. A woman on our tier had pointed her out to me as the craziest bitch on the yard. My heart raced. "What are you looking at?" she asked.

"Nothing," I said, and started to turn away to end it.

She jerked me back by the shoulder. "Are you calling me nothing?"

"No, no. I didn't mean that." I could hear the fear in my voice. So could she, and it made her smile.

"You're going to have to apologize, sweet cheeks." Except for three women who were always with Jasco, people moved away from us as if we were toxic.

"I'm sorry. I didn't mean anything."

"Uh-uh, sweetie. Not here. Just you and me someplace we can work it out in private." She told me where. She told me when. She cupped my chin with a big hand, leaned in, and kissed me. Then she shouldered me aside and went on with her friends, laughing.

The first thing you learn when you go into the system is that the system is not there to help you. If you have a problem with another inmate, you do not go to the COs. You work it out and you live with the consequences.

The cellblocks are mostly empty at four in the afternoon. Inmates are in the yard, at classes or work details. Some of the older women on the ground floor are allowed to rest in their cells, but otherwise no one is there. Four o'clock, Jasco said. I was there at three thirty. I didn't know what I was going to do, but I knew I had to do something, because whatever happened here today would define my life for the next five years, and I wouldn't live long as a victim. I searched frantically for a weapon, any piece of metal or wood I could use to stab or club. The only thing I found was a plastic bucket a janitor had left in a shower room. What the hell was I going to do with a plastic bucket? I filled it most of the way with water. It must have weighed close to fifteen pounds. Okay. Don't think about it as a bucket of water. Think of it as a fifteen-pound weight.

I was on the third tier when Jasco came in with her crew of three at ten to four. My heart was in my mouth, and the bucket was at my feet near the tier railing. Jasco's crew went around the ground-floor tier and cleared out the older women who were in their cells. They didn't like it, but they went. The crew had a few words with Jasco I couldn't make out. There was a burst of laughter at what Jasco said, and then they left. The cellblock was quiet. I could hear the scrape of Jasco's shoes on the concrete below. I edged to the rail and looked down. She was standing just under the tier overhang. I could see part of her shoulder and leg. I would have only one shot at this. I needed her out in the open. I waited. I could feel my heart tripping in my chest. My breath came in gasps.

A couple of minutes later she shifted her position, but she was still covered by the overhang. It was after four now. She was beginning to wonder if I was coming. I heard her say, "Fuck," in annoyance. She didn't like to wait.

Another minute.

She moved out from under the overhang and turned toward the door where I was supposed to enter. She was right below me. I picked up the bucket. I eased it over the railing, being careful not to spill water and warn her. I checked her position. I had one chance here. If I missed, I was finished. I dropped the bucket and watched it fall. She moved. The bucket came down on the side of her head, slammed into her shoulder, and drove her down with a scream of pain and surprise. Then she was still.

I walked down to the ground tier. She was unconscious, sprawled on the concrete. Her head was bleeding. The bucket had torn most of her ear off and smashed her shoulder into a shape it was never meant to have. I went out past her and into the yard. Her three women jerked in surprise when I came out into the sunlight. They ran for the door I had exited and disappeared inside. I began walking my circuits and waited to see if something would happen. One of Jasco's women bolted from the cellblock and crossed the yard running. The adrenaline in me burned away to ash, and I kept walking. An infirmary crew ran a gurney across the yard and into the tier and came out a few minutes later with Jasco strapped down.

The word burned through the yard. On my next circuit, people who had always ignored me stopped what they were doing and watched me go by. There were guards on the catwalk that ringed the yard, but none of them moved. Jasco had a lot of enemies. Maybe no one had reported what had happened to her. Maybe the guards thought she had it coming. Maybe they liked it when the animals ate each other.

When I got to the area Ginger Kitkam used, I stopped. "I want to learn what you can teach me. I want to learn how to fight."

"Okay."

Chapter Nine

෴

Julie's townhouse was in Culver City near the Twenty-First Century lot. There were eight units grouped around a common space with a lawn and a swimming pool with deck chairs on a tiled pool apron. Each townhouse had underground parking. The common area was planted with evergreen hedges and bright flowers in formal beds. Julie's unit was past the far end of the pool.

I used the key my mother gave me.

"Why do you want to go there?" She didn't like it.

"Just to see."

"There's nothing to see."

"Still. I want to see it."

"Do you want me to come with you? We could go on the weekend."

"Today's okay. I'll be in that part of town." She would be impatient to leave from the moment we got there. She would wander around, pick up things, look at them without seeing, put them back, and move to something else. After fifteen minutes, she would ask, *Are you ready to go?*

The key let me into the ground floor. A short flight of stairs led up from a small entry hall to a large open room with a fireplace fronted by an arrangement of comfortable chairs and a sofa around a long, low, black coffee table. I recognized two chairs and the end tables and lamps from our house, casualties of Mom's redecorating. Beyond the living room was an oval dining table with six chairs. A counter separated the dining area from the kitchen, and past the dining area were glass doors leading to a deck big enough for a round table and four chairs.

It was a place for a young lawyer on the way up. There was no mess, no disorder, no dust on the surfaces, because Mom's housekeeper, Carmen, still came once every two weeks to clean, but the air was still and stale. It wouldn't have been like this when Julie lived here. There would have been laughter, and parties, and arguments about why the world worked the way it did, and maybe sex on the dining room table.

Julie's bedroom was at the back of the building, away from any street noise. Framed black-and-white photos of LA in the 1920s and 1930s decorated the walls. There was a queen-size bed with a table and lamp at either side. Our grandmother's chaise longue that Julie had always loved was near the window. It was covered in faded red velvet. The closet was full of clothes neatly arranged. Half were sober lawyer's stuff for work, and half were what Julie wore when she was not at work. She had an eye for style and color, but her taste was cooler than mine.

The bedside table held a box of condoms, a jar of coconut oil, and two vibrators. The batteries were dead.

The bedroom across the hall had been made into a home office. Law books filled the shelves. A slab of polished dark wood held up by two filing cabinets served as a desk. The file cabinets were nearly empty. The few files were personal, not business. They held tax receipts, insurance forms, car information, and other irritants of daily life.

I went out to the car and got the evidence bag with the computer and the police reports. I spread the reports on the dining room table and went through them carefully. The language of the autopsy report was clinical and dry—height, weight, approximate age of the *normally developed white female* who was my sister.

The body is cold and unembalmed. The eyes are open. The irises are blue and corneas are clouded. Petechial hemorrhaging is present in the conjunctival surfaces of the eyes.

Bruising is present on neck below the mandible consistent with manual strangulation, with finger touch pad contusions consistent with complete hand grasp.

The hyoid bone is fractured.

Present are ligature marks on the wrists and ankles.

The genitalia are those of an adult female.
Presence of bruising of vulva.
Presence of bruising on vaginal wall.
Presence in lungs of trace elements of dilution of hypochlorous
acid consistent with swimming pool water.

Immediate Cause of Death: *Asphyxia due to manual strangulation.*
Manner of Death: *Homicide.*

I bolted from the table to the deck beyond the kitchen and leaned on the railing until I could breathe again.

I left the deck door open for air and went back to the table. I pushed the autopsy report away and went through the rest of what Fran Tovar had given me. The report by the two cops Maddie Allen had talked to had nothing in it that she hadn't told me. There was a list of people Gurwitz and Tovar had talked to with summaries of the interviews. They added up to nothing, but I would go talk to them all again.

I plugged in Julie's computer and turned it on. The password window blinked at me. I tried our birth date, our nicknames for each other, the name of a dog we had in grade school. After the fifth guess, the computer warned that it would lock down at the next wrong answer.

I went upstairs and lay down on Julie's bed for a moment to clear my head. When I woke up, it was getting dark and I was due to meet my mother for dinner in an hour. I took a shower and used Julie's soap. I brushed my hair with her brush. I dressed in her clothes, high-waist, wide-legged trousers, a cream linen blouse, and black ankle boots with spike heels. I found a simple gold necklace of hammered links in the upper tray of the wooden jewelry box on her bureau. Her earrings were scattered in the bottom tray—singles, mismatches that were close but not identical, and occasional pairs. There was a pair of small pearl studs I had given her for our fifteenth birthday. Earrings were the only random part of Julie's life. She couldn't hold on to them. She used to say she could put on a pair of earrings, go for a walk down the block, and come back with only one still in her ear. She almost always went out with a mismatched pair—a pearl in one ear, a gold hoop in the other. She said it was a fashion statement, but it was just her making the best of the situation. I found a heavy gold braid and pawed through looking for its twin, knowing I wouldn't find it. I finally settled on two gold hoops of different sizes. When I looked in the mirror, I had to close my eyes for a moment. The house was filled with her presence and her absence.

As I left Julie's house, a woman came out of a townhouse on the other side of the pool. She walked fast toward the front gate. Her head was down as she concentrated on a message she was tapping into her phone. Her hair was cut short and dyed silver. She wore a green metallic dress with a very short skirt that set off her tan. She felt my presence as we closed on the gate and glanced up from the phone.

She stumbled, dropped the phone, and looked at me in horror. "Holy fucking shit." I grabbed her arm to keep her from falling. She took a deep breath and said, "Okay, okay," to steady herself. She looked down at the phone at her feet. "Christ, that better not be broken." She crouched down and picked the phone up and tapped it. "Thank Christ, my whole life's in there." She stood up and examined me with her head cocked to one side. "The twin, right? For a minute I thought I was in some 'Night of the Living Dead' shit."

"Cody."

"Yeah. The jailbird, right? You and I have a lot to talk about. Your sister was the greatest. I loved her ass." A car horn blew on the street. "That's my Uber. I've got to run. I've got a date. If I'm late, he might begin to think he can live without me."

She started to go, then turned and grabbed me in a hug. "We'll talk." She dove a hand into a small green purse that hung on her shoulder and came out with a card. "I'm in number three. Got to run." She went out the gate fast and got into the back seat of the car waiting at the curb.

I looked at the card. It was heavy, expensive, cream-colored stock. The writing was embossed: *Keira*. Under it was a phone number. There was no Keira on the list of people the sheriffs had interviewed.

Chapter Ten

Mom and I ate at a restaurant in Beverly Hills where she was known. Muted lighting, white linen tablecloths, heavy silverware, deferent waiters, and people whom she recognized and who recognized her. She had her favorite table far enough from the door so she could make her entrance and stop to kiss those who deserved it and far enough back that those seated deeper could stop to kiss her.

A Hollywood strategy.

She was in a foul mood. Something had gone wrong on the set, but she didn't want to tell me about it. Her cutlery was spotted. The service was slow. Her steak was overcooked. The wine she wanted wasn't available. When she ran out of targets, she threw a dart at me.

"I wish you wouldn't wear Julie's things. It's too weird."

"Okay."

"And wearing mismatched earrings looks sloppy. It looked sloppy on her and looks sloppy on you."

"Uh-huh."

"You can take my card and go get something of your own."

"Thank you." Don't push back when she's in this mood.

That wasn't what she wanted. She wanted an argument. "What are you going to do with your life now? I trust you're not going to rob another bank."

"Jesus, Mom. Thanks."

Her face was stiff and unrelenting. "Have you thought about it?"

"About robbing another bank? No."

"About what you're going to do." Impatient with me. Nothing new.

"I'm going to find out what happened to Julie."

"Don't be ridiculous. That's a job for the police."

I said nothing.

"What can you do? A girl with no training or anything. Dr. Salavsky says we have to put this behind us. It's over, and there's nothing to be done. We have to move on. Cherish her memory and move on."

"Dr. Salavsky is full of shit. I am not putting it behind me. I am not moving on."

"I forbid you. You will not do this."

"Tell me that you don't care that some man raped and killed your daughter and got away with it. Tell me that you don't care that he's still out there walking around, doing what he does, eating lunch, watching the sun set, going to bed at night, getting up in the morning, seeing his friends, having a drink, alive while Julie is dead. How does Dr. Salavsky suggest we put that behind us?"

She said nothing, and her eyes filled with tears.

"Mom, I'm sorry."

Her face was pale.

"I'm sorry." It was always like that. When she went at Julie, Julie could calm her, deflect her, laugh her out of her moods. If she pushed at me, I pushed back. We would go from zero to sixty in no time.

"You've become hard. You were wild and unthinking, but you weren't hard."

Was that a line from one of her movies? "Prison will do that to you."

"There, that's exactly what I mean. I know prison is a terrible place, but it's over now. You don't have to be so tough."

As if those years, like an acting role, could be discarded when someone said *Cut, that's a wrap*.

The waiter brought the bill and went away with Mom's credit card. As we waited in angry silence, a white-haired couple stopped by the table on their way out to tell her how beautiful she was and how much they enjoyed her movies. The appreciation lightened her mood for a while.

A studio car had dropped her at the restaurant, so she rode home with me. We went in silence. When we got home, she said she had a headache and went up to bed.

I poured myself a glass of single malt at the wet bar in the living room. I turned out the lights and went to stand at the big window that looked out toward the ocean. The lights on the coast highway curved up toward Malibu where someone had killed my sister. Julie had always been there for me, and in the moment when she really needed me, I wasn't there. She was alone. If I had been here, she would still be alive. Whatever happened to her would not have happened if I'd been available. Most people would call that fucked up thinking, but it's not if you're a twin.

I'd thought about it so often lying in my cell that it became the only thing I knew for certain in my life. I owed Julie, not that it would do her any good. But I owed it to her anyway. Julie's murder gave me the liberating gift of rage, purpose for a life that had had no purpose. Was I looking for justice or revenge? Was I looking for redemption? Maybe I'd know the answer when I knew who had killed her and why.

Chapter Eleven

I ate breakfast in the backyard in the warmth of the early spring sun. When I went back into the house, I found the housekeeper, Carmen, standing in the dimness of the living room while she polished a silver plate, already bright, over and over again with a soft cloth. She was fixed on something she could see from the big window that faced the street. I carried my coffee over to see what had hooked her attention.

"There is a man out there. He has been there since before you came down for breakfast." Carmen was a stolid, calm woman from Guatemala who had worked for my mother for ten years. She had been driven from her own country by more violence than most people see in a lifetime. People who live where danger is random and sudden develop an instinct for its presence.

An older sedan of no color at all was parked across the street in front of the ruined house. A man leaned against the driver's door and watched our house.

"*La Migra*?" I asked.

"No, no, not Immigration," Carmen said. "I have my papers. Your mother helped. I am legal for five years."

Footsteps on the stairs, and then my mother was just behind us. "What are you two looking at?"

"Carmen thinks that guy's watching the house."

"Carmen, please. He's a city inspector or something. They come to look at that house across the street all the time. I wish they'd finally get rid of it. It would open up the view." My mother, who spent her working hours in make-believe, thought of herself as a pragmatist and did not move to other people's alarms.

"He came up into the driveway before," Carmen said. "I saw him walking back."

The day's copy of the *Los Angeles Times* lay in the driveway. Mom still got the paper out of habit. "I'll go see." I left my coffee cup on a hall table and went outside. I picked up the paper and looked across the street at him. He looked up from his phone.

"Cody Bonner?"

He pushed himself away from the car. A straw hat with a narrow brim shaded his face. He wore a powder-blue lightweight jacket over a bright, untucked Hawaiian shirt and blue jeans that were short enough to show scuffed black cowboy boots. He was tall and rail thin, and the clothes hung loosely on him.

"Who wants to know?" But I knew. A cop. If you've spent time in the system, you can spot them. The flat way they look at you. The tone of voice meant to bring you to heel.

"Steckley, LAPD Robbery-Homicide." As he walked closer, I could see his face, knobs and angles, a nose like a blade, and a slash of a mouth, too much bone and not enough flesh. He stopped at the end of the drive-way about ten feet from me. He raised his phone, took photos of me, and put the phone away. "I want to talk to you."

"I want to see some ID."

When he went to his pocket for his wallet, I could see the automatic clipped to his belt. He held out a leather case with his badge and ID. If I wanted to examine it, I would have to go down to him. He wasn't going to move. I walked down and took the case out of his hand and tipped it to the light to get a close look. He didn't like it, but fuck him, he didn't get all the control. His name was Aaron Steckley.

"What do you want to talk about?" I gave the ID back.

"Let's go sit in the car."

"You go sit in the car. I'm going back in the house for another cup of coffee." It's a game of who has the high ground.

He brought out a notebook and leafed through the pages until he found the one he wanted. He read off a date. "Where were you that day?" He had a voice like dry sand.

"That's more than six years ago. I have no idea. Where were you? Who remembers dates from then? What's the deal?"

"September sixth, someone robbed the Empire Bank branch in Ocean Park. A lone operator, disguised, female. Showed a gun in her waistband but didn't pull it. Asked for hundreds and fifties, no dye packs." He looked at me with hard eyes.

I said nothing. I hoped my face was calm, because my heart was racing.

"October eleventh, the Los Angeles Credit Union downtown, same MO. Well planned, disguised, nobody saw the getaway."

"Uh-huh."

He folded the notebook and put it back in his pocket. "Almost six years ago. The statute of limitations on a crime punishable by eight or more years in prison is six years. That means I've got till September on the first one and a month more on the last. I like you for both of them."

"Me? I robbed a bank a thousand miles from here. I went in without a disguise, armed with a water pistol, and stuck up the teller next to a deputy paying his mortgage. Does that sound well planned?"

"The last robbery here was a month before you got busted back there. We haven't had another one like it since."

"Maybe the guy made enough to buy the car he wanted. Maybe he moved to Zamboanga. Maybe he just wised up and got a job."

"I still like you for them." He took a striped mint out of his pocket, unwrapped it, and popped it in his mouth.

"Why?"

"Face recognition. Computer programs. A cop's new friends." He sucked wetly on the mint and watched me with hard eyes. "The programs get better and better every year. I've spent a lot of time running the surveillance tapes from those robberies. Each one gives me a little more. A different angle on the face. Or hands, or how you walked. I got the tapes from the bank back east where you went in bare-ass, and that gives me something to compare. I'm building it up piece by piece. Pretty soon I'll have you."

"Have her for what?" I hadn't heard my mother approach, but there she was.

"Bank robbery," Steckley said.

"She already paid the price for that."

"Not for the ones she did here in LA."

"Here? You've been robbing banks here and I didn't see a dime?" She was playing a part, the wisecracking, tough gangster girl.

"Sorry, Mom."

"You want to take this seriously," Stickley said.

"Are you going to arrest my daughter?"

"Not today."

"Then please leave, or I'll call my lawyer and ask them to register a complaint with your superiors about harassment."

He smiled at the threat. "I admire the work you did in *Central Station*, Ms. Bonner, and I loved *Lost in the Whirlwind*. I thought you should have won the Oscar for that one." He touched his hat brim in salute. To me he said, "I'll see you soon." He went back to his car and drove away.

I poured coffee for us in the kitchen, and we carried it out to the backyard and sat at a round glass-topped table under the vine-covered arbor that shaded the patio. Mom looked at me with serious eyes. "Is this real trouble?"

"No."

"You didn't . . . ?"

"He's fishing. I'm a felon, convicted of bank robbery. Cops love felons. The mud sticks easily. They could clear some cases if they could pin them on me."

"Marty Collier is the best entertainment lawyer in town, not exactly what you need, but he knows all the other good lawyers."

"We're nowhere near that, Mom, but thanks."

"You're sure? You don't want me to talk to someone?"

"I'm sure. He'll dig around for a while. He won't find anything. He'll go look someplace else."

"You wouldn't let me help last time either."

"There was nothing to do." She had wanted to hire a big-time criminal lawyer when I was arrested, but I went with a public defender. I pleaded guilty to make the trial go fast. Why? I was tired of who I was.

And I knew if I didn't stop doing what I was doing, it would end badly. I didn't really know how to stop it, but the law did.

She took in a deep breath and let it out. "All right." But her face showed her concern. "I have to go. I hate being late for call. It's such diva shit." She kissed me on the cheek, gave me a hard hug, and left.

The cop had scared me. The dates and banks were right. The robberies were mine. His talk of computer programs sounded real. I could take what money I had and run for it. I could get lost someplace where no one knew me until the statute of limitations on the robberies ran out.

If Steckley was close to nailing me, why come warn me? Maybe he wanted me to run. If he'd had enough evidence for an arrest warrant, he would have taken me today. An arrest warrant had to be issued by the DA's office, and the DA would do that only if they had enough evidence to go to trial. I guessed Steckley didn't have enough for that yet, but if I ran, he could say it was evidence of guilt. A friendly judge might give him a Ramey warrant. A Ramey didn't require the same burden of evidence as an arrest warrant. With it, he could bypass the DA's office. A Ramey would put the statute of limitations on hold until I could be brought in for questioning, even if it took years.

It was one of the things I'd learned working in the prison library for five years. The library was my university. The librarian, Betty Lobel, was a sparrow of a woman with iron-gray hair and an iron will who'd slit her husband's throat one hot summer night when she could no longer stand what he did to her. She decided I was smart and uneducated. She called that a stupid waste. She said I was an empty vessel and she was going to fill me up. She approached the project with the same fierceness Ginger brought to teaching me how to fight. She beat knowledge into me until something cracked open inside and I needed to learn like I had needed drugs. I couldn't get enough.

I don't know how they got to me, what they touched in me, but those two women taught me more in prison than I ever learned on the outside.

How close was Steckley to knowing for sure that the robber on the security tapes was me? How much time did I have?

If I ran, I'd never know what happened to Julie.

Chapter Twelve

❧

The Santa Ana had blown itself out. The onshore breeze pushed the smog back to Pasadena. From the Mitchell, Collier, & Brown reception area on a high floor in a glass tower in Century City, I could see the Hollywood hills in one direction and the ocean in another.

An elegant young woman behind the reception desk offered me a cool smile, took my name and breathed it to someone on the intercom. She showed no signs of recognition, so she must have come to work after Julie died. I refused her offer of water, coffee, or tea and took a seat near one of the big windows until an older and more elegant woman came out and said, "Cody, I'm Carla French, Martin Collier's assistant. Come on, I'll take you back." As we walked down the hall of offices, she looked over her shoulder and said, "I'm so sorry about Julie. She was a wonderful young woman. We miss her."

"Thank you."

She smiled and opened the door at the end of the hall. I went in.

The office was designed to impress. The sofa and four chairs were dark-honey leather, and the coffee table in front of them was a polished oval of dark-green stone shot with lighter veins. Subtle spotlights shone on paintings I recognized—thanks to Mom's creepy artist husband—as two Picassos, a Matisse view of Provence, and an Ed Ruscha of a Texaco gas station.

The man behind the desk said, "Hold my calls, please, Carla." As she left, he pushed a button on the desk, and the heavy door closed behind her with a muted thump. He came around the desk with his hand out. "Cody, I'm Marty Collier." He was broad and thick. His blond hair was beginning to recede. He had a wide, pleasant face, and there was some-thing about his mouth, maybe a lip that had been fixed. It pulled his mouth slightly off center. His eyes were pale blue, cool, and watchful.

He shook my hand and then held it while he looked at me. "I don't believe it. She said you looked alike, but what the hell? If I hadn't known you were coming, I would have thought I was seeing a ghost. I just wish, we all wish, that it hadn't happened, that she was here with us. Let's sit." He waited for me to choose a chair before taking the one opposite, an old-fashioned courtesy. "She talked about you all the time."

"Why not? What better in a law firm than to talk about the felon sister?"

He laughed. "That's one of the things I miss—her humor, always with a little edge to it. She was so bright and smart."

"Yes, she was."

"And tough. She always seemed to know what she needed to do, and she did it, but do you know what she said? She said you were the smart one, the tough one."

"Yeah, well, like you said, she had a sense of humor."

"Okay. What are you going to do now that you're back with us?"

"I'm going to find out who killed my sister."

"How are you going to do that?" He accepted it without comment.

"I don't know exactly. Talk to people she knew. Try to figure out what she did the day she disappeared, where she went, what happened during those couple of days. Talk to the guy she was seeing."

"Tony Riordan. She mentioned him a couple of times."

"Serious?"

"She never talked much about what she did outside the office. And I didn't ask. The police have been over all this. We pushed them hard on it, but they never came up with a solid lead. Do you think you can do better?"

"I knew her. They didn't."

"What if it was random, nobody she knew, no connection?"

"You mean she comes out of Starbucks with a cappuccino. There are a couple of guys in a van at the corner. It's one of the things LA is famous for. I don't see her going that way. You know what the girls used to say in high school? Don't get in the fuck truck."

His laugh was a bark of surprise. "Anything you want from us, let me know."

"What was she working on?"

"Nothing earth shaking. Mostly we deal in the mundane business of contracts, deal structuring, film finance, live performance, sale of literary properties. We'll draw you up a will if you need one. Anything you want except criminal law, and we can refer for that. Speaking of wills, we could go over it right now."

"Over what?"

"Her will. Julie left everything to you. Didn't your mother tell you?"

"No." Mom didn't talk about things that made her uncomfortable: death, wills, bad reviews.

"The townhouse, some investments, bank accounts, life insurance policy. The townhouse is paid for. Your mother bought it for her when Julie came to work here." He went to his desk and brought back a file. I signed papers, and ten minutes later I owned everything Julie had owned. "We'll file the things that need to be filed. You can access the bank accounts today. You'll have to go in, give them the papers, and sign signature cards. There's a vice president at the Wells Fargo branch Julie used named Bob Mitchell. Let me know when you're going in, and I'll give him a heads-up." He slid the papers back into the file and passed it to me. "We were going to lose her. One way or another, she wasn't going to stay with us."

"Why not?"

"We were too . . ." He hesitated. "I was going to say *boring*, but that's not quite right. We try to run a lean operation here. We don't take on a lot of people, and we ask a lot of the ones we do take on. Julie asked about pro bono work. We think that the young lawyers have more than enough work within the firm. We do ask that our people do fifty hours of pro bono work per year, but Julie wanted more than that. She believed, rightly, that the law favors people with money and resources. It's a reality she disliked. She wanted to do more for people without money and resources. I think she would have eventually left us for a firm that was more interested in leveling that playing field, maybe even the public defender's office. In the meantime, I had a feeling that she was doing some sort of pro bono work outside the office."

"Do you know what it was?"

"No. If I asked her about it, I'd have to deal with it. As long as she was doing good work for us, I turned a blind eye. I wanted to keep her happy, because I wanted to keep her here as long as I could."

"I'd like to talk to whoever Julie was working with in the firm. Maybe they'd know. Would that be all right?"

"Sure. I'll set it up."

"Can I do it today?"

"I could make the calls and see what he's up to." He saw my puzzled look. "Julie was shadowing a junior partner, doing whatever he needed done, watching how he went about the business, getting a feel for what we do. We try to link all our young hires to someone who's been around for a while. She got Curtis Whyle."

"Wile E. Coyote? You're kidding."

"What?"

"That's what we used to call him, from the Road Runner cartoons. He was in school with us, preschool all the way through high school. Always a few grades above. Can I talk to him?"

"He doesn't work here anymore. He left pretty soon after Julie died."

"Because . . . ?"

"No, no. Nothing to do with that. Though who knows? Maybe it was a catalyst. Curtis is very ambitious. He was on the fast track here. He was bright as hell and great with clients, but some of the senior partners thought he moved a little too fast, maybe cut a corner of two. We assigned Julie to him because she knew him, and we thought she might get him to tap his brakes every once in a while. I think he found the law as we practice it too confining. He didn't hide that he wanted, at some point, to run a studio. I think he was attracted to the less settled aspects of the movie industry, the high-risk/high-reward part of it. He went to a production company based at Fox called Black Light Films. A bunch of young guys his age. You've been around the Industry all your life. You know what it's like—a gold rush business. You can be living in your car one day, and a year later you're on top of the world. Black Light's one of those. They started with a little Sundance winner. They've got two films out that are big hits, five more in development, and one shooting now. Actually, it's the film your mother's doing, *Injunction*."

"And Curtis is doing their legal work?"

"No. He's chairman. Runs the thing."

"Really?"

Collier nodded in admiration. "Wile E. Coyote."

A discreet knock on the door. Carla to remind him that his lunch appointment was in fifteen minutes. As she walked me to the elevator, she asked if the Sheriff's Department had returned Julie's laptop. "We'd like to clear any work files off it."

"Sure. I'll ask my mother if she has it." I wanted to see what was on that computer before anyone else did.

I thought about Curtis Whyle as I went down in the elevator. He had been one of the few really poor kids in a school of rich kids. I never heard who his father was or what happened to him, but he wasn't around. His mother went back and forth between working checkout at grocery stores or with nighttime office cleaning crews and unemployment. Nobody knew where Curtis lived. No one was ever invited to his home.

He was one of those kids who always knew the angles before the rest of us understood there were angles. In grade school he could get you the weird shoelaces everyone wanted but nobody could find. Later he could get you the primo dope, the answers to the math exam, the back-stage pass at the concert. The teachers loved him because he was polite, enthusiastic, cheerful, prepared. Even people who didn't trust him liked him. He was the cool guy—Wile E. Coyote—voted most likely to run a studio, or most likely to go to jail.

I beat him to that one.

Chapter Thirteen

～

The pawnshop was in Inglewood off South Vermont. The block held a liquor store, a sheet metal workshop, a nail salon, a taqueria, and a tire recapper. All the businesses were in one- or two-story cinder block buildings with heavy metal grates on their windows and doors. The walls were painted with overlapping layers of graffiti. Three ragged men sat on a bench near the door to the pawnshop. One was Black, one was Asian, one was white. They shared something from a bottle in a brown paper bag, a democracy of poverty. The one holding the bag was a whip-thin Black man with a white beard and a twist of a smile. His hand holding the bag was missing the last two fingers. "Nice car," he said, when I got out of Julie's BMW carrying her computer. "Don't see many of them in the neighborhood, 'less it's headed for the chop shop." He grinned.

"If it's still a nice car when I come out, I'll give you ten bucks."

"BMW ought to be worth twenty."

"It's five years old."

"Still, a BMW."

"Okay, twenty." He stuck a hand up, and I slapped it as I went by to seal the deal. "Hey," he called after me. "Whatever you're pawning, don't let that fucker stiff you. He's cheaper than charity."

Inside the shop, fluorescent bulbs glared a harsh white on the locked glass cabinets holding guitars, horns, cameras of different vintages, power tools, ceramic statuettes, watches, jewelry, whatever valuable you could pawn to get you past the looming debt. Two motorized wheelchairs were parked against a wall under a shelf of amplifiers. How deep in the hole do you have to be to give up your wheelchair?

Near the back of the room, a wall of bulletproof glass rose from a cabinet that held a display of guns: a few hunting shotguns, a rifle, and an array of handguns laid out seductively on dark-blue velvet. There were sliding panels in the bulletproof wall for transactions. A tall, thin Black man with hennaed hair done in cornrows stood behind one of them and watched me. He wore a blue one-piece jumpsuit with lots of pockets closed by brass zippers and a heavy gold watch that looked too big for his narrow wrist. He sized me up as I approached the window.

"What you got there, a computer? Look around. You think anyone needs another old computer? Shit."

"I want to talk to Mae."

"Mae? Who the fuck's Mae? What you doing down here? BMW, them clothes. This ain't your neighborhood."

"Tell her Cody wants to talk to her."

"Tell who? I told you, ain't no Mae here."

"Tell her anyway."

"That's an old computer. I could maybe let you have twenty bucks. What you going to do with twenty bucks? Won't even fill that Beemer's tank."

A door opened behind him, and Mae Dasilva came out. She was a large woman in a blue-and-green muumuu. She had a broad, calm face the color of mahogany and dark eyes that had seen more than most people could stand. Gold wire-rimmed glasses were pushed up into her straight brown hair. "Give it a rest, Jerome." Her voice had a soft lilt of the Caribbean. To me, "They let you out."

"Yes."

"Come on back." She pushed a button. The heavy door in the glass wall popped open a couple of inches. I pushed it farther and went in. Jerome reached over and closed it behind me. Mae gave me a hug, and I followed her into the back room. It was a windowless cube crowded with computer equipment, none of it for sale. Even with a big cooling stack vented out through the roof, the room was overheated from the electronics running. Mae took a seat in a chair facing a bank of monitors.

"You're back at it."

"What else am I going to do?" she asked.

Mae had gone to prison for a hack that had looted a retail company of $6 million. According to Mae, her partners had gotten away with most of it. If that bothered her, she never showed it. It was the computer stuff, not the money, that interested her. "What've you got?"

I slipped Julie's computer onto the desk in front of her. "I can't get into it. It's password protected. It's my sister's."

"The dead one?"

"Yes. On the last try it gave me a warning there was only one try left before lockdown."

"What are you looking for?"

"Whatever's in there: Facebook account, Instagram, emails, whatever."

"What about her phone?"

"Her phone's probably in a landfill somewhere, or in the ocean. Whoever took her wouldn't hold on to that."

"Uh-huh," Mae said. "Be a couple of days, depending. If the encryption's good, it might take more. I'm on a project right now I got to finish first."

"Okay."

"Pinky ever get what he wanted from you?"

"He tried again the last day at dress-out. It didn't work out the way he hoped." I told Mae what had happened.

"Well, that's that. Fuck him."

"He had a couple of friends try me at the bus station. They had a room in the basement with a cot."

"Did you hurt them?"

"Yes."

"When are men going to stop messing with the sisters? The day after never, I guess."

"They're not all like that."

"Maybe in your world, honey."

"So who's Jerome?"

"A bad habit."

The door opened, and he slouched in on loose limbs and rubber joints.

"How much do you want, Mae?" I asked.

"A couple hundred."

I pulled out cash and peeled off bills onto Mae's desk. "My phone." I wrote it on a scrap of paper, and she put it in her pocket.

"A couple hundred?" Jerome was outraged. "Shit, woman, I keep telling you, let me do the business. You got no head for it. This bitch has got all the cheese in the world, a Beemer, a pocketful of cheddar. That ain't no insult. Nothing wrong with being rich. Goddamn it, I could use some of that."

Mae waited until he ran down. "Go watch the store, Jerome."

His face tightened in anger for a moment, then he turned and went out the door.

"I'll call when it's done," Mae said.

"Thanks."

"Cody, what are you going to do now?"

"I'm going to find out what happened to my sister."

"Uh-huh. Got some money?"

"Some."

"You're lucky. You're not like most who get out, got no money, looking for a job, trying to explain to some boss that your felony's behind you, that it ain't going to be a problem."

"I know."

"Don't waste it. Don't fuck it up."

"I won't."

Chapter Fourteen

The guard at the Pico gate to the Twenty-First Century studio lot gave me my pass and told me where to park. I left the car and walked down New York Street. It was a couple of blocks of brownstones, a diner, a subway station, all fakes. There was nothing behind the false fronts but empty space. A row of palm trees sprouted past the last of the New York tenements, a reminder of how much of LA was illusion.

Black Light Films was on the third floor of a beige stucco building. Curtis Whyle's office was at the end of a corridor lined with framed posters from movies going back to the thirties. The door to Curtis's office was open. He saw me from his desk and waved me in past his secretary, then went back to blasting someone on the phone.

"Seven million dollars??!! Seven million??!! Are you out of your mind? This part is going to make his career. He's going to go from a pretty face with muscles to someone who can really act. Five million, and not a penny more. Five. Five. Five!" He slammed the phone down and grinned at me. "Goddamn agents. I hate them. Bart Givens. Do you know him? He was in *Live Hard, Die Fast*."

"No."

"Not many movies in the joint, hey?"

"Not many."

"I can't believe I'm begging that squinty-eyed redneck to take five million dollars for a part that's going to make him a star." He got up and came out from behind the desk. "Luckiest dick in the world. By all rights he should be back in Oklahoma pumping gas." Curtis was tall and athletic and had one of those angular faces that missed being pretty by an angle or two. He wore faded blue jeans and an old blue-and-white-striped shirt, running shoes with no socks. Time had been good to him. He was better looking now than when he was in school. He had always been one of those kids who was full of confidence, who talked to the teachers in school as if he were their equal when most of the others in the class were tongue-tied in front of adults, who led rather than followed, went eagerly where others were scared to go. Something had changed about him, or maybe he'd just become more of who he was. A force came off him, heat, or electricity, or maybe it was sex. I didn't know what it was, but it sure as hell was something.

He hugged me and said, "I miss her. I really miss her. What the fuck happened? I still can't believe it." He let me go and stepped back. "Jesus, you look great. If that's what prison does for you, I'm going to go for a couple of years. Let's get out of here. Marcie," he called to his assistant. "What are they shooting on fifteen?"

"The argument," Marcie said. "Axel and Connie kicking each other in the balls."

"Come on, let's go take a look at your mother. A great scene."

I was sucked along by his energy, as I had been when I was sixteen. Not for long. After a while, I hadn't wanted to keep up. He wanted more than I wanted to give. Not sex. The sex was great, teenage gasping excitement, fumbling, exploration, discovery, somewhere between fear and wonder. I didn't know what it was that scared me, but I sensed that it would burn me up. I ran away from it. He wasn't used to people saying no to him, and I thought at the time that he didn't forgive me. Maybe he did and I just didn't know what forgiveness looked like.

* * *

"Don't. Don't touch me. Don't even think about it." My mother, with a clenched jaw and angry eyes. No, not my mother, not Karen Bonner, but Connie French, *Injunction*'s female star role. It was a matter of posture, set of the mouth and jaw, hand movements, eyes, accent, walk, small changes that allowed her to disappear into a part. When I first saw her on a set when I was five, I burst into tears because I did not recognize her.

This set was an expensively furnished living room of a New York City Upper East Side apartment building. I stood with Curtis in the darkness behind the camera looking out at the brightly lit action in sound stage fifteen.

"I'll do what I want, and you'll take it." Jake Gyllenhaal played her young husband, the gold digger with a girl on the side. It was an old story that had been told many times, but Hollywood believed in old wine in new bottles.

"If you hit me again, I'll kill you," she said.

"It might be a relief."

She picked up a letter opener from a desk near the window and advanced on her husband. Axel laughed at the threat and told her to stop being ridiculous. Later in the story Connie would stab Axel in his cheating heart, leading to her trial for murder, the rallying of other abused women, and who knows, perhaps her acquittal. Hollywood loved to jump a trend if there was money to be made.

"Cut."

The lights came up to reveal the army behind the camera who made the film happen. The director got up from his seat behind the video monitor and went onto the set to talk to his actors as wardrobe, hair, and makeup people hurried out to touch up the stars. The lighting crew began to tweak their lights and filters under the lash of the director of photography.

The director came off the set and paused to say something to the first assistant director, a ponytailed stud in blue jeans and a jacket from one of the Star Wars movies.

"Back to one, everybody," the AD called. "We're going again. One more, and then break for lunch."

The director came toward me, grinning. "Cody, Cody, Cody Bonner. How great to see you." Brandon Tower, another schoolmate and, according to my mother, the new hot director on everyone's A-list. Curtis had been the angle player at school. Brandon was the guy who got things done—class president, leader, football captain. He liked to command. His father, Simon Tower, was a successful TV executive who had run a network before starting his own production company, which made

Brandon a Hollywood prince. Brandon was a big man. He had curly blond hair and an open, pink-cheeked face that made people trust him. His blue eyes sparkled with good humor, but I had seen them go cold when things didn't go his way. He kissed me on the cheek and patted my shoulder. "I'm glad you're here. We're going to do one more take and then lunch. Will you stick around?"

"Sure."

He said, "I'll see you at the commissary," to Curtis, and turned back toward the monitor. He nodded to the AD, who yelled, "Places, people. Places. Let's get this done."

Curtis touched me on the arm and jerked his head toward the door. "Let's go." I waved at my mother, who waved back distractedly and went back to talking to her costar. There was no point trying to speak to her. On set she lived in her character and resented any intrusion that might bring her out of it. Julie and I had learned that lesson early.

It was a five-minute walk to the commissary past other sound stages and office buildings, past aliens with their heads tucked under their arms, soldiers carrying fake guns, beautiful young women in evening dresses, stiletto heels, and fake jewelry, bicycle messengers, harried mid-level executives worried about budget overruns, extras in costume for crowd scenes, and occasionally, recognizable stars walking with their assistants and secretaries and others drawn into their orbit by star power. People called to Curtis as they passed, and a couple of executives stopped to talk to him in low voices that emphasized the importance of what they had to say.

A commissary hostess greeted Curtis with a smile and led us to a private room with a table set for eight.

"Who's coming?"

"You never know."

Not Mom. She would have salad and vitamin water in her trailer and go over her lines.

Curtis took a seat in the middle of the table and patted the chair beside him. "Drink?" He raised a hand, and a waitress jumped.

"A Bombay martini, up with a twist, a glass with some ice on the side."

"Alison, make it two."

"Yes, Mr. Whyle." She was a good-looking young woman in a short khaki skirt and a pink button-down shirt. She smiled at Curtis as if he had just offered her the keys to the kingdom and went away fast, a woman with a mission. Hollywood was full of stories of actors and actresses being discovered at a car wash or waiting on tables.

"Do you talk about prison?"

"What do you want to know?"

"Was there sex?"

"Jesus, you haven't changed."

"Come on, come on. Give. I need to know in case I ever end up there. If I remember right, you were the one who said jail was in my future."

"You were being an asshole."

"I was being a teenage boy."

"What's changed?"

"Not much. That's the best part about it. You get out into the world and you discover it's still high school out here. All those mind games people used to play, the jealousies, the smiling knife in the back, all that petty personal shit: Who's on top? Who's moving up? Who's headed down? Who are the cool guys? It still goes on. And your whole deal can turn on one decision, one moment. That's why I love it."

"And you're riding high."

"I am a rocket to the moon."

The waitress brought the drinks, and Brandon banged through the door as she was putting them down. "We're drinking? Well, why not? We're only a week behind and half a million bucks over. Angie, bring me a Manhattan, no cherry."

"Alison," Curtis corrected. "Bring him a bottle of Perrier."

It pissed Brandon off, but he smiled it away. "Right. Someone has to do the work. A bottle of Perrier and a cut-up lime. Thanks." He flicked a *Fuck you* look at Curtis. "Angie."

High school. No one gets away with anything.

It got more so when Terry Gwinn and Mark Siegel barged through the door arguing about a woman one of them had dated, or tried to date, or didn't want to date. It was hard to sort out.

When they saw me, they stopped in shock. "Holy shit!" Mark said. They both stared at me, and finally it penetrated. "Cody?"

"Who else?" I asked. Their reaction was one I was getting used to.

"A fucking ghost, man," Terry said.

Mark threw a look at Curtis. "Dude, you might have told us."

"No spoilers." Curtis's grin showed an edge of mockery.

At school Gwinn and Siegel were known as the Gwingel twins. They both came from vast wealth and inattentive parents who gave them money in place of attention and love. The story at school was Terry Gwinn's grandfather had bought Berkshire Hathaway stock in 1968 while tripping on acid. He never sold it. When he died in the mid-1990s, the stock was worth north of $270 million. His son, Terry Gwinn's father, sold it immediately, quit his job as an insurance adjuster, shed Terry's mother, his wife of fifteen years, bought a yacht, and married a twenty-two-year-old blonde he'd met at his Pilates class.

Another LA story.

He and his new wife died in a plane crash, leaving $183 million to eighteen-year-old Terry.

Mark Siegel's father had built a scholarship at Caltech into eleven software patents that were essential to personal computers and cell phones. He settled a $90 million trust fund on Mark and moved with his boyfriend to an island off Tahiti.

The Gwingel twins were always together. They could have been brothers. They were both stocky, dark haired, and boyish. They were surfers and gym rats, with tight, muscular bodies and nervous energy that kept them bouncing even when they sat down. They reminded me of baby sharks, always swimming forward, looking for something to chew with their sharp little teeth.

"Cody Bonner," Terry said, as if announcing an award winner. "Cody Bonner. Looking good."

"Looking great," Mark Siegel echoed. "Looking really great. Jailbird. Like six fucking years, man."

We used to say that the Gwingels didn't know what to say to girls except *Let me buy that for you.* A pretty good icebreaker in our high school circles.

When they sat down, Mark picked up a roll and threw it across the table at Brandon, who let it bounce off his chest and kept on talking to Curtis. "I can get two pages this afternoon. We can shoot the exteriors of the courthouse tomorrow and do Connie's entrance and her lawyer's stuff to the press outside. If we combine sixty-two and sixty-five, I can shoot them on Thursday, which means we'll pick up two days this week, and by the end of next week we'll only be a day over."

"Yeah, goddamn it," Terry said. "Stop wasting our money or we'll go out and get a competent director who knows what he's doing."

It dawned on me. "You guys are financing Black Light."

"Hell yes," Mark said. "Who else would be stupid enough to give these guys money? Did you see *Slide Area*? It won at Sundance and did a hundred five million domestic gross on a six-million budget, and we plowed profits back into the company."

"I missed it."

"Oh shit. Yeah. You were locked up." Terry was the one who always pushed things too far. "Hey, how about the sex in there? Is it true what they say? Did you have your own bitch?"

"Chill," Curtis said. He checked to see if Terry was getting to me.

"Why? The Bonner girls were always one of the guys. Did you?"

"No bitch for me, Terry," I said. "Because you weren't there."

The others whooped with laughter. Terry flushed, then joined in to save face.

It was like that for the rest of the meal. They cut each other up, called each other dick and asshole and pussy.

Mark's eyes pinned Alison every time she came in the room. When she put his salad down in front of him, he touched her hand lightly. "Hey, Alison," he said. "When are we going on that date we've talked about?"

"You've talked about," she said, and straightened up.

"Okay, so when?"

"When you grow up."

"You'll be an old lady and I won't care anymore."

"Safe at last," she said, and left to the appreciative whoops of laughter from the boys' club. Mark gave her the finger behind her back.

Nothing new, except there was a sharper edge to how they treated each other.

"Curtis and Julie worked together, but did the rest of you guys see much of her?" I asked.

"She'd come by the office with papers to sign and stuff like that," Brandon said. The Gwingels murmured assent.

"I mean out of the office."

"She was going out with someone," Curtis said. "I think his name was Riordan."

"Did anyone meet him?"

None of them had.

"The week when she disappeared, did anyone see her?"

"In the office," Curtis said. "That last day, she and I had a meeting at Warners. She left a little early, as I remember."

"Do you know why? Do you know where she was going?"

"No. She said she had something to do, but she didn't say what." Brandon and the Gwingels watched us back and forth like a tennis match.

"That was the last you saw of her?"

"Yes."

"Did she drive to work?"

"Most days. Why?"

"Her car was found at her place. She must have gone back there before she went out."

"A lot of people use Uber or Lyft now, especially if they're going out to the clubs or something. No one wants a DUI."

"Even if you're just going out for dinner. If you're going to have a couple of glasses of wine, it's better to take one of the ride services," Brandon said. "I take Lyft to the studio probably three days a week just to avoid the hassle."

"Did she go out to the clubs a lot?"

"You should probably ask Riordan about that," Curtis said.

"How do I find him?"

"She said he was an editor. Mostly in TV. You could call the union."

"None of you ever saw her outside the office? You all used to be friends."

"In school," Terry said. "And she was going out with that guy. Things change."

"Okay. I get it. Did she keep a calendar at the office?"

"Her assistant did," Curtis said. "The cops made a copy. There was nothing on it for the day she disappeared except for the meeting at Warners in the morning. Did you ever get her laptop back from the cops? Maybe she kept a calendar on it."

"It's encrypted."

"Did you try to get into it?" Mark asked.

"That's how I learned it was encrypted."

"Sure. Right. Duh."

Brandon said, "I wish we could help more. I'm sorry." He checked his watch. "I've got to get back. If I think of anything, I'll call you."

I punched all their numbers into my phone.

Curtis pushed back his chair. "I've got a meeting in half an hour. Cody, are you ready?"

"Yes."

I walked out with Curtis. A wind had come up, and it blew cotton clouds across the sky. "How can you stand them? Brandon's okay, but the Gwingels, Jesus."

"You make them nervous. You always did. You and Julie. Too smart, too good looking, too tough. They always knew you and Julie thought they were assholes."

"They are assholes. Would you be working with them if they didn't have the money?"

"No, but they do have the money, and in this business money counts. Everyone in the film business runs scared. Every year a movie that looked like a sure hit goes belly-up and no one knows why; the star you were counting on gets arrested; the director dies; the financing falls through; the studio executive in charge of your movie gets fired. The solid ground you were standing on shifts. Mark and Terry have enough money to hedge against disaster. Because of them, Black Light can take a hit and keep going."

"They're still assholes."

"Sure. But they're my assholes."

He walked me to my car.

"Curtis, did Julie talk to you about the pro bono work she was doing outside the office?"

"Not much. A little bit."

"What was it? What was she doing?"

"Keeping streetwalkers on the street." He laughed.

"What?"

"Santa Monica decided there were too many hookers on the streets. Some uptight city father got propositioned and lit a fire under the cops. Julie was representing women who were picked up in the sweeps. She was working with some organization that deals with sex workers, uh, wait a minute, uh, *swap*, something like that."

"Swap?"

"Yeah, Sex Workers of America or something. Google will tell you. Julie always had a cause. All the way back in grade school it was Save the Whales, Save the Bay, save the planet."

"Hey."

"I'm not ranking her. I admired her. Against all evidence she thought she could make the world a better place. And she could get people to do things with just a smile and a couple of words. You're the one who called her Crusader Rabbit."

"Yeah, well, I didn't have a clue." I unlocked the BMW and got in.

Curtis held the door open. "Do you want to have dinner sometime?"

"Sure." Why did my heart speed up?

"I can't tonight, but I'll call you?"

"Yes."

I got in the car and watched him walk away. Come on, Cody, really? I don't know. I don't know.

* * *

The Sex Workers Outreach Project was in a small second-floor office on Wilshire Boulevard. The woman behind the desk looked up when I came in and said, "Jesus Christ."

"I know. I know."

"But you're not her, right? I mean, she's dead, right? I read about it."

"Right."

"Twin."

"Yeah. Cody Bonner."

"Aw, sweetie, I'm sorry. She was the real deal. I really liked her." She came around the desk and gave me a hug. "I'm Angelica." She was a great big sunny woman, over six feet tall. She wore a fire-engine-red wig that fell below her shoulders. Her lipstick was the same color. So were the heart-shaped frames of her glasses. Her tight sleeveless black shirt showed off arms tattooed from wrists to shoulders.

"You want a cup of coffee?"

"Sure."

She went to work a single-service coffeemaker on a table near the window.

"What did she do for you?" I asked.

"Simple legal work. Someone in city government had one of those spasms of morality. You know, get the girls off the streets so the citizens won't be offended. As if. I mean, who do they think our clients are, men from Mars? Anyway, the cops were sweeping for hookers. So, first arrest is usually no big deal, a misdemeanor, but if they're feeling nasty, it can mean jail and a fine of up to a thousand bucks. Second offense is a mandatory minimum of forty-five days in a county jail. After that, it's a mandatory ninety days in jail. Nobody needs that shit. So Julie'd go down to the cop shop and deal. She really cared about the girls. And she was good with the cops. She looked great. She had this, I don't know what—warmth. People liked her. And she had balls." She held up a container of creamer.

"Black, please." I went over and took the coffee cup from her.

"She didn't last that long. Two months. She came in one day and said she'd found something else to do that had more impact."

"Did she say what?"

"She just said she found something that really pissed her off."

"I said, 'Good on you, honey,' and, 'Thanks for what you did here,' but I was running out. I had a date. And that's the last time I saw her. I wish I'd asked what she'd found, but . . ." She shrugged. "I'm sorry."

Chapter Fifteen

The weather changed. The days got cooler. A slate sky threatened. Rain spattered the windshield as I pulled into a parking space in Venice just off Pacific Avenue. Heavy drops chased me toward the building. As I went in under the arcade, thunder crashed, and the rain stopped as if all the energy had been used up in noise.

Venice Studios was at the back of the building. The walls of the reception area held posters from movies and TV shows I'd never heard of. The receptionist was a thin Asian girl with spiked blonde hair and chrome piercings in her face. She was deep into something on her computer screen.

"Is Tony Riordan here?" I asked.

"In the editing bay." She didn't look up.

"I'd like to see him."

She clicked her computer keyboard. "You with the film?"

"No."

"Nobody goes back there unless they're with the film." She looked up. "Oh shit, it's you. I haven't seen you in a while—no surprise. I guess you can go back, though I don't know why the hell you'd want to." She pushed a button, and the door behind her clicked open. "They're in C. You know the way. You going to fuck him over again?"

Why tell her I wasn't Julie?

Editing bay C was a soundproof room with a big window on the hall. Two men were working at an Avid editing setup, a large monitor stacked over smaller monitors, a keyboard, and two elaborate editing racks. One was a rumpled sixty-year-old man with no hair and a paunch. Not Julie's type, so Tony Riordan was the guy manipulating the equipment. Julie had a thing for surfer dudes, and Riordan looked the part—shaggy blond hair, athletic, tanned, dressed in faded jeans and a Hawaiian shirt.

One of the smaller monitors was cut up into eight small screens, each showing a different angle on a city street. A car drove down the eight streets and slammed to a stop, and a man got out and hurried into a building. Sometimes the point of view was from inside the car. Sometimes it was from an angle on the sidewalk, a close-up, or a medium shot. One was an overhead from a helicopter. Riordan worked the keyboard to bring an angle up on the large monitor. The rumpled man, who was probably the director of the show, would study it, ask a question or two, and shake his head, and Riordan would put up another angle. Eventually they decided on one that would go into the finished film. I'd found him by calling the union and telling them I had a job for him but I needed a yes or no answer immediately.

Riordan stood and reached across the desk to turn off one of the racks. I knocked on the window. He looked at me, stumbled, grabbed for a handhold, missed it, lurched backward, and fell over his chair.

"I'm sorry," I said. We were out on the Venice Boardwalk now, the concrete path that ran along the top of the beach. The clouds had broken, and blue sky showed between bands of gray, but it wasn't beach weather and there were only a few people out.

"It's okay. Nothing broken."

"I should have called first."

"Yeah, maybe. That way I wouldn't have had a heart attack. I have fantasies that it was all some sort of weird fuckup and that I would look up one day and there she'd be. And there she was, except it was you. It blew me up." His smile was painful. "I really loved your sister."

We took a table behind the window of a coffee shop that looked out on the beach. A man skated the beach path on Rollerblades. His body gleamed with oil. He wore only a tiny bikini and a backpack. He played an electric guitar as he skated. There must have been an amplifier of some sort in his backpack, because the heavy beat came through the window like a pulse. He noticed us, did a 360 turn for our benefit, and continued on his way.

The waitress brought our coffee.

"I met her surfing," Riordan said. "It was pretty soon after I moved up from San Diego. I was out at Topanga, and some of the locals were being territorial. A couple of guys cut me off, and we were talking it over on the beach after the third time. Julie knew them and in this kind of nice, chill, friendly way told them to fuck off and leave me alone. I begged her to have dinner with me. We ended up talking till they threw us out of the restaurant."

"When was that?"

"Six, seven months before it happened."

"Did you see her the day she disappeared?"

"No. She dumped me before that. I thought we were doing great. We saw each other almost every day. We were talking about moving in together. Then one day she calls me up and says it's over."

"Out of the blue?"

"Yeah. No. I don't know. When I look back, I see there was some stuff going on. She was stressed more than usual. She'd get pissed off at little things. I asked her about it, but she said it was her job. You hear about people going into those big law firms and working twenty-hour days, so that seemed right. She missed a few dates. She'd call at the last minute and say she couldn't make it. Okay, that happens, right? But she wouldn't talk about it. I kept after her. That was probably a mistake. She told me to back off."

"Do you think she was seeing someone else?"

"I thought about it. I hated thinking about it, but I did. You can't help yourself." He shut his eyes for a moment. "We were going to have dinner one night. She canceled with some half-assed excuse. I went out and had a few drinks, maybe more than a few, and thought fuck it, I'm going to go over to her place and find out."

He waited for a reaction, but I said nothing.

"Being an asshole and half in the bag, I brought a pair of binoculars so I could get a close look at who she was ditching me for. I parked a couple of blocks away and found a place I could watch from. About half an hour later, she came out. You know how she dressed. Cool, not flashy. Not that night. She was wearing a really short dress made of some silver material. Barely covered her butt. Spike heels. Her hair was up in some fancy way, and she was wearing a lot of makeup."

It didn't sound like anything Julie would wear, and I hadn't seen anything like what he described in her closet.

"A car pulled up. I figured it would be a good idea to go over and cause a scene."

"Display your wounded pride. She'd take one look at and come to her senses, dump the other guy, and come back to you."

"Right." A twist of a smile at the way the heart works.

"You've been editing too many low-budget movies."

"Hey, I was drunk. How many good ideas have you had drunk?"

"Even more when I was high. So how'd it go, the scene?"

"Never happened. I checked through the binoculars. It wasn't some guy. It was an Uber chick."

"Disappointing."

"Yeah, well . . . I followed them. I figured I'd get my chance when she dropped her off. You ever tried to follow a car in LA? Drunk?"

"No."

"If you hang back a little so they won't see, you get guys cutting in front. You get caught at a light, 'cause the asshole in front of you is on his phone. I followed them up into the Brentwood hills but lost them, drove around a few blocks, and caught the Uber coming back the other way. I flagged her down, but she wouldn't tell me where she dropped her— company policy. I know the block but not the house."

"The next time you saw her, did you bust her?"

"No. I was embarrassed. I was trying to hang on with her. If she knew I was spying on her, she'd cut me loose."

"How long after that did she dump you?"

"A couple of weeks, I guess."

"Did she give you a reason?"

"She admitted she was seeing someone else."

"The guy from the Uber date?"

"I don't know. I wasn't even sure it was true. Like maybe she made it up to let me down easy."

He had an hour before he had to be back in the editing room. We drove up into the Brentwood hills above Sunset. The houses there were big and expensive, and the backyards held swimming pools and tennis courts. We wound around until we found the block where he thought the Uber driver had dropped Julie. We drove the block a couple of times, but the houses presented blank faces to the street and offered no clues to what went on behind their walls.

Tony drove me back to Venice and dropped me at my car.

"Thanks for your help."

"I wish I could do more."

We were awkward now. We didn't know each other, but Julie tied us together. I offered my hand, and he shook it. "Could we get together for a drink or something sometime? Or is that too weird?" he asked.

"I don't know. It might be. Let me think about it."

"You have my number."

"Yes." But I probably wouldn't call. No matter what I looked like, I couldn't be Julie for Tony Riordan.

* * *

The three ragged men sitting on the bench in front of the pawnshop in Inglewood watched the car pull to the curb. Whatever color it had been when new, they agreed as they passed the bottle, it was not that color anymore. Puke green, piss yellow, something ugly. They spotted the tall, thin driver in the cowboy boots as a cop. Cops were a part of life, like bad wine, cold rain, hunger, or cockroaches. They were always there and didn't signify one way or the other. This cop was so thin it looked like he was built of wood slats and wire hangers. Steckley touched the brim of his hat in salute to the drinkers and went into the pawn.

Jerome stood behind the bullet glass and watched the cop approach. No sweat. Nothing hot in the cases. Everything legit. As long as he didn't get in the back room.

"Help you, Officer?"

Steckley turned on his phone and held it where Jerome could see the screen and the photo of Cody Bonner Steckley had taken outside the Bonner house. "This woman was in here last week."

Jerome didn't deny it. The man had a way of looking at you that went to the bone. "Yeah. So?" Fuck knows how the cops knew stuff, but there was no point in lying unless it was really necessary.

"What was she doing here?"

"Had an old computer. I offered her twenty bucks. She didn't take it."

"Anybody with her?"

"No."

"Did she talk to anyone?"

"Talked to me."

"Anyone else?"

"Nobody else around." The cop studied him, but Jerome had been skating lies past cops since he was six. Practice made perfect.

"Did she talk to you about buying a gun?"

"No, sir. And I ain't sold a gun in two weeks. Got the inventory list goes back a while. They're all in the case here, if you want to check."

"Let me see it."

Jerome found the list in a drawer and slid it through the service slot in the glass. Steckley checked the list descriptions against the pistols in the case. They were all there, as far as he could see without running the serial numbers.

"Why'd she come in here?"

"I don't know. Driving by, got it in her mind to pawn the laptop. Came on in. How the hell would I know?"

Steckley put the phone in his pocket and left. Jerome watched him go. What'd the rich bitch do, bring a cop like that down on her? Got to be cheese for the taking there someplace. Might need some figuring.

Chapter Sixteen

～

"I don't want you moving over there," Mom said. "There is no reason to go to Julie's. This is your home."

"You'll be away on location for a week. You won't be here anyway."

"That's not the point."

"What is the point?"

"I know you're safe here. Everything you need is here. I'll feel better knowing you're here. I don't want you over there."

"Safe?"

"Yes."

"No one's safe anywhere."

"Why didn't you let me see you while you were there? I flew all that way and you wouldn't see me."

"Mom . . ."

"I was working. I took time off. They had to shoot around me that week, and they hate doing that. I was there for three days. I went to that awful place every day, and you never let me see you."

"I didn't want you to see me like that. I was trying to change. I was afraid if I saw you or Julie, I'd slip back to being who I had been."

"Oh, for Christ's sake, I'm your mother." That was always meant to be the end of any argument.

She pushed things around on her desk in agitation. "Where is my glasses case? I just had it here. Did you move it?"

"No."

"Well, don't just stand there. Help me find it."

"It's on the floor by your foot."

"Oh." She picked it up and slammed it on the desk to punish it. "I'm going to sell it."

"Mom, the place is mine. You can't sell it."

"I paid for it."

"You gave it to Julie. She left it to me. It's in my name."

"Get rid of it. We'll find you some other place."

"No."

"It's morbid. I won't let you do it."

An hour after she left, I moved into Julie's place—well, my place now, I guess. I moved because I needed Julie's presence. Maybe if I lived in her skin for a while, she would rise up to help me find who had killed her and why.

Weird thinking if you're not a twin.

I searched all Julie's closets and drawers, but I didn't find anything like the metallic silver dress Tony Riordan described.

*   *   *

An hour in the LA County Hall of Records downtown got me the names of the people who owned the four houses on the Brentwood street where Julie had been dropped by the Uber driver. Google told me more. They were owned by a cosmetic surgeon, a UCLA professor of medieval history, the owner of a chain of car dealerships, and something called Coldwater LLC, a limited liability company that sheltered the name of the house's owner. I wanted to know who hid behind the LLC.

I drove back up to the Brentwood. The four houses were on one side of the street. On the other side the land fell away steeply and was covered with brush and tall grass. All the houses had signs on their lawns or on their walls announcing the name of the security service that protected them: HawkEye Security—Armed Response. The street was quiet. Few cars passed. I parked where I could see the houses.

A few minutes before three thirty, a car pulled to the curb in front of the surgeon's house, and two middle school children, a boy and girl, got out and chased each other up the walk. The car left carrying three more children—a carpool. The boy opened the front door with a key. A housekeeper was waiting for them. Half an hour later, a Mercedes convertible pulled into the drive. A woman in gym clothes carried shopping bags from Neiman Marcus into the house. She used a key to get in. Cautious people. They kept the door locked even when they were home.

A white-and-gray sedan marked HAWKEYE SECURITY drove by. It had a light bar on the roof, and the two men in it wore gray uniforms. Rent-a-cops. The break-in artists in prison considered them pests, like mice in the kitchen, but they admitted you had to watch out for them. They were armed. "Don't fuck with them," a burglar named Cynda said to me. "They're wannabe cops, and they will shoot you if they can."

An older Volvo station wagon pulled into the UCLA professor's drive. A man and a woman got out. The man's hair was gray. He carried a worn leather briefcase and was dressed in khakis and a tweed jacket. His wife was a matronly woman in a denim skirt, cotton blouse, and sensible shoes. She got a grocery bag out of the back seat. The man made a gesture to take it from her. She slapped at his hand playfully, and through the open window I heard her say, "I can carry it and you too if I have to." He laughed, and they went up the path hand in hand and into the house. They were not people my sister would be visiting in a silver dress and spike heels.

A few minutes later, the man came out and crossed the lawn to the house owned by the car dealer. He checked the mailbox and removed a couple of envelopes, then went up to the front door and collected some brochures that had been thrown there. Burglars look for houses with uncollected mail or newspapers on the front lawn. They drive through neighborhoods and leave a couple of empty cans or other minor trash in front of the house and then come back the next day to see if it's still there. If it is, they go in. The professor opened the front door with a key. He left the door open while he went into the front hall to add the mail to a growing pile on a table there. He came out, shut the door, locked it, and went back to his house. No alarm there. Some owners are too cheap to pay for the service but they put the sign up anyway. Guys on the prowl look for the easiest score. An ARMED RESPONSE sign might be enough to turn them away.

The patrol would be back on its rounds. They'd notice a woman sitting in a car on this street for more than an hour. They'd remember me. Time to go. I started the car and let it roll down to the last house on the street, the one that belonged to the LLC. The other three houses were on big lots, but this house took up two lots and was much larger than the others. It was a modern design of stacked concrete boxes and expanses of glass. The ground-floor box ran straight back from the street. The second-floor box ran at right angles across the top of the ground floor. It was a rich man's house designed for maximum *curb appeal*, the LA realtor's term to describe a house's impact from the outside when you drove by it. Was this the house Julie visited?

I drove to a sporting goods store on Wilshire and bought a black lightweight jacket and a black baseball cap to cover my hair. I stopped at the Starbucks in Brentwood Village and sat outside on the patio with a cup of coffee and ate a power bar to raise my blood sugar.

By the time I got back up into the Brentwood hills, lights were on in the houses and the sky was deep purple in the west. I parked on one of the bigger streets where my car wouldn't be noticed among the other cars at the curb. I locked it and jogged back to the block and the four houses that interested me.

The patrol car passed me going the other way. The passenger turned to look at me as they went by. I waved. Just another resident back from work taking her evening run.

Lights shone from every window in the surgeon's house and from the ground-floor windows of the professor's house next door. There was one light on upstairs and one downstairs at the car dealer's. They were probably on a timer to make people think someone was home. The only light at the LLC was an automatic one over the front door. Whoever owned it wasn't home yet.

The driveways to the car dealer's house and the LLC's ran next to each other. A tall stucco wall separated them. A gate blocked the LLC's drive, and I couldn't see into the backyard. I walked back along the dealer's drive, hoping to find something to stand on to look over the wall. A wash of light flared along the stucco as a car turned into the street. I stepped back into the shadow of a doorway until it passed.

The HawkEye patrol car stopped at the curb across the street from the driveway. The driver's window was down, and I could hear the squawk of the radio. Had someone spotted me and called it in?

The driver got out of the car.

My dark clothes would hide me in the shadowed doorway, but I'd stand out if I went down the drive along the white stucco wall or the house.

I tried the door behind me, but it was locked.

The driver started to cross the street.

His partner said something, and the driver turned back to the car. When he leaned in the open window to talk, I went across the drive in two strides, up on the curb of the flower bed that ran along the wall, and jumped high enough to get my hands on the top of the wall. I pulled hard, got a leg up on top, and rolled over into the yard of the LLC. I landed in a bush with a thump and crunch of branches. Did he hear the noise? I rolled out onto to the lawn and scuttled away from the wall into the dark shadows of a pool house.

A flashlight played across the upper stories of the house next door, and I could hear the guard's footsteps as he walked down the drive. How stupid was this? A convicted felon caught on a breaking-and-entering charge. Stupid, stupid. The smart ones in prison taught the same thing: plan, plan, plan, then plan for when the plan went wrong.

Of course, all my teachers were locked up. So much for plans.

The light swept along the top of the wall. Had I left a mark when I went over?

The light dropped away. The footsteps stopped. A click and a metallic scrape, and then the smell of a cigarette. The footsteps went back up the drive. A car door slammed. The engine started, and the HawkEye car drove away.

Chapter Seventeen

There were underwater lights in the swimming pool. It was a blue rectangle in the darkness. A light mist rose from it in the cool night air. A filter burbled and swished near the hot tub built into the corner of the pool. Beyond the pool was a tennis court. Patio furniture clustered around a glass-topped table on the pool apron. A big chrome gas grill bulked next to a tiled counter with a sink and a built-in refrigerator. The back wall of the house was glass, with glass doors framed in wood that gave out on a grouping of chairs and sofas under the protective overhang of the second story.

I went to the glass wall and looked in. There was enough light to show me a large living room with a high ceiling. A river-rock fireplace dominated one wall. An elaborate bar took up a corner. There were groups of leather sofas and chairs, one near the fireplace and the other looking out toward the backyard. It was a man's room, heavy, comfortable, and expensive.

A car slowed on the street. The tires thumped as the car pulled into the driveway. The driver got out and shut the door. I could hear his shoes scrape on the pavement as he walked back up the drive. My heart sped up.

The smart move for me would be to go back over the wall and get out of there before he came into the house, but I wanted to see who Julie might have come here to meet. Once I saw him, I'd go. I took cover behind a clump of leafy trees in big terra cotta pots to one side of the pool. I heard the front door slam. Moments later the lights in the living room turned on, and he came in through the arch that led to the front hall.

He was a big man in a well-cut black suit and a white shirt with no tie. He shed his jacket and tossed it at a chair as he crossed to the bar to make himself a drink. He carried the glass to the big window and looked out at the yard. He had a big round head with thick curly brown hair going gray at the temples. His face was heavily fleshed. His eyes were small and deep set. He had heavy sloping shoulders and a deep chest going down to a barrel of a gut. He stood with his legs apart and one hand behind his back, thick from top to bottom, heavy, powerful.

He took a slug of the drink and rolled his head around as if to relieve tension in his neck. He looked out at the yard, and for a moment his eyes seemed to stop on me. Unsettled, I stepped back, though I was sure he couldn't see me in my dark clothes through the screen of trees.

The doorbell rang. He checked his watch and nodded in satisfaction. Someone was on time. He picked up his cell phone from the coffee table and stabbed it with a thick finger. It must have opened the front door, because moments later a woman walked into the room. She was a tall, beautiful redhead in a small red dress and spike heels. She walked as if all the cameras were on her and this was her big moment—heat, sex, and confidence. He met her halfway across the room. She put out a hand to shake his. So they didn't know each other, at least not well. Then she leaned in and kissed him on the mouth. Maybe they did know each other. He made a gesture toward the bar, and when they went there, he kept one hand on her hip.

He made her a drink and refilled his. She said something that made him laugh. Then she put her hand down to his crotch and cupped his balls through the cloth. He put his drink on the bar and reached down and ran his hand up under her dress. She spread her legs to oblige him. He brought his free hand up to squeeze her breast hard enough to make her wince. She unzipped his fly and went down on him until he pulled her up and shoved her toward the leather sofa. He bent her down over the wide arm, lifted her skirt, and pulled her panties down. He went into her like a man trying to batter down a door with a ram.

When he was finished, he put himself back in his pants and zipped up. He walked back to the bar and took a slug of his drink. The redhead straightened, kicked her panties off her foot, pulled her skirt down, and went to join him. He passed her drink to her. She took a sip, then leaned forward and kissed him on the mouth. They talked for a while. Her face was animated and bright, and she said things that made him nod and smile, and he said something that made her laugh. What the hell could he say to make her laugh after that hammering?

He gestured toward the glass wall and backyard beyond it, and she nodded and smiled. He began to strip off his clothes. She took the hem of her dress in both hands and lifted it up and off in one motion. She wore a black push-up bra underneath. Her hands went behind her for a moment, and then it fell to the floor. He stopped what he was doing long enough to reach over and pinch her nipple hard and massage her breast like he was kneading dough. He smiled at her while he did it. When he turned away to finish taking off his clothes, her face twisted in pain.

He had a pelt like a bear, hairy shoulders, chest, belly, and groin. Thick arms, thick legs, big hands. He walked over to open the door to the patio. Shit, they were going skinny-dipping. I was watching a fucked up caricature of a date. Who were these people?

I didn't have time to make a run for the pool house, so I moved to put the trees between the pool and me. The pool was lighted underwater and shone bright blue in the night, but the rest of the yard was dark. My clothes were dark. The trees were thick with leaves. I was all right where I was.

Then he turned on the outside lights.

Suddenly the backyard was bright as a movie set. He would pass close by when he walked to the pool, and if he looked in my direction, he would see me.

He stepped out the door.

My heart raced. We're all scared when we're operating. I was scared every time I went into a bank. You learn how to push the fear down so it doesn't scream. Go slower. Think out the steps. Don't rush. Speed kills when you're operating. Slow it down.

"Hey, let's go. I'm freezing my ass off here." He turned in the doorway to see what she was doing. "And bring the bottle of tequila."

There was a piece of machinery near me, a vented cylinder about three feet high and three across, some sort of pump for the house air conditioning. I went down on my belly and crawled back behind it.

He walked past where I was hiding and lumbered down the steps into the shallow end of the pool, pushed off into the water, and did a clumsy breaststroke out and back.

The redhead came out of the house carrying a bottle and two glasses. She put them on the pool apron and walked down the steps into the water. They swam out to where it was deeper and fooled around for a while, their hands working underwater. He said, "Jesus Christ," once in a strangled voice.

"Want me to stop?" she teased. In answer he pushed her head underwater and held it there, and for a moment I thought he was going to drown her. I started up from where I was hiding without any plan beyond *Do something*, but then he tipped his head back and howled, and pulled her up into the air.

He pushed her back to the shallow end and up onto the steps and then rammed into her again like a meat hammer. It was brutal, ugly, a beating, not sex. I could see both their faces. His lips pulled back from his teeth. His eyes bulged. Every once in a while he slapped the side of her butt hard.

She moaned and squealed and gave him all the sounds of pleasure, but her eyes were half-closed. Her face was slack and blank, distanced from what was going on at the other end of her body.

He put his hands around her throat and began to choke her. Her eyes went wide. Her hands came up and grabbed his wrists. Her face turned red and her mouth strained open. I started to move out from hiding.

He finished with a gasp, let go of her, and fell backward into the water with his arms outstretched. She got up and walked stiffly into the house like the survivor of a car crash. Her side was red from where he'd slapped her. One of her breasts was livid. Her knees were raw from the rubbing on the stone steps. Her face clenched like a fist. Her breath came in gasps.

I didn't know what to do with my rage. I wanted a gun. Walk out and shoot him once in the balls while he floated. The surprise, the pain. Shoot him again. Shoot him till it was empty. Lucky for him I didn't have a gun. Lucky for me.

By the time he got out of the pool, she was dressed. Her wet hair was combed. She wore her spike heels and carried her small purse on a chain over one shoulder. Except for the raw knees, she looked untouched by what had happened. How could that be? She was a better actor than a lot of the famous ones in Hollywood.

He went into the house with a towel around his waist. She touched him on the cheek, smiled, and kissed him lightly. She said something I couldn't hear and took a cell phone from her purse. He went to the bar and came back with his phone. They tapped their keyboards and then touched the screens together.

Payment. She was a pro.

He tossed his phone on the bar and walked her out with a hand on her hip. Just another fun couple at the end of a great date.

I wanted his phone. Mae would crack it for me. His phone numbers, his schedule, his emails, his texts—I'd know his life inside out. Go fast. There weren't going to be any sweet, lingering good-bye kisses at the front door. He'd be back soon. Go, go. In, grab it, out, over the wall.

Anger made me stupid. I went in as fast as I could, but I was only halfway to the bar when I heard the front door slam. Turn around. Get out.

No time. He would see me going out the door. I grabbed for the phone. Too fast. I knocked it back, and it fell behind the bar. No time to get it. He was coming. I went to ground behind a big leather chair in the corner near the fireplace. Farce heading fast toward disaster.

I heard the pad of his bare feet as he came through the arch and crossed the living room to the bar. A rattle of ice into a glass. The clink of a bottle on the glass rim. The scrape of bottles pushed around on the bar top. "Shit, what the hell?" He couldn't find the phone.

I looked past the corner of the chair. He pawed through the bottles and glasses on the bar, stopped and thought about it. He went around the corner of the bar and stooped out of sight to pick up the phone. I pulled back behind the chair as he stood up. I heard him tap the keyboard. A moment later, "Brenda, see if Brad can do lunch tomorrow at one thirty, and cancel that four o'clock with Willerstein. Find a time next week." He was moving away from me while he spoke.

He tucked the phone in his towel while he closed the doors to the patio. Then he punched in the alarm code on the pad near the door. He turned off the outside lights, bundled his discarded clothes under one arm, and left the room, turning out the lights as he went.

I could hear his heavy footfalls as he lumbered around upstairs. He could come back any moment, to get another drink, to look for something he'd forgotten. Don't push your luck. Get out now. The front door or the back door? Both were alarmed. Was there an advantage of one over the other? The front door put me out on the street quickly, but the footsteps upstairs seemed to come from the front of the house. If his bedroom was on the front, he might get a look at me as I ran. How much would he see? Not much. Still, better to go out the back door, over the wall, around to the other side of the car dealer's house, and no one would see me. Okay, the back door.

I used the hem of my jacket to unlock the back door without touching the brass. No fingerprints. I was in the system and easy to find. I gripped the doorknob through the cloth.

Wait.

Why leave? This might be my only chance here. When he leaves in the morning, the place is mine. It's a big house. Find a place to hide.

Are you crazy? Get out. Get out now. Don't be stupid.

Why do I say yes when I should say no? Why do I go forward when I should run away?

Chapter Eighteen

～

My rubber-soled shoes made no noise as I crossed the living room. I could hear the muted sounds of a TV coming from upstairs. There was enough light from the stairwell for me to find the open door to a study. Light through the front window showed me a desk with a desktop computer, built-in bookcases, a flat-screen TV fixed to a wall, and two leather easy chairs flanking a round wooden table facing the TV. No place to hide.

I went along the hall to the kitchen at the back of the house. I turned on my phone's flashlight, shaded the beam to a sliver with my hand, and looked around. The first door opened to a closet holding brooms, mops, and cleaning supplies. The next was a laundry room with a washer and dryer and a large table for folding clean linen. The third showed narrow stairs that led down to a small cellar with a concrete floor. A wine rack was bolted to the cellar wall at the bottom of the stairs. A stack of old patio furniture cushions was piled near a furnace. It was no worse than my cell. And here I had wine.

I had left the cellar door open.

I climbed up to close it. A light went on in the kitchen. I heard a cough and the pad of bare feet on the tile floor. The big man wore a short, dark-blue silk robe. He opened the refrigerator and took out a bottle of water. When he turned, he saw the open door to the cellar. He was looking right at me, but I was in darkness and he was in light, and he couldn't see me unless he got closer.

The open door puzzled him. He put the bottle on the counter and started across the kitchen toward me.

I backed down the stairs quietly. Would he see me if I hid behind the furnace? He would if he came down the stairs. I slipped a bottle out of the wine rack and gripped it by the neck.

He opened the door. A click. Light flooded the cellar from a single naked bulb in a fixture on the wall above the wine. He walked down the stairs. I held my breath. He stopped halfway down and bent over to see to the back of the room. His thick calves were six inches from my face where I crouched in the space under the stairway. I could smell him. Sex, sweat, and chlorine. He took another step down, and then another. I'd have to go for him when he took the last step to the floor, because if he turned and saw me, it would be too late. He was too big, and the space was too small to maneuver in. If he got his hands on me, I was done. I took a hard grip on the wine bottleneck and tried to think how I would take him. The cellar ceiling was low. He was tall. There wasn't enough room for an overhead strike. Fake a blow to his balls to keep his hands down, and then a backhand to the face. Hurt him fast. Get him down and hurt him again.

He took another step down.

Adrenaline pumped me up the way it did before one of the gladiator fights in the yard. Eyes focused. Muscles cocked. Ready. Ready now. Let's go.

He straightened with a grunt, went back up the stairs, turned off the cellar light, and shut the door. I began to breathe again.

The rattle of silverware, the clink of plates and a glass, the opening and shutting of the refrigerator as he banged around the kitchen for a few minutes. Then the bar of light under the cellar door went out. His bare feet were silent on the kitchen floor. Had he walked away, or was he standing there waiting?

I didn't move for half an hour. Then I turned on my flashlight and pulled the patio cushions out onto the floor near the furnace. I lay down and turned off the light. My heart slowed. I retreated deeper into myself.

Black darkness, silence, the walls crowding in. I slowed my breathing. It was something I had taught myself at night in my cell, a way of going into a trance and stilling the panic that sometimes hit me. This was a shade of where Julie was, somewhere out there in nothingness, unhearing, unseeing, unfeeling. The rage went out of me, and I was left with nothing but sorrow to the bone. I cried until my stomach hurt and my breath came in gasps.

Chapter Nineteen

～

I woke up with an urgent need to piss.

I didn't know how long I had slept. In the darkness and silence of the cellar, time had no meaning. I felt around on the floor until I found my phone. It was six in the morning.

At seven he fed himself in the kitchen. I heard him dump the china and cutlery in the sink and the whisper of his bare feet on the tile floor as he left.

An hour later I heard the distant slamming of the front door. I gave him fifteen more minutes in case he had forgotten something. I piled the cushions where they belonged and put the bottle back in the wine rack. I climbed the stairs and opened the door to daylight.

First things first. I used the powder room in the front hall and splashed water on my face to drive away the last of sleep.

I went into the study and searched the desk, using a piece of tissue to avoid leaving fingerprints. The man's name was Harry Groban. He banked with Wells Fargo and still got printed statements, old-school. He had $78,869.06 in his checking account, more than most people made in a year. He kept a short-barreled revolver in a bottom desk drawer. Under it was a photograph of a naked woman. Her hands and feet were tied with white rope, and there was a black cloth bag over her head. She lay on the hearth of the living room down the hall. She was not Julie. I could tell that much.

My rage was back.

I turned on the computer. It asked for a password, so I shut it down.

I went upstairs. There were four bedrooms with adjoining baths. Three of them had the decorated sterility of an expensive hotel and were probably guest rooms, because I had seen no evidence of family in the house. The fourth bedroom was Groban's. It was a huge room with a high ceiling. Groban's clothes from last night were on the floor near the walk-in closet, left for someone else to pick up. The bedclothes were a tangle on the king-size bed. There was a mirrored headboard and a mirror on the ceiling. Heavy, dark-green curtains that could black out the room were drawn aside at the windows that overlooked the street and the canyon beyond it. The top of a large, built-in dresser held a set of silver-backed brushes, a wooden tray with six or seven pairs of cuff links, and a couple of expensive watches. There was a framed photograph of a younger, trimmer Groban on a paddleboard and a smaller, silver-framed photo from an earlier era of a man and a woman standing together with a small boy between them in front of a frame house with a porch. The woman had a pinched, narrow face. Her mouth turned down at the corners in a look of discontent. The man smiled at the camera. He looked like a milder version of what the son had become.

I searched the bureau drawers and found nothing except an envelope of hundred-dollar bills under a pile of cashmere sweaters. The bedside table held a box of condoms, a pair of handcuffs, a prescription bottle of Viagra, and a glass jar with a silver top that held two inches of white powder. I dipped a wet fingertip in and tasted it. Cocaine. Even that tiny bit on my tongue slammed open all my receptors, dormant all those years but happy to get back in the game if that's where I wanted to go. I weighed the jar in my hand for a minute and then put it back in the drawer.

A car stopped out front. I went to the window and saw an old minivan at the curb. A middle-aged Hispanic woman got out and stood at the window for a moment, talking to the driver. She waved to the other neighborhood housekeepers in the back seats and then walked up the drive. I heard her key in the lock. The front door opened and closed, and then she took a few quick steps across the hall and tapped in the disarm code for the alarm system. I peeked down from the top of the stairs. She stood in the front hall wearing a cotton coat and a scarf that covered her hair. She recoded the alarm and went down the hall toward the kitchen. A woman alone in a big house—maybe she felt safer with the alarm on.

Maybe Groban required it. It left me with a problem. When I opened the door to leave, the alarm would go off. I didn't want Groban to know I had been there. I wanted him to feel safe and unwatched. But I had to get out of there before the housekeeper found me.

I went back to the upstairs hall window and looked out. Just after Groban's house, the street made a sharp turn and went down to a bigger street that led farther up into the hills or down to Sunset.

I went quietly down the stairs. I could hear the housekeeper humming a song in the kitchen. I pulled my sleeve down over my hand so I wouldn't leave fingerprints on the door handle. Something fell to the floor in the kitchen with a metal bang, and the housekeeper said, "*Coño*," in annoyance. I opened the door. The alarm shrilled, a high, piercing noise. I slipped out quickly and closed the door as quietly as possible. The alarm continued to shriek. I sprinted for the corner without looking back and ran fast down to the next street. I slowed there and jogged away at the calm, steady pace of a dedicated morning runner.

A block from my car, a HawkEye Security car passed quickly, lights and siren. What would they find? No sign of entry. With luck they would put it down to a glitch in the alarm system.

I started the car and headed home. Who was Harry Groban? Why had Julie shown up at that house in a silver metallic minidress and spike heels like a high-priced hooker? I was the one who jumped off the cliff without looking. I bent the rules. I was the one who stuck my hand in the flame. Not Julie. Never Julie.

*   *   *

Steckley was up early. He checked his computer. The tracker he had attached to Cody Bonner's car the day he saw her at her mother's house showed the car was still parked on the street in Brentwood where she had parked it the evening before. He drank a cup of coffee while he went over the security tapes from the bank robberies in LA and the one where she got caught back east.

He knew he was obsessed by the Credit Union robbery, but he couldn't help it. The Credit Union was a five-block walk from police headquarters. It was where Steckley had banked since joining the force.

And every time he ran the Credit Union robbery tape, there *he* was, walking across the bank floor, putting money he had just withdrawn into his wallet, and right behind him, the woman robber walked toward the teller she would rob.

The first time they played the tape in the squad room, Lieutenant Beasley said, "Jesus Christ, Steckley, isn't that you? All you had to do was turn around and shoot her." The rest of the cops in the room broke up, and they ran the tape on a loop on squad room monitors for days until Steckley busted one with a hammer. Lieutenant Beasley was right, of course. All he would have had to do was turn around. Every time he watched the tape, it tore the scab off the wound.

He got into his car and drove to Brentwood and watched Bonner's car from a block away. He'd been there for more than an hour and was about to give up and head downtown.

She jogged out of a side street dressed in black. Was that to make her invisible at night? What the hell was she up to? Where had she gone? What the fuck was she doing?

What was wrong with her? He understood guys who came out of nothing, guys who knew life was stacked against them and felt they had to go out and grab what they wanted. They were assholes, but at least they had an excuse. Cody Bonner had had everything from the get-go: money, brains, education, looks, a movie star mother. What was she doing robbing banks? It upset the natural order of things. Why did she do it? She had no right. It pissed him off. And every time he began to calm down about it, he ran the Credit Union tape and watched himself walk past her.

At least with the tracker, whatever the hell she was going for now, he'd be there when she fell.

Chapter Twenty

⌒

Every day I rang the doorbell of unit number three across the pool from
Julie's, hoping to talk to Keira about my sister. I tried the phone number on the card she gave me. There was an announcement in Keira's
voice: "I'm in Antigua getting tanned and more beautiful. Back soon
and dying to talk to you, whoever you are."

*   *   *

I spent a couple of days with death certificates and copies of Julie's
will, switching her stuff to my name: the car, the townhouse, the bank
accounts. I took the written test at the DMV, and they gave me a tem-
porary license.

Between those errands, I mined the internet for information on
Harry Groban.

Groban ran a talent agency called, with unusual modesty, The
Agency. He and his two partners, Anson Lewis and Colin Fimrite, had
been agents at William Morris Endeavor until a night five years ago
when they downloaded all their files, wiped their computers clean, and
stole away to surface the next day in offices in Beverly Hills. They also
stole a core group of A-list actors, directors, and writers. My mother was
one of them.

The Agency was now the most powerful one in Hollywood. They
could make or break careers. The word most used about Groban and his
agency was *ruthless*. It was said with admiration.

Three years ago a young actress client named Sandra Gallimore had
accused Groban of raping her in his office. According to the stories I

found on the internet, she went there to discuss a role on a long-running TV series. Groban made it clear that she could have the part in return for oral sex. She agreed and did it. He wanted more. She refused. He raped her. She went to the cops. There was a trial. He was found innocent. He sued her for defamation of character. He won. The judgment against her ran to six figures. It bankrupted her. A month later she died in a crash. She was alone in the car when it hit a bridge abutment. Her blood alcohol level was three times the legal limit. Her friends were sure it was suicide.

* * *

Curtis took me for dinner to a hole-in-the-wall in Chinatown. Was it a date? He presented it in such an offhand way, I wasn't sure. No one else from our part of town would have known the place existed. It was a typical Wile E. Coyote deal to find something great that everyone else walked by without noticing. There were twelve Formica-topped tables with mismatched wooden chairs. The walls were painted dingy mustard yellow. The paint had chipped off in places to show the plaster underneath. The floor was covered with small, worn black-and-white tiles. There were Chinese movie posters on the walls. We picked up a bottle of white wine in the adjoining bar, a narrow room whose dim, greenish light made the few serious drinkers there look like they were underwater. The other tables in the dining room were occupied by Chinese who checked us out once and then ignored us. A stooped, quick-moving woman whose age was somewhere between fifty and a hundred hustled the food to us. She banged down plates, said something in Chinese, and scurried off with plates for other tables. "This is going to be the best food you ever tasted," Curtis said. He snapped up a piece of something with his chopsticks and held it out until I opened my mouth and took it. "Is that good? Is that the best thing you've had in forever?"

"You've never tasted prison chop suey."

"Hey, hey, hey, seriously. Here try this." He poked another piece into my mouth. His enthusiasm was irresistible.

"It's really good."

"Yes, it is. I hope nobody discovers it and fucks it up." He used his chopsticks to dip a piece of shrimp into a pale-yellow sauce and then ate it while he looked at me. Something was going on behind his eyes. He was building up to saying something.

"Go ahead," I said. "Say it. Ask me. I don't mind."

He smiled. "What happened to you? One day I see you laughing outside the library at school. The next thing I know, they say you're strung out on the street. I went looking for you."

"You did?" That surprised me. "Why?"

"To see if there was anything, you know, like I could do. Something you needed or anything."

I had never seen Curtis so awkward. Even when we were teenagers, he was never out of control. I reached over and touched his hand. "Thank you."

"Yeah, well, for nothing. I never found you. I asked Julie once about it, and she just shook her head and walked away. Then I heard rehab. Then nothing. Then I heard you were gone, left town. Then you robbed a bank. Why the fuck did you rob a bank?"

" 'Cause that's where the money is." Wisdom I'd been told in prison that came from some famous old bank robber. Curtis gave me a little smile, but he wanted more. "I don't know. I can't talk about all that with you right now. I'm still trying to figure it out."

"Will there be a time?"

"I don't know. Maybe."

"I hope so," he said.

"So do I." I surprised myself by saying it.

We ate until the food was gone. He emptied the last of the wine into our glasses. "Do you want anything else? Dessert?"

"No, thanks. Curtis, tell me what you know about Julie's pro bono work."

"I told you," he said. "She was doing legal work for the working girls."

"After that."

"What do you mean, after that?" He waved to the old woman and made a sign of paying.

"She stopped doing that after a couple of months. The woman she was working with said she found something that really pissed her off and that she was going to do something about it."

"What was it?"

"I'm asking you."

"She never said a thing to me."

"You've known her forever. You weren't close?"

"Julie and me?" He was surprised at the question.

"You never went out with her?"

"Cody, Julie was the one who named me Wile E. Coyote. It wasn't a compliment. She saw right through all my bullshit, and she wanted no part of it."

"I thought maybe since you guys were working together . . ."

"Uh-uh. Just work, nothing more. We were a good team. Marty Collier put her on me to make me stick to the speed limit. She was great on detail. We worked well together, but her and me, uh-uh." He shrugged. "I knew she was doing something outside the firm, but I thought it was the streetwalker thing, which wasn't exactly Mitchell, Collier, and Brown's thing. It didn't add to the bottom line."

I asked him a few more questions, but it was clear that I had all his information. Maybe I'd find out more on Julie's computer once Mae got into it.

"I think she knew the guy who killed her."

"Why? Why not some random serial wacko? LA grows them like weeds. Half the guys driving vans around town have really bad fantasies." The old woman came with a scrawled piece of paper. He glanced at it, handed her some bills. She was surprised by how much he had given her and tried to give some back. He refused, and she smiled and went away.

"Who goes to the trouble of tying a cinder block to her and dumping her in the ocean? Someone who really doesn't want to get caught. The fuck truck guys dump her in the hills and hope the birds and animals clean up their mess. A mugger leaves her in a dumpster. Someone with a lot to lose if she was found did this to her, someone connected to her."

"The Riordan guy?"

"No. He was in San Diego cutting a commercial for the Del Mar racetrack."

"Are you sure?"

"Yes. I checked. I've been calling people we went to school with to see if any of them knew anything. Had she said anything to anyone about being creeped out by someone? Nobody I've talked to remembers anything. Some lost touch. Some moved away. Amy Martin's dead. Did you know that?"

"Yes. Skiing. Crashed into a tree." He paused. "Do you think someone we knew at school did it? Jesus, I can't think of one who's that weird. Well, maybe Lyle Wolnitz. He became an army sniper. I'm pretty sure he was in Afghanistan when she disappeared."

"No. No. I just thought she might have said something to one of her old friends, maybe just something in passing. I don't know. I don't know."

And then I began to cry. I didn't want to. I was too tough to cry, wasn't I? But there it was.

Curtis got me up out of the chair and walked me out with his arm around my waist while I leaned on him. My eyes blurred with tears. I stumbled over the doorsill and nearly went down, but Curtis held me up. He got me out onto the street and held me. I heard a woman say, "Is she all right?"

"None of our business," the man with her said.

"She lost someone," Curtis said. "It just hit her. She'll be okay."

"Oh. All right. Sorry," the woman said.

I leaned on Curtis, and he held me and patted my back and talked to me in soothing tones.

"I'm okay." I stood up and wiped my eyes with my sleeve.

"Sure?" My tears unsettled him. They made him feel helpless, something he was not used to.

"Yeah. God. I don't know. Every once in a while it just knocks me down. Bang."

We walked without talking the four blocks to where we had left Curtis's car. The valet went off to find it.

"Tell me about Harry Groban," I said.

He looked at me quizzically. "Huh, that's a jump. Where the hell did Harry Groban come from?"

"Do you know him?"

"Sure. If you're in the business, you know Harry. The Agency is the big dog in town. There are a couple of places nipping at his heels, but Harry's still the stud." He stopped.

"More."

"Why?"

"Did Mitchell, Collier do work for him?"

"Sure."

"Did you when you were still there?"

"Some. Not much. Harry likes to deal with principals, not junior partners. Mostly he worked with Adrian Mitchell. I see more of him now because of Black Light."

"Did Julie know him?"

"What the fuck, Cody? What's going on here?"

"Did she?"

"Maybe. He came into the office sometimes. He's your mother's agent. They probably met. I don't know. She never said anything, but why would she?"

"What do you know about him personally? Outside of work."

"Not much. The usual grapevine crap. Ruthless. A bully to work for. Charming when he wants to be. Friends with people on the way up or on top, not so much with people on the way down."

"Family?"

"No. Married and divorced, once, I think. The rumor is he likes younger women, but that's not exactly out of the mainstream in this town."

"Three years ago he was accused of rape. What do you know about that?"

"He was tried. Not guilty." He shrugged.

"That's it?"

"I didn't really follow it. I mean, like everyone in the business, I knew it was happening, but once the verdict came in, it was pretty much over. I think a lot of guys breathed a sigh of relief that finally someone got through one of these things without losing his ass."

"Oh, good. I'm so glad they all feel better. Poor boys waiting for the other shoe to drop."

He held up his hands in defense. "Okay. Okay."

"He sued her and won. She committed suicide."

"How does this connect to Julie?"

"I don't think it does," I lied.

He read something in my face. "Uh-uh. No. Julie and Harry Groban. No. Not a chance." He waved it away.

"Why not?"

"Oh, for Christ's sake, why would she go anywhere near him?"

"I don't know. But that doesn't mean she didn't."

"Come on. Where the hell did you get this idea?"

"He beats women."

"How do you know?"

"I know, okay? I know."

"And he killed her? Why would he do that? You're out of your mind. Harry Groban's much too smart. He's not some wacko killer. He's a calculator, an odds reader, a strategist. He didn't kill Julie. Not because he isn't an asshole and a pig, but because he's too smart to do something that stupid."

"What if they got into something and he got too enthusiastic? What if it was a mistake, an accident? Rough sex that went too far."

"Come on."

"It's possible."

"It's not possible. It's too weird. Julie wouldn't go near him."

I couldn't tell him that I broke into Groban's house.

"You have no evidence."

"Not yet."

"But you're going to find some?"

"I don't know."

He looked at me seriously for a long time and then shook his head. "This is nuts."

He drove me home in his Porsche as if red lights were options and cops didn't exist. He walked me to the door. He didn't have to tell me that he wanted to come in, and for a long moment, I wanted him to. I started to say it, but then I kissed him on the cheek and went in alone.

Chapter Twenty-One

〜

I called Lara Jannicky, the *L.A. Times* reporter who'd covered the Groban rape trial. I got passed to three different extensions and finally got her voice mail. I left a message and my number, and she called me back an hour later.

"Cody Bonner? Lara Jannicky here. Five years in prison for bank robbery. Daughter of a movie star. Twin sister of murdered lawyer. It's already a good story."

"Not if you live it." But I admired her efficiency.

"Yeah. Right. Sorry. You want to talk about Harry Groban. So let's talk."

"Can we meet?"

She thought about it. "Okay. Where are you, the west side?"

"Culver City."

"Halfway? I've got to be downtown this morning. The Farmers Market? I have a low-down craving for Ya-Ya at the Gumbo Pot."

"One o'clock?"

"See you there."

Lara Jannicky was a tall Black woman in her forties with an open face and an easy manner. Her hair was cut to a half inch like a dark cap on her skull. She wore tailored khaki pants and a dark-red shirt and carried a small leather backpack instead of a purse. She said something to the counter man that made him laugh, and she watched me come through crowded tables as she did. I suspected she was a woman who didn't miss much.

"Lara Jannicky, I'm Cody Bonner."

"Yes." Her handshake was firm. "We'll order and sit down. Clinton," she said to the man at the counter. "I'll have the Gumbo Ya-Ya and a Barq's root beer."

"As usual," he said with a grin, and looked to me.

"I'll have the shrimp po' boy and the root beer, please."

"I'll bring 'em over."

We found a table for two far enough from the other tables to talk without being overheard. "What's your interest in Harry Groban's rape trial?" Jannicky asked.

"He's my mother's agent. I want to know more about him."

"Do you think he might rape your mother?" Her tone said it wasn't a serious question.

"No."

"So what, then? It's a three-year-old story. Why the interest now?"

"Because I don't think the whole story is in the papers."

Clinton brought our food. I started to speak again, but Jannicky put up a hand to stop me and dug into her gumbo. After a few bites, she came up for air. "I've been thinking about that since I got up this morning. I had to get some of it in me. Go ahead."

"I've been in the system," I said. She nodded encouragement and went back to eating. "The system grinds slowly, and most people want it to grind slowly, because if it's going to eat them up, they want to postpone when that starts. From what I could figure from your stories, Harry Groban didn't want it to grind slowly. He pushed hard for an early trial. Am I wrong?"

"No, you're not." She took another bite of gumbo and studied me across the table. "Your sister was murdered."

"Yes."

"Do you think Harry Groban had something to do with that?"

"I don't see how."

"Uh-huh." I couldn't tell if she believed me or not. We ate while she thought about it. When she finished, she pushed her bowl away reluctantly. "God, that's good." She dabbed her mouth with her napkin. "Do you want coffee? It's got chicory in it."

"Sure."

She caught Clinton's eye and raised two fingers. "You're the first person who's noticed that Harry Groban was in court a couple of weeks after the rape accusation. I couldn't get the DA or the judge or Groban's lawyer to admit it was unusual. They all gave me the same answer, quoted the Constitution about the right to a speedy trial. Bullshit. Groban's smart. He saw what happened to Harvey Weinstein and those other guys. They let it drag out. More women spoke up. That gave others the courage to speak. Pretty soon those guys were swamped. Groban decided to get out in front of it. The guy knows everybody in town. He pulled strings to jump the line for trial. They got the judge they wanted and the DA they wanted. Groban's lawyer asked for a bench trial, just the judge, no jury. The DA went along. Sandra Gallimore turned out to be a lousy witness. She got the date of the meeting wrong. She got the name of Groban's assistant wrong. She couldn't remember much of the salient details about Groban's office, no paintings, nothing about the furniture. She said she was drugged, which would explain that, but she failed to go to the hospital or the cops for over a week. By that time any drugs in her system were gone, and there was no useful evidence of forced sex. And she had a skeleton in her closet. Maybe Groban got lucky with that, or maybe it came up in their research."

"What was it?"

"When she was in college, Gallimore accused a classmate of date rape. The college decided there wasn't enough evidence to support her claim."

"Shit."

"Yeah. Groban's defense team painted her as a screw-and-sue kind of girl. The judge bought it."

Clinton brought our coffees and went away. "All the cellblock lawyers I talked to said a defendant asks for a bench trial in front of a judge because she thinks she'll do better without a jury. If the defendant does that, the DA almost always presses for a jury. Why didn't the prosecutor do it in the Groban case?"

"Who knows?" Jannicky said with a twisted smile. "But six months later the prosecutor quit the DA's office and went into private practice with the law firm that defended Groban. Probably doesn't mean a thing."

"What about the judge? Does he have his own TV show now?"

"Girl, prison made you cynical. No, no show of his own, but he consults on a couple of lawyer shows, and he's had a couple of small roles in movies. That all started about a year after the trial. Probably no connection. Just an LA story." She gave me the smile again. "Now you can bullshit me all you want, Cody Bonner, but there's something here, and I want it."

I didn't say anything.

"Okay, fine," she said. "But when it's time, it's mine."

"If something comes up."

"Uh-uh. *When* something comes up." She took a card from her pocket, wrote something on the back, and slid it to me. "My direct dial at the paper and my cell. When it breaks, give me a call."

* * *

Curtis called me from his car as he drove to the studio. "Hi. I had a great time the other night. I'd forgotten what it was like to be with you."

"I had a great time too."

"I was thinking about what we were talking about. Let's just say for the sake of discussion that Groban did it. What could he have left as evidence that would let you prove it?"

"I don't know."

"Did you know any murderers in prison?"

"Sure."

"What got them caught?"

"Usually stupidity. Most of them did it on the spur of the moment. It wasn't planned. It was usually someone they knew. They got angry, they did it; then they'd try to figure out how to get away with it afterwards. Too late."

"There must have been somebody who was at least half smart. Even if they didn't get away with it, they must have tried."

"Hmm. Yeah. Maybe."

"So what tripped them up?"

I thought about it for a moment. "Well, there was one. Mostly people kill people they know, but she didn't. She hitchhiked and killed people who picked her up. Just men on the road she didn't know. She kept trophies—an engraved cigarette lighter, a key ring, a handkerchief, one guy's false teeth."

"No, that's really wack," Curtis said. "Harry's not that reckless. Why would he? It would be so dangerous. What if someone found them?"

"The cops never found her clothes or her purse," I said. "Maybe he kept them."

He was silent for a moment. "Come on. First of all, he didn't do it. Second, he's not that stupid."

"Not stupid, twisted. One of those arrogant bastards who thinks the rules don't apply to him."

"You don't really believe that."

"No. Probably not."

"Speaking of clothes, I have a photo of what she was wearing the last day at the office."

"You do? How come?"

"We were at Warners that day, and she took the lead in a negotiation with the business affairs guy, a real asshole named Buckner who treated her like she was my secretary. It pissed her off, and she nailed him on three points. She wanted a victory picture in the parking lot. I'll send it to you. Anyway, forget that trophy stuff, but I know someone who worked for Groban. Something happened and she quit. You might want to talk to her."

"What kind of something?"

"I don't know. She said something shitty happened, but she wouldn't tell me what. Maybe she'll tell you. I'll call her and let her know you'll call."

He gave me her name, Carol Greene, and her number.

The photo of Julie hit my computer a moment later. She was grinning at the camera with her arms raised in triumph. She wore a green sheath dress with a cowl neck. She looked happy, alive.

*   *   *

"You sure you don't want to order anything more?" Carol Greene asked. "Almost everything's gluten-free, and it's all organic."

"No, thanks," I said. "Coffee's fine. I had something before I left." We were in Superfood Café on Wilshire.

"I'm a doer, you know? High energy. If my blood sugar gets low, I'm fucked." She was working her way through an Acai Brazilian Bowl, enough food to feed a family of four as long as they didn't eat meat. She was blonde and pretty with those big blue eyes men think are innocent. She wore a light-blue-and-cream patterned sleeveless dress with a tightly fitted top.

"How long did you work for Harry Groban?"

"See, like I worked at the Agency for a year, but I only worked for Harry for about a couple of months once I figured that shit out."

"What shit?"

"This is on deep background, right? I don't want to be quoted. Harry throws a lot of shade in this town."

"I never met you. We never talked."

She looked me over carefully and decided to trust me. Or maybe she just needed to tell the story. "Okay. Well, like if you're Harry's assistant, you're pretty much fast-tracking to become an agent. And he makes that clear. Like the unspoken thing is, do what I want and you're on the way. And that's what I wanted. I really wanted to be an agent."

"What did he want?"

Carol chewed and swallowed a mouthful of Acai Brazilian Bowl and washed the last bits down with a sip of ginger–rose hip tea. She checked her cell. It was a stall while she decided whether she was really going to tell me. Then she gave a little nod and said, "Like an actress is coming in to talk about representation, and I'm supposed to meet her and take her up to Harry—but not at the office, at the suite he keeps at the Intercontinental. And she thinks I'll be there to take notes, but after ten minutes my phone rings, and I say I have to go."

"And she gets to stay with Harry in the hotel suite."

"Yeah."

"How many times did that happen?"

"I don't know, two or three."

"In a couple of months."

"Yeah. And once it was me."

"You?"

"Yeah. One evening Harry's staying late, and I'm staying late, 'cause if you're his assistant and he's staying late, like you're staying late. So after a while, he calls me into the office. I go in, and the door shuts and locks, 'cause he's got one of those buttons under his desk that does that. He's at his desk. His jacket's on the back of the chair, but he's wearing a shirt and tie. Then he stands up, and he's not wearing pants or anything."

I laughed. I couldn't help it.

"Yeah, laugh," she said. "You weren't in there."

"I'm sorry."

"It's okay. Now it's funny, but it wasn't too funny then."

"What happened then?"

"He says his lower back is killing him and he needs me to give him a massage. His back may be killing him, but his dick's pointed at his chin, and it's not his back I'm going to be massaging. I tell him no, I can't do that. It wouldn't be like appropriate. He keeps after me, but I just keep talking and walking, and then he's jerking off into a potted plant that's next to his desk."

"Jesus Christ. A potted plant? What the hell's that?"

"I don't know. It sure as hell isn't sex. Jesus, men. So that's it for me. I take out my phone and tell him I'm dialing 911, which I do, but I don't hit the send button. I just keep my finger over it and ask him to let me out. He finishes up, pushes the button, the door unlocks, and out I go."

"You should've taken a video."

"Yeah? I don't think so. I've seen him angry. I think he might have killed me."

"Are you serious?"

"I don't know. Maybe. You know what they say: men are afraid women will laugh at them; women are afraid men will kill them. I've got a theory about that. You know why men are so pissed off at us? Because they may be the big strong guys running the world, but deep down they know we're in charge of the mystery. We're the ones who bring new life into the world. They're like, you know, the second assistant directors in the process. All that antiabortion shit, how they believe in the sanctity of life. The same guys can't wait to beat up their wives, bomb some city, or send a bunch of kids to war. No wonder they're jerking off into plants."

"So you quit."

"Not right away. They owed me money. I come in the next day, it's like nothing happened. It's like hi, Carol, how are you? Get me Mel Tucker over at Warners, then Stan Hough at MGM, then see if Liam can do lunch at one thirty rather than one. A couple of days later I'm transferred to a junior agent who came to work two months after I did. I got the message. I gave my notice, worked a couple more weeks, signed the confidentiality agreement, and got the hell out of there."

"Confidentiality agreement?"

"Yeah. Do you think I just broke it? Fuck them. Just don't quote me."

"They won't hear anything from me. When did this happen? Before or after the rape trial?"

"Before."

"Did you ever tell anyone?"

"A few of my girlfriends, but, you know, Harry's a big deal, and I was going to go look for a job. I needed the reference. And I was lucky. Nothing really happened."

"What are you doing now?"

"I'm brand manager for Carstairs Communications, and I love it. I always wanted to be in the movie business, but working at the Agency beat that out of me. You know what they say: the culture comes from the top down. They weren't all pigs working there, but enough of them were." She finished the bowl and drained her tea. "I've got to run."

I left money on the table, and we went out to get our cars from the valet. "Can you give me the names of any of the women Groban saw in the hotel who might talk to me?"

"Let me think about it. I might give you a couple who had some stuff happen. I don't know if they'll talk. Harry scares people."

"Thanks."

"I'll text you."

Chapter Twenty-Two

~

"I told you on the phone I don't want to talk to you," Selene Wilson said. She was moving fast toward the Lyft car waiting outside the LA Models building on Sunset in West Hollywood. Her stiletto heels clicked the pavement as she hurried. She held a big black leather portfolio in her left hand as if to shield herself from me. She was tall, with honey-tan skin and dark eyes. Asian blood gave her hair so black and smooth it looked like it would shed water. In a city of beautiful women, she stood out.

"Just give me a minute. I won't use your name. No one will know."

"I signed the agreement. I took the money. I'm not talking. I'm still working in this town. I'm up for three movies. What do you think happens if Harry Groban blackballs me?"

"He's going to do it again unless women who know step up to stop him. You could help."

"Yeah? Well, where were you when I needed help? Where were you when I was up in that room with Groban?" She jerked open the car door, threw her portfolio in, and slid in after it. "Leave me alone." She slammed the door, started the car, and left with an angry yelp of tires.

* * *

Randi Porter was the second name Carol Greene had given me. The cell number Carol gave me didn't work anymore, but I had the address, and it wasn't far. It was an old-fashioned bungalow court south of Fountain that had escaped redevelopment. Two rows of whitewashed stucco units with red-tiled roofs faced each other across winding brick paths and a narrow garden that ran from just inside the wrought-iron street gate to a larger unit that blocked off the far end. Orange-beaked birds of paradise grew up next to the buildings.

A woman was planting bright flowers in a bed near one of the dwarf palms that formed a small oasis around a shallow concrete pool with a green bottom. She saw me coming and stood up. She took off her gloves and dropped them. She put her hands in the small of her back and bent backward, trying to stretch out the kinks. She was wearing a one-piece paisley jumpsuit of some shiny material that might have been the thing for six minutes in the 1980s. It had a big brass zipper that ran from her throat to her crotch. Her hair was a dark red unknown in nature. She wore fabulously long fake eyelashes and makeup in thick layers that did nothing to conceal her age.

"Sorry, honey, we're full up, and we've got a waiting list. I can put your name down if you like." She peered at me more closely through the underbrush of her lashes. "Wait a minute. I know you. Don't tell me, don't tell me. I'm real good on names. It begins with a G or a J. Gracie? No. Jenny?" She shut her eyes for a moment. "Got it. Jackie."

"Julie."

"Well, I was close. I've got a real good memory. I could always learn my part cold. I never went up on my lines. Never. Once I learned them, they were in there. And I learned my whole part beginning to end, not like these kids today. They only learn the scene they're doing that day. No continuity. That's the problem with actors today. No sense of the whole." She knelt again and pulled on her gardening gloves. She took a flower out of its small plastic pot and stuck it in a hole she had dug with a trowel. She patted the dirt down around it and dug another hole.

"I'm sorry," I said. "I don't remember your name."

"Misty Franklin. It says so right on my driver's license. I made it legal when I first came out to LA in 1975."

"I was hoping to talk to Randi Porter, Misty."

"No can do. She left. It was maybe a month after you talked to her the last time. I remember, 'cause I had a couple of weeks' work on that movie *Scattershot* just about then. Did you see it? I played Myrna, the old broad who helps the kids after they get away with the money."

"I missed it. I'm sorry."

"Randi was just unlucky, I guess." She pushed another flower into the dirt and pressed the earth down around it. "She met one of the big-time agents. She thought that was going to be her break. I don't use an agent anymore. All the casting directors know me. If they've got a part that fits, they call me up and I go in. I'm up for one right now. The great-grandmother on a CBS sitcom. They say it might be a recurring role." She smiled at the thought of steady work.

"Who was the agent Randi met?" I asked, trying to pull her back on track.

"Somebody at the Agency. That's right up there at the top of the heap. She was on her way, but then she had the accident." She put the last two flowers in and collected a stack of the little plastic pots they came in.

"What accident?"

"Fell down stairs." She pulled off her gloves and got up to stretch again.

"Fell down stairs? How did that happen?"

She thought for a moment. "She didn't tell me. Must have been a department store or something, 'cause they were quick with the insurance check. I guess they didn't want any publicity. Delivered it right to her here in person."

"Really?"

"Yup. The guy had to ask me which unit she was in. I didn't much like him, but I liked that he brought the check. There was something about him. It wasn't 'cause he wasn't good looking, 'cause he was. He could've been an actor. He was that handsome. Except he had one of those red birthmarks on his forehead. Kind of like a spider or something. Still, they can cover those up with makeup, no problem. Handsome but mean looking. Still, he could've played a villain."

"Do you know what insurance company he came from?"

She thought for a moment. "No. I don't know if he actually told me the name, but he brought the check." She looked longingly toward the unit at the end of the garden. "Can I offer you a cold beer? I'm kind of parched."

"Sure. Why not? Thanks."

I sat at a round green metal table on the dark-red concrete patio in front of her unit while she went in and got two beers. Half of hers was gone by the time she sat down and pushed mine across the table. "That insurance check sure came in handy. She owed me a couple of months' back rent. She paid me two days later. A few days after that she was packed up and gone."

"Do you know where she went?"

"She had people back east someplace, so maybe she went there. She didn't give me a forwarding address. No reason to leave at all. When she fell, she didn't hurt her face, not even a scratch. Bruises all over, but not on her face. Still a beautiful girl." She finished her beer in one long swallow and stood up. "Want another?"

"No thanks, I've got to go. Misty, is there anyone living here who knew Randi?"

"Nope. That's like more than two years ago, and I get quite a turnover." She picked up the two empty bottles. "Nice to see you again." She started toward the bungalow door.

"Misty, did Randi ever tell you what she and I talked about?"

"No. No, she didn't."

"Do you have a phone number for her? The one I have doesn't work."

"I might. Let me go look."

She came back a few minutes later with a number scrawled on a piece of paper. It was different from the one Carol had given me. It was an LA area code, but that meant nothing with cell phones. Randi could be anywhere in the country.

I called the number while I drove back to Julie's. It went to message after four rings. I left my name and number and asked her to call me.

I drove back west against the rush hour traffic and stopped at the gym to work out with Sakchai for an hour. Then I went home.

When I opened the door and stepped in, the hair stood up on the back of my neck. Someone was in the house.

Chapter Twenty-Three

～

I'd left the hall light on when I went out, but it was off now. I heard the whisper of a shoe on the rug upstairs. It stopped.

Silence.

Whoever it was must have heard the key in the lock or the door when I closed it. He knew I was here. Unless he wanted to jump from the terrace, the only way out was down the stairs past me or down the back stairs from the kitchen.

I had come in through the front. I took off my shoes and barefooted along the hall to the rear of the house and the narrow stairway that went up to the kitchen. I opened the stairway door and listened. I heard nothing. I threw one of my shoes the length of the hall. It banged against the front door and clattered to the floor. I went up the back stairs as quickly and quietly as I could while he was worrying about the noise down in front.

A little light came in from the street, not enough to see by. If I couldn't see him, he couldn't see me. I wanted a weapon, but the knives were in a drawer that made noise when you opened it. There was a big frying pan on the back of the stove, but it would be clumsy to swing. Working by feel, I found an empty wine bottle I had left on the counter near the sink. Sometimes it pays to be a bad housekeeper. I gripped the bottle by the neck and slipped along the wall to its end. I crouched down as low as I could get and eased my head out until I could see toward the living room. If he was looking for me, I hoped he was looking high, where a head would normally be. What light that came in the front windows threw deep shadows around the furniture. He could be anywhere.

I waited.

People don't like to wait. Waiting makes them impatient. Impatience makes them careless. The occasional hum of traffic penetrated from the street. I could hear the blood flow in my head. I breathed steadily in, out, in, out in a hypnotic rhythm that removed me from time.

He moved. He was standing in shadow next to the short wall that separated the living room from the dining room. He was across from the small hall at the top of the front stairs where he expected me to appear. When he moved away from the wall, toward the hall, I saw that he carried something in his right hand. A poker from the fireplace. It outgunned my wine bottle. The weapon made him brave. He decided to hunt me.

He took a few careful steps toward the stairs. He held the poker in front of him like a sword. He wore dark clothes. I couldn't see his face. I couldn't tell anything about him except that he was a medium-size man. He moved to get a better view of the stairs. When he did, he made a quarter turn away from me.

I went for him.

My bare feet made almost no noise, and he didn't sense me until I was almost there. I swung the bottle at his head. As he jerked around toward me, he backhanded the poker at me. The bottle hit him hard on the forearm. He grunted at the pain, and the poker flew from his hand. The bottle flew from mine and shattered on the hall floor. I tried a fist strike, hoping for his face, but got him high on the shoulder. I stabbed a straight kick that knocked him back against the wall. The breath blew out of him. I had him now. I took a step forward to finish him.

Something hard hit me in the back. If I hadn't been moving forward, it would have hit me on the head.

He wasn't alone.

I tried to turn. One of them hit me again. My legs gave way, and I went down. Someone kicked me twice in the side, then delivered a glancing blow to my head. I slid down into a gray world. I dimly heard them stampede down the stairs. The door slammed, and they were gone. And then so was I.

I wasn't out long. I came back in time to hear the roar of a car engine starting and then the squeal of tires as they got out of there in a hurry. I hurt too much to try to make it to the window. I rolled over on my back and assessed the damage. My back hurt from where the guy had hit me, and my ribs were sore from his kicks. My head rang, but my probing fingers found no blood. I took a deep breath. There was no sharp pain, so I figured no ribs were broken. I pulled myself up using a chair and turned on the lights. The poker lay near the top of the stairs. The second guy had hit me with the fireplace shovel. It was on the floor near where I had fallen.

I looked around the living room but couldn't see that they had taken anything. I dragged myself upstairs to the bathroom, where I took off my shirt and inspected myself in the full-length mirror. My side was livid. Tomorrow I'd have a spectacular bruise. I craned around to see my back. There were two bright-red marks the size and shape of the shovel blade. I was going to be stiff and sore, but I was lucky I'd been stepping forward when he hit me the first time. If he'd gotten me in the head, I'd still be out. Or dead.

I threw my shirt at the laundry basket, splashed cold water on my face, and took four Advil from the medicine cabinet. Then I went to see what they had stolen.

Julie's jewelry box was still in the bureau drawer. Nothing had been taken from it. The $500 in cash I had left under the box was untouched. The only thing the thieves grabbed was my computer. Maybe I had interrupted them before they had a chance to get to anything else. No. They were already downstairs in the living room when I came in. They were on their way out with the computer. Why did they want it? The most they could get for a hot laptop was a few hundred bucks. The jewelry was worth more than that.

I went downstairs and poured bourbon over ice and carried it to the living room. I kicked the shovel toward the fireplace on the way to my chair. I drank a jolt of the liquor and leaned my head against the cushion.

They'd stolen my computer, but they'd come for Julie's. Mine was the only one in the house, and they'd taken it thinking it was hers. The pissed-off Sheriff's homicide investigator, Gurwitz, must have told the Mitchell, Collier office that I had Julie's computer. The lawyers hadn't sent the thieves. They would have sent a process server with a court order to turn it over. But they'd told someone I had it, and someone told someone, and pretty soon I had a couple of guys hitting me with fireplace tools. Were they the men who had killed Julie, or had someone sent them? What was in the computer that was so important?

How did they get in? I went downstairs and examined the front door. It was intact, but at the back door I found scratches around the dead bolt keyhole where they had picked the lock.

Chapter Twenty-Four

෪

The three ragged men were back on the bench in front of the pawnshop on South Vermont, drinking from their bottomless bottle in its brown paper bag. "A fucked up world when a girl like you shows up again at a place like this," the thin Black man said.

"Same deal?" I asked, and showed him a twenty to watch the car.

"Oh yeah. And if you're buying in there, whatever that asshole says, cut it in half. The man would cheat his mother out of her last dime."

"Cheat a baby out of her diaper," the fat white one in the middle said.

"Cheat Christ out of his cross," the Asian said, and spat on the pavement between his feet.

"Fucking guy," the bottle holder said.

"Fucking guy," the others agreed as I went into the shop.

Jerome watched me from behind the bulletproof glass as I crossed the floor. He opened the door to let me in behind the glass. "A cop come by asking about you."

"A cop? What'd he want?"

A sly smile. "Gotta be worth something."

I showed him a twenty. He sneered. I showed him another. He looked insulted. "Sixty. That's it. It's not worth anything more to me."

He reached out and took the money out of my hand, folded it, and put it in his back pocket.

"What'd he want?"

"Wanted to know what you were doing in here."

"What'd you tell him?"

"That you came in to hock a laptop. Told him I offered you twenty bucks for it."

"A tall guy? Thin, bony. Maybe wearing a straw hat with a narrow brim."

"That's him."

"Did he talk to Mae?"

"I ain't nobody's fool."

"Okay. Thanks."

Steckley. He'd followed me down here. He wasn't going to let up. Well, now I knew. I'd have to pay attention.

Jerome pushed a button below the counter, and the door to the back room clicked open. I went in, and the door closed and locked behind me.

The electronics were humming, and the back room was as hot as a sauna. Mae was dressed in a green-and-red muumuu. Her hair was in a yellow turban. Her gold-rimmed glasses were down on her nose, and she was examining a screen full of code on the monitor in front of her. She raised a hand without looking up, and I took a chair near her and watched her work. After a while she typed something in, hit save, and put the computer to sleep. She swiveled her chair, pulled Julie's laptop from a shelf, and handed it to me.

"The password took a while. A bunch of work stuff, legal language. I don't know if that signifies. Just looks like office stuff, but you'll know better. Then there was a file inside that was even more heavily encrypted. That took longer."

"What was it?"

"Photographs with stuff written."

"And?"

"There's a date under each photo, and then a short note written in some language I don't know and I couldn't find in any online translator. Maybe you can figure it out, sisters and all."

"What are the photographs?"

"One of her, your sister. Others, I don't know. I could run facial recognition on them. Might get some hits if they're people who get photographed in public. Nasty."

"The photos?"

"Yeah."

"Do I owe you more?"

"Uh-uh."

"Thanks, Mae."

"Stay out of trouble, Cody. You don't belong back in a shithole like that. You remember what I told you. Don't be a fool. Make a difference."

"I'll try."

She walked me out. Jerome was out in the main room rearranging the watch display in one of the glass cases. "Want to talk to you," he said to me. "Got a business proposition."

"Jerome," Mae said, and her voice held a warning.

"Shut up, woman. Got nothing to do with you. Go on back in there and do what you do."

"I'll stay."

His open hand cracked across her face. She stumbled and went down before I could grab her.

He turned to me. "Got some photos of you, some of your friends. Bare-assed. Tits and everything. Be a shame for them to show up on the internet." He grinned.

Mae moaned and tried to get up.

I put the computer on a display case. Then I hit Jerome with a back-fist that broke his nose and knocked him back two steps. Then I hit him with an elbow strike. He slammed back against a display case and dropped to the floor in a shower of glass. He was hurt but still conscious. I knelt down with one knee on his chest and grabbed his face so he had to look at me. "Those photos aren't me. They're my sister. She's dead. If you put them or anything else you lifted off that computer on the internet, I'll come back for you. Do you understand?" He looked at me with sick eyes. I banged his head against the floor. "Do you understand?" He nodded against my hand.

I went to Mae and helped her up from the floor. "Are you all right?" There was a red imprint of his hand on her face.

"Yes." She turned away and went into the back room. When she came back, she was carrying a small, black automatic. She stood over Jerome and aimed the gun at his face.

"Get up, and get out," she said. He groaned but didn't move. She bent down and touched the gun to his cheek. "I said, get up. And get out."

He tried and fell back. She jabbed him in the neck with the gun barrel. He rolled over and got up on his hands and knees. Glass crunched under him as he crawled toward the door. His hands left blood smears on the floor. Mae walked with him, pacing him. She opened the door and held it as he crawled out. I could hear the hoots of laughter from the old men on the bench. One of them said, "Crawl away, you miserable motherfucker. Crawl away." And then more laughter cut off by the closing door.

"Mae, are you going to be all right?"

She put the gun down on a counter. "I'm going to be fine. Should've done that months ago."

"Will he come back?"

"He'll think about it. Try to work up the courage. Might even try it. He'll only try it once. I'll be all right."

*   *   *

When I got home, I took the laptop up to Julie's desk and turned it on. The photos popped up.

A young woman stood in bright light looking at the camera. She was probably pretty, but someone had blacked her eye and broken her nose. Her jaw was swollen. There were more shots of her in profile, right and left. The images were close-ups showing her from the neck up. The background was blurred by the tight focus. There was no way to tell where the photos had been taken. Her face was thick with pain.

The next young woman was naked except for green bikini panties. Someone had hit her in the stomach hard enough to leave a bruise the size of his fist. Someone had split her lips. The stitches were a dark line against her fair skin. They began just under her right nostril and slanted down across her mouth, pulling it to one side. The beginning of Frankenstein makeup, except it wasn't makeup.

There were more photographs of women. One had red choking marks on her neck. One had livid welts on her back, butt, and thighs.

The rest were unmarked. What happened to them was internal, wounds that didn't show on the flesh. Beaten or unmarked, they all corroded the camera with looks of debasement and humiliation. Julie had written dates on each photo. They began about three months before she died. There was a note after the last one. As Mae had said, it was in a strange language. I couldn't decipher it, but I knew what it was.

When Julie and I were little, we had our own language, something a lot of twins did. We could understand each other. No one could understand us. We called it *shabway*. Our parents thought it was cute at first, but then they hated it, and when we were seven or eight, Julie said she didn't want to speak it anymore for the exact reason I wanted to keep going—our parents didn't like it. If I spoke to her in *shabway*, she answered in English. I gave up. After a while, I forgot the language except for a few words. Julie obviously hadn't.

The last photo was Julie.

She stood naked in front of the mirror on the bathroom door I could see from where I sat. The silvery dress and spike heels Tony Riordan had described from the night he had followed Julie to Brentwood lay puddled at her feet. Her hair, which he said had been pinned up, was in disarray, half pinned and half falling haphazardly. What remained of her makeup was smeared. She held the cell phone with which she was taking the photograph. One of her breasts was red and sore. There was a red hand mark from a slap on her side. She had turned in the next photo to show the red marks of hard blows on her butt and back. They were the same marks Harry Groban had smashed on the body of the call girl. There was a longer note on her photo.

Julie did not look debased or humiliated. She looked enraged.

Chapter
Twenty-Five

~

"Pick me up in an hour," Curtis said. I was driving, because his house was on the way to the party, wherever that was. When he called, the only thing he'd told me was that he was taking me to a party and that I would find it *interesting*. Curtis amusing himself by being mysterious.

"I don't even know what we're doing. What am I supposed to wear?"

"Late-afternoon Malibu beach party, swimming not required unless you're an actress showing the goods. Wear something elegant, fashionable, something sexy in a way that says you may be available if the guy is a god, says that you're smart, wildly interesting, serious, but a lot of fun, cool, *and* hot."

"I've got just the thing."

Curtis laughed, but from his look I must have gotten it right. "Wow. Come on in. I'll be ready in ten minutes. I'm just going to jump in the pool. I lost track of time." A lie. Curtis never lost track of anything. He was barefoot and wore only yoga pants. His body was tanned, muscular, and sheened with sweat. I had an urge to lick some of it off him. The night with Alex Ames from the dance club was a long time ago. Did Curtis know me that well? Or was he just testing?

I followed him out to the pool. He stripped off his yoga pants and went naked into the water in a flat dive. He swam a quick, effortless freestyle to the shallow end, got out, grabbed a towel from one of the deck chairs, and went into the house. "I'll be quick."

Disappointed. At least he could have hit on me so I could say no.

Curtis's house was a beautiful two-story white stucco with a red-tiled roof, bought, I assume, after he fell into money at Black Light. It was tucked into the side of a hill above the Pacific Coast Highway. There were no houses close by, and there was a spectacular view of the ocean from the deck where I stood. I went back into the large living room. Money had been spent to furnish it with comfortable sofas and chairs covered in gray-blue heavyweight cotton enlivened by colored throw pillows. The floor was dark-red terra cotta tiles softened in places by bright-patterned Mexican throw rugs. The mantel over the big fireplace at one end of the room was made from a roughly carved piece of weathered wood. There were a few abstract paintings on the walls, and one big photorealist painting of a blue-green wave with a curling white break. A long dark-wood table held a scatter of magazines and books and a pair of running shoes. A leather jacket was tossed carelessly on one of the chairs. It was a comfortable room, but aside from the jacket and running shoes, it didn't look lived in. I wondered where Curtis hung out. His bedroom?

He was good to his word, out in ten minutes with his hair still wet. He wore khaki-colored linen pants and a dark-blue shirt. He said, "Let's go," so we went.

* * *

The party house was toward the far end of the Malibu Colony, about a mile from where Julie's body washed ashore. A valet parker took my car away. A security man in a sharply tailored dark suit asked to examine Curtis's invitation and gave us a steely look to remind us that he would shoot us if he had to. We went in through the gate to the court-yard, where a blonde waitress in a short-skirted black-and-white uniform offered us champagne or sparking water.

"Whose house is this?" I asked. "Whose party?"

"Wait for the story to unfold. Don't ask for the ending first. It's the journey that's important." Curtis grinned.

It was a two-story modern house of glass and wood. The living room was furnished with wicker sofas and chairs with bright cushions and glass-topped tables on complicated metal stands. A stone fireplace was laid decoratively with driftwood. Men and women in expensive casual clothes were talking quietly at a table near the glass wall that gave out on the backyard.

I stopped in the middle of the living room. Curtis went on a couple of steps before he realized I wasn't with him. He turned back toward me.

"Are you all right?" he asked.

"I don't know." I held on to the back of a chair to steady myself. Sweat burst out on my forehead.

"You're pale. Cody, what's wrong?"

"I suddenly feel weird." Terrified was a better word, a lurching fear, as if I was about to fall. I didn't know where it came from, but suddenly I was so scared I couldn't breathe. My heart hammered.

"Do you want to sit down?" Curtis put a comforting hand on my arm.

"Don't touch me." Fast and angry.

"What's wrong?"

"I don't know. Something dark and awful is here."

"Sylvester Stallone?"

"Don't do that." I pushed back from the chair. "I need some air."

We went out into the sunshine. "Do you want a glass of water or something?" Curtis asked. He watched me closely.

"No thanks."

"Are you sure?"

"I'm all right." A little sharp, because I couldn't shake a feeling of dread as strong as the one I'd felt in the prison yard the day Julie was killed. As we moved away from the house, it slid to a queasiness. Stop being an idiot. You're in Malibu on a bright sunny day, and you're about to have a glass of champagne. Get over yourself. My pulse slowed. My breathing evened out.

Curtis stopped a waitress and took two glasses of champagne. He gave me one. "Here. The bubbles will lift you up."

I took a sip and moved out onto the lawn. The further I moved from the house, the better I felt. There was a lap pool and Jacuzzi near the high brick wall that defined one side of the yard. The lawn swept to a pale-wood deck that was blocked from the beach by a low glass wall set into polished wood posts. At one end of the wall, stairs went down to the sand.

There must have been at least fifty people milling around the lawn and deck. I recognized a small herd of major movie stars. Agents and producers with ready smiles and cool eyes were in animated conversation with each other while looking over the shoulders of the people they were talking to in case someone more important came close enough to snag. Brandon Tower waved from a group that included an aging action hero with a face like leather and a young actress more famous for her public drunkenness than for any movie she had made.

Terry Gwinn and Mark Siegel, the Gwingel twins, were talking fast to three young actresses in skirts so short they were practically belts. Mark made swooping movements with his hands, demonstrating something that made everyone laugh. One of the girls slapped him playfully on the chest.

My mother sat on an outdoor sofa with bright-pink cushions and talked to a distinguished gray-haired man in a wheelchair, a Polish director she had worked with fifteen years ago who had treated adolescent Julie and me with grave consideration, as if we were people whose thoughts and opinions he valued. I started to go over to say hello, but Curtis said, "Turn around."

When I did, Harry Groban was coming toward us with a grin on his face.

I felt the blood rise hot in my face.

"Curtis, you made it. Great. Great. I've been trying to get you out here for months," Groban said. "Your rat pack practically lives here." He flapped a hand at the Gwingels and Brandon. "But you've been avoiding me, you dick." High energy and good cheer. He clapped Curtis on the shoulder with one hand and shook his hand with the other while looking at me with eyes that weighed and cataloged.

Curtis, smiling but cool. "Revenge for all the times I couldn't get you on the phone."

"Hey, you were a punk lawyer. Now you're a movie mogul. From now on, you call, I pick up." He put out his hand to me. "Harry Groban. And you must be Cody Bonner." Practiced charm.

I barely found my voice. "Yes." I did not like touching his hand.

"I knew your twin sister a little bit. She used to work with Curtis over at Mitchell, Collier. She was clearly a wonderful girl. I was so sorry to hear what happened to her. We all were. And of course, your mother's been a client for a long time. Karen's one of the great talents in the business. We're lucky to have her."

He was so good I almost believed he was sincere. I wanted to scream. I tugged, and he let go of my hand.

"Are you an actress? Following your mother's footsteps?"

"No."

"The camera would love you. I'm usually right about this. Call me. We could set up a couple of quick videos if you're interested. See what we've got. Curtis has my number."

My heart kicked. My throat was closing, but neither Groban nor Curtis seemed to notice. "I'll think about it."

"Great. If there's anything I can do to help you, please let me know. Karen also has my direct number." He slapped Curtis on the shoulder and moved off toward a group that was just arriving.

In my mind I could see him hammering into the woman in his pool, his hand slapping her hard.

Curtis was watching me. A smile tugged at the corner of his mouth. Fucking Wile E. Coyote. "You shit."

"Hey, you said you wanted to meet him."

"Not like that. That was an ambush. How could you do that? I told you what I think he did."

He raised his hands in surrender. "I'm sorry."

"You didn't believe me, did you? You think I'm nuts."

"Look, Cody. I don't know. In daylight it just doesn't make sense to me."

"Is this his house?"

He could see how twisted up I was, and it worried him. "On the books the Agency owns it, but Harry is the Agency. It's the party place like today. And big clients get to use it if they want to be at the beach, that kind of thing."

"If they want privacy."

"Okay. Sure."

"I'm going to look around."

"Cody . . . I don't know if that's a good idea. Harry doesn't like people getting into his shit."

"Are you scared of him?"

"Bet your ass I am. You know the business. You need to be able to get to the actors and directors you want. Harry's the gatekeeper. If he shuts you out, you're out."

"I'm just going to look."

"For what?"

"I don't know. Whatever I find. Where do you go if you bring someone here?"

He shrugged. "I don't know."

I checked him with a look.

"There are rooms upstairs."

"I want to see them."

"I'll go with you."

"Why?"

"I don't know, to watch your back."

We went back into the house. The moment I stepped inside, the feeling of dread came back.

We went upstairs. The door to the first bedroom was open. Two women and two men were snorting lines off a glass-topped table under the window. One of the women saw us pause at the door and said, "Want some? Plenty for all," as she wiped her nose with the back of her hand.

God, maybe. Just a taste to take the edge off. It pulled me into the doorway. One of the men offered a lopsided grin in recognition of my need. It stopped me.

We moved on.

There were three more bedrooms on the second floor. One had been turned into a home gym. A couple of guys were making out in another. One of them came up for air and said, "Please close the door when you get the fuck out."

The next bedroom was sterile as a motel room but ten times more expensively furnished. The closet held only a pair of swim fins and a diving mask with a broken strap. The only thing in the bureau was a box of Kleenex.

The last bedroom was a corner room at the end of the hall. An outside staircase ran down to the backyard. When I walked into the room, I stopped breathing. The hair stood up on the back of my neck. Julie had been here. No. Julie was here.

Chapter
Twenty-Six

⟋

"What's wrong?" Curtis asked. He put a hand on my arm. "You're really pale."

"Julie was in this room."

"How do you know?"

"I can feel her."

He raised an eyebrow.

"Get out of here," I said.

"Cody, come on."

"No. Get out of here now. Leave me alone. Go."

He started to protest, but he read my face and went.

I locked the door and searched the room for something that would prove I wasn't crazy. The drawers in the bureau were empty. A couple of bathrobes hung in the closet. There was nothing in their pockets. I touched the smaller one, hoping my fingertips might sense some presence of my sister. I got nothing. I smelled the cloth for a trace of her perfume. It smelled of laundry soap.

Someone tried the door handle.

"Go away," I yelled. "We're using it." A woman laughed. A man said something, and footsteps went back along the hall.

A large platform bed jutted out from the wide wall opposite the door. It was covered with a black velvet throw, and the sheets and pillowcases were pale-blue silk. There was a mirror on the ceiling above it. A couple of drawers were built into the headboard. The first one held a ball gag with a black leather strap, a leather collar with metal studs, and a couple of pairs of restraints. The second drawer was empty, but when I closed it, something in it rattled. I opened it again and tried to pull it out of its slot, but there was a catch of some kind, and I couldn't figure it out. I felt into the drawer with my hand. My finger brushed something way at the back. I pinched it and brought it out.

It was a single earring, a heavy braid of gold with a wire for a pierced ear. I held it up to the light from the nearby window. I knew where I had seen its twin—in the wooden box on Julie's bureau.

I went into the bathroom, wrapped the earring in toilet paper, and put it in my pocket. I would take it back to Julie's to compare it to the one there, but I already knew it would match. The medicine cabinet held a bottle of Advil, a half-full box of Tampax, and a nail file. There were towels on the racks. The soaps in the shower and on the sink were new. The house was unlived in, a place to visit, a party space that was cleaned regularly. But Julie had been here, and she was still here. I could feel her. Where? Somewhere in this room. Somewhere close.

As I turned to leave, I noticed a panel under the sink that gave access to the plumbing. I crouched down to look at it. The paint was scarred around the four screws that held it to the wall. I used the nail file from the medicine cabinet to unscrew the screws. I pried the top of the panel out from the wall with the file until I could get my fingers in the gap. I pulled the panel loose and leaned it against the wall.

The pipes for the sink took up most of the space. I reached in. The space to the left wasn't deep, and my fingers touched nothing but dust. I reached into the other side and touched something soft, something wrapped in plastic.

I pulled a plastic bag out into the light. I opened the bag and pulled out a roll of cloth. A pair of panties and a bra fell out as the cloth unrolled. I stood up and held the cloth against me while I turned to the long mirror on the back of the door. I was holding a pale-green cowl-neck silk sheath dress. It was the dress Julie was wearing the last day at the office, the dress in the photo Curtis had sent me.

There was a dark smear of blood on the hem of the dress. I lurched against the door, my knees gave way, and I slid down until I was sitting on the floor with my legs splayed out. The dress was in my lap. The panties and bra were on the floor between my knees. There was more blood on the panties. I couldn't breathe.

She died in this house. She left the office one afternoon, came here, and he killed her.

I don't know how long I sat there. At some point someone knocked on the door and then went away without saying anything. I got up and stuffed the clothes back in the plastic bag. I put the panel back up and refastened the screws. I couldn't leave the clothes there for her killer to gloat over. I doused my face in cold water from the sink to shock it back into life, but when I looked in the mirror, a ghost looked back at me.

I went down the outside stairs into the backyard with the bag of Julie's clothes under my arm. I had to think.

Curtis was talking to the leather-faced action star near the pool. I didn't want him to see me. I didn't want to talk. I had to get out of there. I skirted the edges of the crowd on the lawn. My mother waved to me. I waved back but didn't stop.

I went out onto the deck, where steps led down to the beach. Halfway down, a covered rack held three surfboards and a paddleboard. There was a photograph in Groban's house of him on a paddleboard. I had told the Sheriff Department's investigator Fran Tovar that Julie's killer didn't need a boat to get her out to deep water; a surfboard or a paddleboard would work.

A group of people, glasses in hand, stood near the bottom of the stairs, talking. They moved to let me by. I took my high heels off so I could walk in the sand toward the public-access path that led from the beach to Malibu Road.

Just before I came out onto the road, I stopped to put my shoes on. A colorless older car was parked on the other side of the road. The cop Steckley sat with his back against the passenger door, watching the Agency house. I stepped back into the shadows of the tall bushes that framed the beach access and watched while Steckley smoked a cigarette down to the butt and then flicked it out the open window. He must have picked me up at Julie's and followed me to Curtis's and then here. Why? On the off chance that I was going to rob another bank? Fuck him. He could wait for me here till he grew roots. I got out my phone and called Lyft. The driver would meet me in front of Becker Surfboards in the shopping center, a five-minute walk away.

As I was about to leave, a low-slung Italian sports car growled up and parked, a Ferrari or Lamborghini, one of those 180-mile-an-hour cars that men buy to drive around LA, where the average speed on the freeways is about twenty-five. The doors swung up, and a man and a woman got out. She complained, "Jesus Christ, Jimmy, now we're going to have to walk all the way up there. Why can't you use the valet parker like everyone else?"

"I don't like to wait twenty minutes for my car when I want to leave," Jimmy said. "You run four miles a day. You spend half your life in the gym. I think you can make it a hundred yards."

"Bullshit. You're just too cheap to tip the valet."

I stepped back so the bushes masked me as they came along the sidewalk. The man had the thick, muscular build of a weight lifter. His head was shaved smooth and polished. He had a mouth that would be mean even when he smiled.

The woman wore a short yellow-and-white silk dress that showed off her body and stiletto heels that made her legs look impossibly long. Her hair was strawberry blonde. Her makeup was so well done you had to look hard to see it was there. I was pretty sure she was one of the women in the photographs on Julie's computer. What was she doing here?

There was a red birthmark on Jimmy's tanned forehead. It was shaped like a small spider. He was the man who had delivered the check to the young actress Randi Porter after she "fell down stairs."

Chapter
Twenty-Seven

∽

Curtis kept calling and texting me, but I didn't answer, and I didn't call him back, so he stopped.

My mother asked me for dinner, but I told her I was busy. "Too busy to even say hello the other day at Harry Groban's? Kurt Nowak was disappointed."

"I'm sorry."

"So were Kurt and I." The needle of guilt.

I spent a lot of time lying on the living room floor thinking about Julie and what had happened to her. Harry Groban was a violent sexual shit who abused women. His agency had a house on the beach not far from where Julie washed up. Clothes she had worn were hidden upstairs. He was a paddleboarder with the equipment to take her body out to deep water. My guess was that the bald guy, Jimmy somebody, was his fixer who made sure the women he violated would keep their mouths shut. Did he help Groban with Julie? Who was the woman with him? How did she end up in Julie's photos?

Why had Julie gone there? She must have heard the rumors about Groban. What could have gotten her there?

Every once in a while, I would pull her computer from its hiding place and stare at the photos of the women and the captions in the language I couldn't understand. Did she write them that way to confuse others who might read them, or had she left them for me because she thought I would know what she had written? If so, I was failing her again.

* * *

My car was still out in Malibu, so I used Lyft to get around. There were only two dealerships in Beverly Hills selling really expensive exotic cars. I found Alex Ames at the one off Olympic. An eager salesman with a mahogany tan and the white-on-white smile of a movie star overcame his disappointment that I wasn't there to buy a $200,000 car and told me Alex was out with a customer but would be back soon. He offered me bottled water, tea, or espresso, then lost interest in me when I said no thanks. I went outside to wait.

Ten minutes later a red Ferrari convertible announced its arrival with exhaust rumble. It came up into the lot fast and then jerked to a stop with a yip of braked tires. The driver revved the engine a last time and turned it off. Alex Ames and the driver got out and met near the front of the car. Alex saw me and his eyes widened in surprise, but he concentrated on the driver, a middle-aged stud using the windshield as a mirror to recomb his hair. He wore a black shirt three buttons open at the throat, black silky trousers, and black ankle boots. His glasses looked too dark to see through. He stroked the fender of the Ferrari like he would a horse while he and Alex talked. He nodded a few times, laughed at something Alex said, shrugged, shook his head once, stroked the car one last time, pumped Alex's hand, walked to a Corvette, and drove away.

Alex walked over to where I waited at a table under an umbrella on the small patio outside the showroom door.

"Hi."

"Hi yourself, the mysterious Cody no-name." He stood with his hands on the back of a chair looking down at me.

"Is he going to buy the car?" I pointed a finger at the Ferrari.

"He is. He just doesn't know it yet. It'll take him a couple of days to persuade himself that he owes it to himself to have it." He pulled out the chair and sat down and looked at me across the table with his chin resting on his palm. "You seduced me without shame; you used me for your pleasure and threw me away when you were done with me."

"And loved every minute of it."

"You've been haunted by the memory, and now you're back to ask for forgiveness and for a small place in a corner of my heart."

"That, of course. And less importantly, I need your help with something."

"Aha." He sat up straight in the chair. "What?"

"Did you sell a Lamborghini to a man named Jimmy, last name unknown? He's about six feet tall, muscles, shaved head, and a birthmark sort of like a spider on his forehead."

"No."

"Shit. I went to the other dealer in Beverly Hills, and they didn't know him. There's one out in the Valley and another in Torrance. He probably bought it in Phoenix or someplace. Dead end."

"I sold him two Lamborghinis. He cracked one up and bought another after he got out of the hospital and the insurance kicked in. When he came to pick it up, he was still in a cast. Jimmy Lasker."

"That's great. Will you give me his address, phone, whatever you've got?"

"Why do you need this? What did he do? What do you want from him?"

"Does it matter?"

He thought about it. Then he stood up. "Okay, Cody Mysteriosa, I'm going to do this for you. No, you know, quid pro quo, give-and-take. I'm going to do it because I like you. And, uh, I'd like you to keep me in mind."

"Alex, I'm kind of with someone."

He nodded. "How could you not be? But hey, this is LA. Marriages only last a couple of weeks. I'm an optimist." He took out his phone and ran through his contacts. "Give me your number. I'll text it to you."

"I can copy it."

"Damn. Okay." He held out his phone, and I copied it onto mine.

"Thank you." I kissed him on the cheek.

"Keep me in mind."

"I will."

Jimmy Lasker lived in a big high-rise building on Wilshire Boulevard in Westwood. I waited outside in a rental car for two days before I spotted him. In the early afternoon a valet brought his car up to the entrance driveway. Ten minutes later Lasker came out. He said something to the doorman, who was dressed in a uniform that would make an admiral proud, got in the car, and blasted out onto Wilshire. I almost lost him at the first light, but I squeezed through on the yellow and followed him into Beverly Hills. He turned north on Rodeo Drive and then east again on Sunset. I hung back just in case he was in a suspicious mood. He drove a car that could go two hundred miles an hour, but in LA traffic I could have kept up with him on roller skates. Just after we crossed into West Hollywood, he pulled in under the portico of the five-story building set back from Sunset. I drove up the block and parked. I watched in the mirror as a valet in a dark-green uniform came out and ran around to open the car door. Lasker got out and went into the building. The valet revved the Lamborghini's engine and popped the clutch, and the car darted forward. He drove by me, threw the car into a right turn, and disappeared down the hill toward the parking lot behind the building.

Before I got out of my car, I put on dark glasses and a scarf to cover my hair. At a quick glance I looked like half the young women on the street and no more memorable. As I walked back, I saw the building had no windows fronting the street, but there must have been a camera somewhere, because seconds after I stepped in under the portico, the massive carved wood door opened and a man came out. He wore a black suit and a white shirt. His gray tie with small red clocks was his only sign of wildness. He was compact, with even features and seriously short hair. He looked like a cross between a funeral director and a bouncer.

"Can I help you?" A low voice without much affect, polite in case I was somebody, cool in case I wasn't.

"I was walking, and I thought I saw Jimmy Lasker go in."

"Yes." Not yes, he did, but yes, I'm listening.

"What is this place?" I had my voice pitched toward the brainless end of the spectrum. It comforts tough guys to feel they're not only stronger but smarter.

"Asgard House is a private club."

"Cool. Like a sports club or something?"

"No."

"What's an Asgard?"

"In Norse mythology, it's where Valhalla is. It's the place where heroes go when they die."

"Wow. Heroes. Okay. Listen, tell Jimmy Annie says hi."

"Annie who?"

I slapped him on the arm and laughed at the silliness of the question. "Don't worry. He'll know." I went off down the street. When I looked back, he had gone back inside to report. Guys like Jimmy Lasker always had Annies in their lives. He wouldn't give it a minute of thought.

*   *   *

I spent a lot of time at the Muay Thai gym the next few days trying to sweat out anger and bullshit until the day Sakchai, the owner, told me to go home before I hurt someone or hurt myself.

Curtis was waiting outside the townhouse. My traitor heart jumped when I saw him.

"I brought your car back."

"Thanks."

"May I come in?" Curtis asked.

"What for?"

"To grovel. If I do it out here on the pavement, I'll ruin the knees of my pants."

"You're an asshole." I didn't want to give up my anger at him. I should have told him to fuck off. Instead, I unlocked the door and went in, leaving it open. He came in and closed it behind him. "I'm going to go take a shower. There's beer and wine in the fridge, tequila in the cabinet."

When I came downstairs twenty minutes later, Curtis was on his knees in the hall. "What the hell, Curtis?"

"I don't know what happened out in Malibu, but whatever it was is my fault. I took you there. I should have told you where we were going, but I was being a smartass. Whatever happened is on me. I apologize." His face was serious.

"Get up."

"I'm sorry."

"I heard you. Get up." He didn't move. "Apology accepted. Get up."

I reached out. He didn't need a hand up. It was a gesture of forgiveness. He took my hand and stood.

"I still think he killed Julie." I told him about the clothes I had found and the earring that matched the one upstairs on Julie's dresser.

"Jesus. Don't you think you should call the cops?"

"I'm a convicted felon. Groban runs an important company and is friends with half the weight in LA. Can I prove the clothes belong to Julie? I don't know. I guess if they have her DNA on them, it would be something, but how do I prove she was there to see Groban? How do I prove he was there at the same time? You said lots of people in the business use the house. What do I tell the cops about how I found the clothes? That's probably illegal search."

He followed me into the kitchen. I opened two cold beers from the fridge and handed him one.

"Okay, take me through it. Tell me how you think it happened."

"He abuses women. Something went wrong. Something went too far. I don't know."

"But Julie? Why would Julie go anywhere near him?"

"Mitchell, Collier, and Brown were his lawyers. Maybe she went to his house on something legal."

He shook his head. "I don't think so."

"Why not?"

"Harry Groban has a reputation. No one comes right out and says it, but everyone kind of knows."

"You mean the men know but they don't say anything. I'll bet you the women talk about it."

"Marty Collier would never send someone like Julie to Groban's house," he said.

"A good-looking, young woman."

He shrugged. "If someone else in the firm had sent her there the day she disappeared, it would have been on the calendar. Someone would have mentioned it."

"Maybe she wasn't sent. Maybe she ran into him after work."

"Okay, but why would she go to his house?"

"I don't know. Maybe he asked her to come pick up some papers." I wasn't going to tell him she had been there before. Share the information and you lose control of it. I had to know why Julie had gone there before I did that.

"There were no papers to pick up. That would have come up somewhere in the investigation."

I said nothing.

"Okay. I get it," Curtis said. "An excuse to get her to the house. And things got out of hand."

I waited while he thought about it.

"How are you going to find out for sure?" he asked.

"I don't know."

I drove him back to his house. He said he could take Lyft or Uber, but I owed him, both for bringing my car back and for my anger, which was greater than his crime.

And I wanted to be with him.

We headed west against the headlight stream of rush hour traffic going the other way. When we hit the Pacific Coast Highway, the last of the sun had sunk to the ocean and the horizon was a band of scarlet and gold. We traveled in silence. Curtis had pushed his seat back and his head rested against the window. He closed his eyes, and in sleep he looked about fifteen years old. When I stopped in front of his house, he opened his eyes. "Do you want to come in?"

I did. I wanted to go in. I wanted to stay. I didn't know for how long, but I wanted it then. Refuge. A place away. Away from what? Away from whatever it was I was doing. Away from wherever it was going to take me.

He waited.

"Yes."

We went up to his bedroom and had sex. Or fucked. Or made love. Sometimes what you call something has no meaning compared to the thing itself.

* * *

Steckley parked his car up the road past Curtis Whyle's driveway where he could watch the entrance. He had missed the Bonner woman when she left the party house in Malibu. He had watched her car being delivered to the front of the house by the valet, but the guy she had come with had come out and driven away in it. She hadn't left by the front door, so she had taken off up or down the beach, and he had wondered why she sneaked out like that. The car had led him to Whyle's house. He ran the address to get Whyle's name and then had spent time on the internet to find out who he was: formerly a lawyer at Mitchell, Collier, & Brown, a big entertainment law firm, and now the president of Black Light Films at Twenty-First Century. The little fucker had jumped from around two hundred thousand bucks a year at the law firm to somewhere over a million at Black Light, according to Steckley's brother, Harvin, who was vice president for doodah and bullshit over at Universal Studios. Harvin was the go-to guy if you wanted news and rumors about what went on in the movie world. Steckley thought his brother was an asshole, a dreamer, a believer in miracles—perfect for the movie business, where nobody seemed to know what the hell they were doing. To Steckley, making movies looked like throwing stuff against the wall and hoping it would stick. Sometimes it did. Sometimes they took the same stuff, the same stars, same director, same writers, threw it against the wall, and it slid to the bottom like a pile of crap. When it worked, everyone was a genius. When it didn't work, all the fingers pointed at some idiot who had fucked it up despite all the geniuses.

Steckley was a man for rules and straight lines, no cutting corners, one foot in front of the other until you get to where you're supposed to go. The movie business was full of people like Curtis Whyle, people who got where they wanted to go without doing the work. They chapped his ass. The moment someone began cutting corners, he was on his way to breaking the law. Whyle and Bonner deserved each other. Cody Bonner. Jesus, he wanted her under the lights. Her car was still at Whyle's at midnight, so he went home.

He poured some rye over ice and stood at the window of his Boyle Heights apartment and looked out at the lights of the city. The neighborhood was changing. Gentrification. The bodegas were giving way to coffee shops where they sold you a six-dollar latte made with almond milk. Half the people on the street wore yoga pants. He wanted to smack them.

From somewhere farther to the south came the pop, pop, pop of gunfire—the assholes in Shootin' Newton at play. Not his problem just then. Cody Bonner was his problem.

Chapter Twenty-Eight

～

Curtis took me to Asgard House on a Saturday night. Paparazzi and celebrity junkies snapped photos as we drove into the parking lot. The valet took Curtis's Porsche and parked it in a corner where it wouldn't embarrass the really expensive cars. The man at the door wore a black suit and a blue silk shirt open at the collar. He was built like a linebacker and had one of those secret service earbuds in his ear. He nodded to Curtis and opened the door.

"Why the hell do you want to go there?" Curtis had asked when I brought up Asgard House. We had been in his pool and lying naked on pads, absorbing a dose of cancer.

"Somebody told me it was a cool place."

"Check his credentials."

"Do you know a member, someone who can get us in?" I tried to keep it light so he wouldn't wonder why it was important to me.

"I'm a member."

"You're a member of someplace that's not cool?"

"Hey, I'm the head of a successful film company. I have obligations." He dropped the mock indignation. "It's the movie business. If the herd joins the new hot place and you don't, everyone begins to wonder if maybe you're no longer hot. If you're no longer hot, they think maybe they should take their projects somewhere else. Pretty soon you are no longer hot because all the projects went away. So you join, and every once in a while you go, have a couple of drinks, and kiss the people you're supposed to kiss."

"Let's go kiss some people. I want to see it."

"Okay."

One of LA's beautiful young women perched at a desk in the entry hall. "Good evening, Mr. Whyle. It's nice to see you again."

"How are you, Blake?"

"I'm fine. Thank you. What can we do for you this evening?"

"I think we'll start out downstairs."

The room was called Valhalla, but this wasn't the kind of place that felt it had to put up old swords and drinking horns. The booths were deep and private, the chairs were comfortable, the lighting discreet, the service quiet and efficient. The men and women servers were all beautiful.

Curtis ordered a Rusty Nail.

"What is that?"

"Drambuie and Scotch. It's not too sweet. The Scotch gives it some bite. Want to try it?"

"Sure."

"Two. On the rocks." The waitress went away.

I hadn't been in a club like this before. I went off to prison a year before I could legally drink, and kids with false IDs don't go into places that look like big money and serious adults. There can't be fun in a place like that. And if you're on the street, you're not going to pay bar prices. You're going to liquor stores where they'll sell you a quart of malt without giving a damn about your age.

Almost all the tables were full. A rumble of conversation, the occasional spike of laughter or shriek of delight, but on the whole, the noise level was low. I looked around the room. Channing Tatum and five friends were seated a respectable distance from Ryan Gosling and his three, and Justin Timberlake was all the way across the room with three women and another man. Margot Robbie was in a booth near us. She leaned in to talk quietly with a good-looking bearded man who reached over to touch her cheek. She turned her face to kiss his palm.

The waitress brought our drinks. I took a sip. Curtis waited to see how I liked it.

I raised the glass in appreciation. "I guess nobody comes in here to rip it up."

"Hey, you haven't seen the whole place yet. The dance floor and the big bar are upstairs. Some bedrooms on the floors above that. And a roof garden on top. Do you mind if I leave you for a few minutes? I need to work the room."

"Go work. Go kiss somebody."

Jimmy Lasker came out of the back room and stopped to talk to a waitress for a minute. He crossed to the bar, and by the time he got there, the bartender was pouring his drink. Lasker picked it up, said something to the bartender, and went out the door we had entered and up the stairs.

Curtis was talking to a Black man and an Asian woman at a table across the room. He saw me get up from our table. I pointed at myself and then at the ceiling. He nodded, and I went out and went upstairs.

I didn't hear the music till I opened the big, padded doors. Then it knocked me back. The bass beat was heavy enough to change your heart rhythm. The crowd here was younger, and the dance floor was packed. Most of the women knew what they were doing on the floor, but for every man who could dance there were three who looked like they needed antiseizure drugs. Brandon was dancing with a stunning Black woman a couple of inches taller than his six one. Trust Brandon to be one of the good ones. He didn't do things in public he wasn't good at. Terry Gwinn and Mark Siegel were with three women in one of the booths that lined the wall. One of them looked familiar, but the light was low and they were across the room and I couldn't tell who it was. They didn't see me, and I made no move to go to them.

Jimmy Lasker was leaning on the bar, talking to the bartender.

I took a stool next to him. "What can I get you?" the bartender asked. When Lasker glanced at me, he jerked in surprise.

"A Bombay martini, up, not too dry, a twist."

"You got it."

Lasker was looking into his drink as if he might find an answer to something at the bottom of the glass. "You knew my sister," I said.

He looked at me as if for the first time. "Who's your sister?"

"Julie Bonner."

He pretended to think about it and then shook his head. "Uh-uh, I don't think so." His head was newly shaved. Maybe he waxed it, because it shone under the bar lights. The red spider on his forehead stood out. His hands were stubby and thickly padded with muscle.

"If you didn't know her, I'm just another woman sitting at a bar. If you did know her, then you know she's dead, and looking at me gives you one of those Walking Dead moments, 'cause I look just like her. You flinched when you saw me. Dead giveaway."

"Sure. Whatever you say." I could smell the heavy cologne he wore. It couldn't quite cover his body musk, a whiff of the zoo. His eyes were like stones set deep in his head. When he looked at me, it was like being watched by an animal from the darkness of his cave.

He scared me.

The bartender put my drink down in front of me. "Account name?"

"Curtis Whyle."

He nodded and went away.

"What about Randi Porter?" I asked Lasker. "Do you know her?"

"No."

"Somebody beat her up. You delivered the *Get out of town* check, and she got out of town."

Nothing changed in his face. "Huh. When I was about ten, I found a hornets' nest. I started poking at it with a stick to see what would happen. I found out. You kind of remind me of that. Why don't you fuck off like a good girl?"

I raised my glass to Lasker. "Have it your way, Jimmy." I picked up my drink and walked away from him. Go when you've had the last word, an exit strategy I learned from my mother. I'd confirmed that Jimmy Lasker knew Julie. Now I had to find out why that was important. And I had seen one of the women at the twins' table get up and walk toward the ladies' room. It was a woman from Julie's photos, the strawberry blonde I had seen with Lasker in Malibu outside Groban's house.

Two of the stalls were in use. I put my glass on the shelf above the sinks and washed my hands while I waited. One of the stall doors crashed open, and a rail-thin woman with scarlet hair wearing a tight black dress stilted out on stiletto heels. She closed her purse with a snap, pinched her nose and snorted, gave me a scorching look, and banged out through door. Sometimes I missed that chemical urgency to get somewhere fast to do something that couldn't wait.

A moment later the other door opened and the strawberry blonde came out. She didn't really notice me until she was at the sink and saw me in the mirror. Her eyes widened and her face paled. She grabbed the sink to steady herself. "It's okay," I said. "I'm her sister, not a ghost."

"Jesus. For a minute there, I don't know. It freaked me out." She looked me over closely. "Okay. Wow."

"I'm Cody Bonner. What's your name?"

"Ashley." She started to say her last name and then stopped. "How'd you know I knew your sister?"

"I've seen the photograph on her computer."

She tightened up. "What photograph?"

"The one where you had a black eye and a busted mouth."

"I don't know what you're talking about." She was scared.

"You don't know?"

"No. Whoever it was, it wasn't me. Nobody puts a hand to me."

"Uh-huh. She has photographs of a bunch of women nobody puts a hand on—except whoever beat the crap out of them. Who are they?"

"I don't know what you're talking about. I saw your sister a couple of times around town. I had coffee with her maybe twice. That's it." She had recovered enough to come up with the lie.

"Okay. All right. Do you know Harry Groban?"

"I know who he is. Everybody in the business knows who he is. I'm an actress." She felt she was on safer ground.

"Have you ever met him?"

"No, I don't think so. I'd remember. He can really do you some good if you're an actress." She took a brush out of her purse and began to fix her hair.

"I saw you going into his party in Malibu with Jimmy Lasker."

Her face closed up. "Okay, that's fucking sneaky. I'm not going to talk to you anymore."

"Who are the other women in the photos? What happened to them? What was my sister doing? Why did she take those pictures?"

"Fuck you. I don't know what you're talking about. Leave me alone." Then she was gone.

Chapter Twenty-Nine

⸜

I had downloaded all the decrypted files from Julie's computer to the new laptop I had bought to replace the stolen one. I hid Julie's computer behind a panel in the kitchen broom closet. I worked at the dining room table to translate the text she had written in our twin language below the photos. Day after day I failed. Some of the words were familiar and their meanings were just below the surface in my brain, but I couldn't pull them up.

I became angry with Julie. Why hadn't she told me she was preserving the language? Why had she locked me out?

Why had I done it to her? Why hadn't I told her what I was going to do? Maybe because I didn't really know myself.

Julie was driving us home from school that day. We were headed west along Pico. She was complaining about how Mr. Barker always called on the boys first in science class, something I thought was a blessing. It allowed me to sit in the back row and read trashy novels. That month I was into the Twilight series by Stephenie Meyer—vampires, sexual tension, and teen alienation. I sucked them up, and reading them beat listening to Mr. Barker drone on about plant classifications.

Our school should have been named The Academy of Spoiled Children. We were the kids of movie stars, producers, directors, software billionaires, high-priced lawyers. Half the kids had tutors for every subject. The tutors were paid to do their homework. The cars in the students' parking lot were worth more than all the yearly salaries of the teachers combined. For diversity, we had kids whose families made less than a quarter of a million a year.

And Curtis.

That Monday Brandon Tower had shown up with a new BMW convertible. The word went around that Terry Gwinn had bought it for him. The word went that Terry, Mark Siegel, and Brandon had stomped a homeless guy they found in an alley in Ocean Park.

For kicks.

Kicks for the homeless guy. Kicks for the boys. The word went around that Mark and Brandon had been picked up by the cops. Terry got away. The cops knew there were three of them, but Mark and Brandon weren't talking. Expensive lawyers were brought in by Brandon's father and by the people who handled Mark's trust fund. Mark and Brandon were still juveniles. Terry was already eighteen, an adult by some measure that had nothing to do with impulse control but everything to do with going to jail as a grown-up. Mark would never have ratted Terry out, but Brandon had to figure out where his loyalty lay and what his price was. A new BMW simplified his choices. So the word went.

The homeless guy disappeared. A bus ticket out of town and an envelope of cash, so the word went. This too was an LA story. Maybe it was the truth.

I asked Curtis about it, because Curtis always knew the secrets, but he wasn't talking. He was like that. Sometimes he retailed the rumors. Sometimes he leaked them out in a strategy whose purpose only he knew. Sometimes all you got was a knowing smile. That's what he gave me that day. That and "You're very cool, Cody Bonner, the best. But try not to care so much. Nobody else does." He pressed his finger to my forehead like a blessing, smiled that smile, and walked away.

What made three boys who had everything kick the shit out of a man who had nothing? I thought about that, but I didn't come up with an answer that would have passed with people who believe that every effect can be traced to a discernible cause. Maybe they just wanted to do it and acted before they thought out the consequences.

I knew how that went. I was doing that over and over again those days. Maybe it was the drugs I was using. Maybe the drugs were another symptom of what was wrong with me.

We stopped for the light at Lincoln Boulevard. Julie looked over at me, having picked up on my silence. "Are you all right?"

"No." I got out of the car.

"Where are you going?" She was startled by my sudden exit.

"I don't know." I shut the door and walked away into my first night on the street.

Why did I do it? I sure as hell didn't know what the consequences would be.

At the time I wanted to get away from everything I knew, everything familiar, everything that made me *me*. I wanted to shed the skin of who I was. I didn't want to be the me I had been brought up to be. I wanted to get away from expectations, from responsibilities, from the bullshit everyone passes off as reality, from being told it's one thing when you already know it's something else. I wanted to get away from the Academy of Spoiled Children, from the cliques, the cruelty, the rules of cool, from my mother and the confusion in her eyes when she looked at me. I wanted to go where no one knew me, where I could be who *I* wanted to be.

Laughable now, but that's what I had to have then.

Mom hired detectives. They eventually found me and scooped me off the street. Mom sent me to a tough-love rehab camp in the hills above Ojai. It was run by a hot-shit, charismatic ex–Green Beret, the go-to guy for LA parents with kids like me. He ran it like a boot camp—early-morning runs, physical exhaustion, a twelve-step program, Spartan quarters, daily chores to help run the camp. I went with it until they believed I had turned the corner and sent me home.

I fooled everyone but Julie. "Is there anything I can do?"

"I wish there was," I said.

"You just have to ask."

"I know."

I made it through high school graduation. Then Julie went to San Francisco for a summer internship before starting Stanford. I ran into a guy I'd known in rehab. He had some primo stuff. I thought I'd give it a try just to see. A week later I was back on the streets.

I make no complaints about what happened to me. I did it to myself. I grew up in privilege, and I threw it away. I don't know why, but that's what I did.

I got what I wanted. Life on the street peels you down to the core fast. Where do you sleep? How do you get food? Which do you need more, food or drugs? What will you do to get them? Who do you trust? Survive, or don't.

You get down to the place where a pair of clean socks is the best thing in the world. Weird to think of bank robbery as a way up from the bottom.

Chapter Thirty

It isn't hard to kill someone. People do it all the time. I spent years locked up with a bunch of them. There was a woman named Callie Brown I used to walk with on the yard. She had a hitch in her step from the time her husband broke her leg with a crowbar. She'd used a ball peen hammer to drive a tenpenny nail into his temple while he slept. "Easier than driving a finishing nail into soft wood," she said with some satisfaction. "He kept complaining I wasn't handy, but I was handy enough that day." Betty Lobel, the librarian who decided I needed an education, had slit her husband's throat with a knife he'd stolen from Outback Steakhouse. I knew poisoners, shooters, and a woman who ran down her boyfriend with his own pickup truck in the driveway of his side girl's house. She kept rolling over him backward and forward till he stopped moving. Killing was easy. Getting away with it was the problem. I knew a lot of efficient killers, and they were all behind walls.

Harry Groban was one of those guys with power and money who gets away with things. He had already proved that when he sued the woman who had accused him of abuse. He had killed my sister. I was going to kill Harry Groban, and I had to get away with it, because I was never going back inside again.

All I had to do was figure out how.

The first rule: never tell anyone you're going to commit a crime. The women I knew in prison had been betrayed by family, friends, and lovers. A secret between two people remains a secret only if one of them is dead.

The second rule: don't leave a trail. Don't buy a gun from the brother of the dude you used to sleep with. He will trade you out for a lighter sentence when he gets caught with a pound of crank. Don't ask the chemistry guy about untraceable poisons. Don't bring your friend's car back with a dented fender and blood on the hood. Don't tell anyone about how you've figured out the perfect way to dispose of a body.

Trust no one.

Even Curtis?

I had told him Groban killed my sister. What would he think if Groban turned up dead? Would he think of me? Wile E. Coyote would definitely think of me. Keep that in mind. Make it part of the equation. Trust no one.

* * *

I rode the train into downtown LA, got off at the Seventh Street station, and walked the few blocks to Central Public Library. If you're going to plan a murder, listen to your paranoid self. Mine was telling me to put distance between where I lived and what I was hoping to find. I would do no research on my own computer, none at the Santa Monica library.

I used a different computer terminal every day. I wore crappy clothes and running shoes I bought at Goodwill to blend in with the homeless and street people who were the daily users of the library.

I learned about poisons.

White arsenic is a tasteless, water-soluble solid you can easily add to drinks.

Strychnine is extracted from the seeds of the Southeast Asian nux vomica tree. It is used in rat poisons and available from hardware stores and pest control websites.

Cyanide is the fastest-acting poison and the favored suicide pill for spies.

Thallium sulfate is water soluble and tasteless, and the symptoms often mimic symptoms of other illnesses.

They all leave a residue in the body that will show up in an autopsy. They all indicate the killer knew the victim well enough to get close enough to him to give him the stuff.

I read about sniper rifles, about men who could hit a target the size of a playing card from a mile away. The advantage was distance—no DNA at the scene of the crime. No indication of passion that would suggest the killer knew the victim well enough to get close. It could be a random killing.

I'd never shot a rifle. Hiring someone else to use one broke the basic rule—trust no one.

I read case after case of murders made to look like accidents, murders made to look like suicides, murders made to look like robberies gone wrong, murders made to look like home invasions.

Every one I read about failed in one crucial aspect: the murderer had been caught. What the hell good was the internet if it couldn't tell me how to kill Groban and get away with it? Maybe I wasn't smart enough. Maybe Harry Groban was smarter. He was getting away with murder.

Chapter
Thirty-One

If you're going to kill a man, learn his habits.

I spent days following Groban. I'd pick him up at his house in the morning and follow him to his office. The Agency was on Colorado Boulevard in Santa Monica in a football-shaped building of curved milky-glass panels that looked like an alien space pod.

Groban drove a gray Maybach sedan. Google revealed that it had cost him just over $350,000.00. The perfect car for a Hollywood prince, it was elegant in an understated way, but it told those who knew what things cost that he was breathing the pure air near the top of the mountain. Some days he drove it into the underground garage. If he left it in the semicircular driveway, it meant he would drive himself to appointments. Hollywood is feudal. Harry Groban was a powerful man. People who had less power came to him. Men and women who had more power summoned him, though there weren't many women who could do that. Mom might have been one for a while after she won the Oscar. On the days he left the car out front, he was going to see someone with more weight. Or he was going to see someone with less weight whom he wanted to flatter with a visit.

LA calculations.

I followed him wherever I could. I wasn't good at it. I lost him at red lights. I lost him when cars cut in front of me and blocked me from seeing him make a turn. I lost him at studio entrances. You don't get on studio lots without a pass. Twice in one week he went onto the Twenty-First Century lot, the only studio he visited more than once.

I asked Curtis for a pass from Black Light.

"What kind of pass?"

"An employee pass so I can get on the lot whenever I want."

"Why do you want that?"

"I'm not going to tell you."

We were in bed at his house. He raised himself on one elbow to see me better. "Why not?"

"Because you don't have to know."

"Hmmm." He studied me like a man trying to figure out which piece of the puzzle to move first. Then he sighed and fell back on the pillow. "Clever woman. First sex, then ask for the favor."

"Will you do it?"

"Of course. But you've cheapened our relationship. You've made it transactional."

I put my hand on him. "Want to do it again?"

"What'll it cost me?"

"I haven't decided yet."

"Ah, what the hell. How much lower can we sink?" He rolled toward me.

* * *

Two days later, I used my new employee's sticker to follow Groban onto the Twenty-First lot. He had a meeting in one of the buildings that housed independent productions. I missed him when he came out, but I found him in the commissary. He was sitting with my mother. She laughed at something he said and reached across the table to touch his arm. It was a gesture of intimacy that made my skin crawl.

"Hi, Mom." I leaned in to kiss her on the cheek.

"Cody, what are you doing here?" My ear picked up the slight accusation in her voice. My mother did not like surprises.

"I had to get something from Curtis. Hello, Harry. How are you? Nice to see you again." He rose and kissed me on the cheek.

"Cody. Hey, great. Sit down. Sit down. Can I get you something to eat?" He raised a hand for a waiter.

"No, thanks. I've eaten." I took a chair with my back to the window.

Groban waved off the waiter and stood. "Karen, I've got to run. Have you read the script yet? I'd like to let Warners know you're interested."

"I'm not interested."

"It's an Academy Award part." His look didn't change, but now there was something hard under the calm.

"I'm not old enough to play someone's grandmother."

"She's not a grandmother."

"She sure as hell acts and talks like one. 'A woman of a certain age'—that's how she's described in the script. 'A certain age.' Do you know what that means? It means old. Once a woman takes one of those parts, she's done doing anything else. I'm not doing it."

"Nicole does parts like that."

"Nicole is Australian."

"What the hell does that have to do with it?"

"I don't know, but it must be something."

I laughed, but her look slapped me quiet.

"Meryl Streep," Groban said.

"Meryl's a freak of nature. She could play a hundred or fifteen. No one else can do what she does. But look, Julia's still getting laid on-screen. Julianne spends half her time in front of the camera naked. If they can do it, so can I. We talked about this. I am not playing the mother of anyone over the age of ten." She pointed a finger at me just in case I had something to say. "That time will come, but it is not here now."

"It's a great part. It's going to be an important film."

"Fine. Then there'll be plenty of your other clients who'll jump to do it. Not me."

"Okay," Groban said, but he wasn't happy. "We'll find you something else. Cody, it's good to see you again. Have you thought about my offer?"

"I'm thinking about it."

"Whenever you want, just call my office." He nodded to me, touched Mom affectionately on the shoulder, and left.

"Way to go, Mom."

She looked startled for a moment at my praise, then smiled at me. "He doesn't like it when people say no to him, but you've got to stick up for yourself. No one else will."

"Did he ever hit on you?" I asked.

"Who? Harry?" She laughed. "Cody, almost every man in the business hit on me. Even some of the women. On my first feature the crew had a pool on when the makeup lady would nail me." She laughed again. "You looked shocked."

"I'm trying to think of my follow-up question."

"The obvious one is, who succeeded?"

"Well?"

She waved that away. "You know, sometimes it was just flirting, no pressure, just attraction. And sometimes it wasn't. Sometimes it was obvious and ugly and it was *Do this for me and maybe I'll do that for you.*"

"And?"

She shrugged. "If I went back and thought about it, I could find times things happened that shouldn't have. But I don't go back. And now? Maybe I'm getting too old to be a target. I talk to other women, and they say it's still out there."

"Even after Harvey Weinstein?"

"Men have the memory of a radish when it suits them. You'd think they'd learn, but every day you hear about some idiot at a college who's hitting on his students or some middle-management fool who thinks his secretary should spend time under his desk."

"So did Harry hit on you?"

"Harry's a wonderful agent, but he's a shit, and I stopped sleeping with shits, even beautiful ones, which he is not, before he became my agent." She stood up. "I have call in fifteen minutes. Walk with me."

Outside the sun was bright, but the air was cool. We walked to the sound stage where they were shooting *Injunction* and went into her trailer, parked near the stage door.

"What was the offer Harry mentioned?" Mom asked. She threw her purse on a chair and began to take off her clothes.

"He said he'd set up a screen test if I wanted. He thinks I should go back into acting. I bet he says that to all the girls."

"Only the ones who look like you. You should do it. You were very good in *Family Feeling.*" She put on a ratty flannel bathrobe and tied her hair back tight.

I poked around a counter covered with makeup. "No, Mom. Julie was good. I just looked exactly like her, so they could use me to get around the child labor laws."

"Julie was good, but it was technique. You had something the camera loved. It can't be taught."

"Julie was great. I was a huge pain in the ass." I found a lipstick and drew myself a heavy red mouth and made a face at myself in the mirror the way I used to when I was a kid and Mom took us to the set. "Half the time I didn't know my lines. I was always getting my costume dirty. Sometimes they couldn't find me when it was time to shoot. They wanted to fire me. The only reason they kept me on was 'cause I was her double."

"No. Three different directors and the producer told me that they would use Julie for all the stuff that bored you and save the emotion scene for you, because you gave them something they couldn't get from her."

"Yeah, yeah, yeah. Come on." I smeared on thick eyeliner, rouge, and a metallic green eye shadow until I looked like Cleopatra after a very bad night.

"And Julie knew it. That's why she wanted to quit after the third season."

"What? Wait. She quit because *I* wanted to."

"No. She quit because you were better at it than she was. She wasn't used to that, and she didn't like it."

It stunned me. "She never told me that. I thought she quit because of me."

"Nobody tells everything. Everyone has something they don't want you to know."

"Not Julie. Not with me."

She looked at me seriously. "Maybe you didn't know your sister as well as you thought you did. I always wondered if Julie held back because you were so out there. You were always leaping without looking, and she decided she wasn't going to do that too. Then you went to prison. And she thought, okay, I'm by myself now. Cody's gone. I'll do what *I* want. I'll let some of that out."

"And that's what got her killed?" My heart raced. "I went to prison, and so she went out and did something stupid that got her killed?" My face was hot and I had trouble breathing.

"No, no." My mother looked like I had hit her. She reached out to me, but I knocked her hand away. "That's not what I meant at all. I was just saying that I think she suddenly wanted to be different. She didn't want to be cautious anymore. She didn't want to always obey all the rules."

"She didn't obey all the rules when we were kids either. You just didn't know about it. And whenever something went wrong, you blamed it on me. You decided she was the good one and I was the bad one, and that was it."

"No, Cody, no. I never thought that." She reached out to hug me. I tried to fend her off, but she got her arms around me and drew me in. I stood there stiffly. I could feel her heart. It was racing as fast as mine. Her hair was in my face, and I could smell the shampoo she always used, a smell from our childhood. I began to cry silently, but she sensed it. She stroked my back and held me close. "It wasn't you," she said. "You're not to blame."

"Then who is? Who is?" Why was I wailing like a child? I knew who was to blame.

Chapter Thirty-Two

～

I woke up in the middle of the night with a plan on how to kill Harry Groban and get away with it.

Anything thought of at three o'clock in the morning is probably fucked up, but when I examined it in daylight, it still looked good. Of course, if one little thing went sideways . . . Don't think about that. Put it in motion. See how it feels. You can always stop if things start to go bad. Can't you?

The first thing was to get back into Groban's house to check out the gun in his desk drawer.

I put on the dark clothes I had bought for the first time I scouted his house. I made coffee and forced myself to eat a couple of eggs for the energy. I went out in the early-morning light and stopped at the twenty-four-hour Ralph's on Olympic to buy a large bunch of cut flowers. Then I drove up into Brentwood and waited on a street a half a mile from Groban's house on the route he took to work. At eight thirty he drove by me in the Maybach. He was talking on the phone. I waited ten more minutes to make sure he wasn't coming back to pick up something he'd forgotten. Then I drove up to his house and parked in front. If the house-keeper was on the same schedule, she wasn't due for another half hour. I got out of the car and walked boldly up to the front door and rang the bell as if I were delivering the flowers, a charade for anyone watching from another house. While I waited for someone to answer, I examined the front door lock. It was a Kwikset. I rang the bell again, waited, and then walked back to the car with the flowers and drove away.

Don't buy anything with a credit card or an ATM card when you're buying for a job. Plastic can be traced. Leave your cell phone at home. It works like a GPS. They can tell where you are and where you've been. Even if it's supposedly untrackable like mine, why take the chance? Don't buy all your burglar tools in the same store. It makes it too easy for the cops to gather evidence.

I bought a Kwikset lock like the one on Groban's front door with keys to fit it and two extra blanks at a locksmith's on Lincoln. Then I walked to a hardware store on Olympic and bought a slim taper triangular file and small vise. I found a mallet with a hard rubber head in a hobby store on Wilshire. On the way home I stopped at another locksmith shop and bought a Schlage lock, keys, and two blanks for about the same price as the Kwikset. I couldn't remember what the lock was on the glass door into Groban's living room from the pool area, and I wasn't going back over the wall to find out. Schlage and Kwikset are the most popular locks with contractors. I figured one or the other would be on the yard door.

* * *

Steckley stepped out of his Boyle Heights building at five thirty in the morning. The owners of the bodega on the corner were rolling up the metal shutters in front of the store. At least three times a week he stopped in for a breakfast burrito. The word was that they had sold out to a developer. Well, good for them, but bad for him. Where was he going to find something to eat in the morning? He hated change. He got his car out of the garage space behind the apartment building and drove out East First Street to pick up the 10, headed west. Not even six o'clock and the traffic was heavy. No point in fighting it. Just get in a lane and go with the flow. He got off at Overland and went up to Pico and found a parking space where he could watch the exit from Bonner's place.

She came out in the BMW a few minutes after seven thirty. He let a few cars go by and then pulled out to follow her. He wasn't worried about losing her. The tracker would tell him where she was going. Ten minutes later she parked at a twenty-four-hour Ralph's. He parked where he could watch her car. She went into the store. Was she meeting someone? Nothing he could do about that. He couldn't take a chance on her seeing him. A few minutes later she came out carrying a large bunch of flowers.

He followed her into the Brentwood hills. She parked for half an hour and didn't get out of the car. Then she moved again. She turned onto a short street, and he couldn't follow without being conspicuous. His mapping system showed there were only four houses on it. The tracker showed that she parked near the end of the street. Five minutes later she drove back out, and he followed her down into Santa Monica. What the hell was so interesting about Brentwood? What was she doing up there? Was she shadowing a banker? There'd been a robbery a few years ago in the Valley where the robbers did a house invasion at the bank president's. They left a couple of guys with the man's wife and children and drove him to the bank and made him open the vault when the time lock went off. Got away with over four hundred thousand. Maybe she was planning the same kind of thing.

He lost her at a light on Wilshire, but the tracker let him find the car parked at a meter on Lincoln just south of Pico. She had put in enough money for an hour.

She was back in half that time carrying a heavy shopping bag. She pulled out into traffic, took the first left, and the tracker showed her headed east on Pico. Steckley got out of his car, locked it, and stretched until his back cracked. He pulled his phone, found the photo of Bonner, and went into the first store south of where Bonner had parked, a dry cleaners. They had never seen her.

He got lucky with the sixth place, a hardware store with a display of nonstick pots and pans and kitchen gadgets crowding the front window. He showed his badge and the phone photo of Cody Bonner to the clerk behind the counter. "Was this woman in here?"

The clerk looked at the photo over the top of his glasses. "Yeah. Sure. I remember. Don't get many who look like her. Most of the cleavage I see around here is plumber's butt crack."

"What did she buy?"

"What'd she do?"

Steckley put hard eyes on the man.

"Uh, a Kwikset lock and a couple of extra key blanks."

"That's it?"

"Yeah."

"Did she say what she needed the lock for?"

"Lock a door, I figured. What else do you want a lock for?"

"How'd she pay?"

"Cash. What's up? She some sort of terrorist or something?"

"Did you see which way she turned when she left?"

"No. Hey, you ever hear the one about the three plumbers and three electricians taking the train to a convention?" But Steckley was already out the door.

He spent an impatient half hour canvassing stores until he found a hobby shop that had sold Cody a mallet with a hard rubber head.

A lock and a mallet with a rubber head. She was up to something. What the fuck was it? Back in the car, he checked the tracker. Bonner's car was back at her place. The phone rang. He picked it up off the passenger seat. "Steckley."

"Where are you? We're due in court in an hour," assistant DA Paprocki said.

"I'll be there."

"I need you there in forty-five to go over testimony."

Paprocki was a nervous dick. "I'll be there."

Steckley cut the connection. He'd have to pick up Bonner another day.

* * *

I set up in the kitchen at Julie's. I attached the vise to the counter overhang near the sink and spread newspaper to catch the crap from the work I was about to do. I laid out the two locks, the keys to each, the four blanks, the triangular file, and a fine permanent marker I found in Julie's desk. Then I set out to make two bump keys.

A bump key works with most common door locks. It pops all the lock pins up at the same time and separates the upper and lower pin to allow the key to turn. Locksmiths, cops, repo men use them for fast entry to locks without keys. So do burglars.

I took a key for the Kwikset lock, lined it up with a key blank, and traced the serrated edge onto the blank with the marker. I tightened the marked blank into the vise and spent a tedious fifteen minutes filing the blank into a rough shape of the original key. I had to make sure that I got the depth of the grooves right. You don't want to go past the maximum depth of the original key. Then I filed down the peaks until they were lower than the peaks of the original and were all the same height so the bump key looked like a miniature saw.

I pulled the key and put the Kwikset lock in the vise. I pushed the bump key all the way into the lock and then pulled it back slowly till I felt a click. I twisted the key to put pressure on it and bumped the back end with the rubber mallet. Nothing happened. I tried again. Nothing. Shit. I pulled the key out and filed the peaks down a little more. Key in. Pull back to click. Twist. Bump. Nothing.

File down the peaks and do it again. Cynda, the thief who taught me, said you had to have patience. File a little and try again. If you file too much off the peaks, they won't work, and you'll have to start again.

The fourth time, *click*. The lock popped open.

The key for the Schlage lock worked on the third try. I colored the back end of it with the marker so I knew which bump key was which.

I put the vise in a drawer with the few tools Julie had kept for household chores. I put the bump keys in a dish on the bureau in the bedroom with a bunch of Julie's keys. I wiped the locks and everything else for fingerprints, put the file, the locks, keys, and extra blanks on the newspaper that held the filings, wrapped it tight, and taped it shut. There was a dumpster at a construction site a couple of blocks away where I could throw the bundle. Maybe I was being overly cautious, but I had eaten breakfast, lunch, and dinner for five years with too many people who had let the small things slide until they became the big thing.

Chapter Thirty-Three

The wind woke me in the middle of the night. It took me a moment to remember that I was at Curtis's. He was asleep on his stomach on the other side of the bed, one arm thrown up across the pillow. The Santa Ana was back. Palm fronds scraped against the outside wall, and a loose shutter banged somewhere on the house. The night had been cool when we went to bed, and we had left a terrace door open a few inches to take advantage. The air that blew in now smelled of desert and dust. It lifted the curtains and made the screen door rattle.

I slipped out of bed and pushed the door open wide and went out onto the terrace. I was naked, and the dry wind was hot on my skin. A full moon hung over the ocean. It left a path of silver light on the dark water. The trees below me on the hill swayed back and forth in the wind, and a frond banged down from a palm on the far side of the terrace. I heard a soft step behind me, and then Curtis put his arms around me and touched his face to my hair. "I tried not to wake you," I said.

"It wasn't you. It was the wind." His body was warm from the bed.

"I like the dryness and the heat. I like the way it blows the smog out to sea."

"Santa Anas, they say it makes people act weird. Hey," he said, and then stopped.

"What?"

"What would you think about moving in here?"

I froze for a moment. "So they're right. The red wind does make people act weird."

"Don't do that," he said. I turned in his arms. His face was set and serious. "Don't joke. Just tell me."

He waited.

I was scared to answer. The idea frightened me as much as anything I'd ever done.

I waited too long. He let go of me and stepped back. "Okay." A shrug and a twist of a smile. He started to turn away.

"Yes."

He stopped.

"Yes. I think so. Yes." Moonlight and the Santa Ana wind. I leaped at him. He caught me, and I wrapped my arms and legs around him. "Yes."

I was throwing myself off a cliff, hoping I would soar, not fall.

* * *

The next day Curtis called his office and said he wouldn't be in. We drove up to Rincon Beach and rented a small house north of the oil company pier on a sand beach. We had three magical days. We swam, and surfed the small break just up from the house. Curtis thought we should go up to Rincon Point just past the Ventura–Santa Barbara County line to surf the big break at Indicator, but I didn't want to mess with the crowds, and we stayed where we were. We grilled things to eat, wore no clothes in the house, made love, and slept. We were out of the loop of our real lives. We were happy.

The last night there I dreamed about Julie. In the dream she waited for me. I hurried, but every time I thought I was close to her, something happened and she was farther away.

We got up early Monday morning and drove back down to the city.

That first week in his house was weird for me, and maybe for him. I had known him most of my life, but this was different. It was like going back to someplace familiar and discovering the details had changed in your absence. I was in a rush to know everything about him. I was impatient. I wanted to know him from the inside out. I wanted to invade him, wear him like a second skin.

Three or four times in those first days I found myself on the edge of telling him what I was planning. I wanted him to know. I wanted him to help me. But I didn't tell him. The old rule still applied: trust no one.

I needed to creep Groban's house, and to do that I had to be there in the window after Groban left and before the housekeeper arrived. Curtis usually didn't leave for work until after nine. By that time, the window was closed.

At the end of the week, the movie moved to Connecticut for a week of shooting on location. They were over budget, and Curtis went with them to ride herd. "Goddamn Brandon wants to do thirty takes on every scene. Shoot ten miles of film and then figure it out in the editing room. The first movie he did he practically cut in the camera, and it came in a half a million under budget. Now he's an artist." He wanted me to come, but I said no.

"Why not?"

"You'll be on the set all day. Then you'll watch dailies. I'll never see you."

"Come to the set."

"I've been on movie sets. There is nothing more boring unless you're working on the movie. You stand around half the day while the DP fiddles with the lights. I have things to do here."

"What things?"

"Just things."

"I'll miss you." But he didn't push. We were both new to this. We didn't yet know the boundaries and didn't want to test them.

I moved back to Julie's for the week he was gone.

Chapter
Thirty-Four

~

At seven o'clock, the traffic was already thick on Sunset when I crossed at North Kenter and drove up into the Brentwood hills against the tide of cars headed down in the morning commute. I parked and drank take-out coffee while I waited. Groban's Maybach went by just before eight. I gave it fifteen more minutes and then got out and jogged to the house. In scouting Groban over the last couple of weeks, I'd learned that his housekeeper arrived around eight thirty. Sometimes she got dropped earlier, sometimes later. Everyone in LA is subject to the uncertainties of traffic. I had to be there when she went in.

I had the bump keys, gloves, and the rubber mallet in my pockets, right for the mallet and the keys for the Kwikset lock on the front door, left for the Schlage in case there was a different lock on the back door. That was the door I had to use.

As I jogged toward Groban's short street, the professor and his wife passed me in their car. There was no car in front of the house with children. It was the mother's week for morning carpool, and they would already be on their way to school. I had never seen anyone at the car dealer's house, and now there was a real estate dealer's FOR SALE sign on a white wooden post on the lawn.

A swimming pool service truck was parked in front of Groban's. That wasn't right. Pool service was Wednesday, tomorrow. Why had it changed?

Reboot? Do it tomorrow? No. The housekeeper didn't come tomorrow. That would put it off until Thursday. If something went wrong on

Thursday, it would have to wait till next week. Curtis would be back. I'd have to lie about where I was going some morning at sunrise. Maybe the pool guy was almost finished. Wait and see.

I had to get off the street. I went down the driveway of the house for sale next to Groban's and stood in the doorway to the back door. From there I could see when the pool guy left and the housekeeper arrived.

Eight twenty. Ten minutes until the housekeeper arrived if she was on time. If she was early, I was screwed.

How long did the pool service take?

A couple of minutes later I heard a car, first distant and low, then growing as it approached the bottom of the street. I wouldn't be able to see it until it passed the driveway where I stood. If it was the house-keeper, I was done for the day.

The HawkEye security service car. I pulled back into the doorway out of sight. The car stopped. They were scoping the pool service truck, checking it against the list of approved services. A minute later it rolled on.

Eight thirty. She'd arrive any minute. The pool guy was still there. The plan was screwed for the day. I started out of the doorway, then stepped back as the pool man came out of the gate to Groban's backyard dragging a long articulated hose and carrying a couple of pieces of equip-ment. He carried the stuff to his pickup truck and loaded it into the back. Okay. Okay. Get out of here. He opened the driver's door. Then he shook his head and went back down the drive, opened the gate, and went into the backyard to get whatever he had forgotten.

I heard the housekeeper van before I saw it. It pulled to a stop behind the pool service truck. Groban's housekeeper got out, and the van pulled away. My window slammed shut.

The pool man came out of Groban's backyard and closed the gate. He saw the housekeeper as he started toward his truck. He raised a hand and called out, "*Maria, espera un momento.*"

"*Hola, Carlos. ¿Qué tal, guapo?*" She smiled and waited for him to cross the lawn to her.

I went up and over the wall into Groban's backyard.

The red alarm light blinked next to the back door. When the house-keeper came in through the front door, she'd have thirty seconds to a minute to punch in the code to disarm the alarm. She'd wait a moment and then rearm it. When I had watched her do it the last time I was in the house, she had waited about fifteen seconds. During those fifteen seconds, the alarm would be dead. I had to unlock the back door, get in the house, and close the door before she rearmed.

The back door lock was a Kwikset. I pulled on surgical gloves, took the Kwikset bump key and rubber-headed mallet from my pocket, and pushed the key into the lock. I couldn't test it. I didn't know how sensitive the alarm was. Bumping the key with the mallet might set it off. Fifteen seconds, plenty of time to get it done. Unless she rearmed it faster. Call it ten seconds to be safe. If I couldn't do it in that time, I'd have to quit.

I waited.

The alarm light blinked off. I had ten seconds.

One.

Pressure on the key. Bump it with the mallet. It didn't turn.

Two seconds gone.

Bump it again. Nothing. Pull it out a little. Push it back in. Hit it with the mallet. Nothing.

Four seconds gone. Try again.

Click. The lock opened. I pulled the key, turned the handle, and opened the door.

Eight seconds gone.

I slipped into the living room.

Ten seconds gone.

The red light was still off. Hurry. Close the door. Lock it from the inside. Just as I finished, the red light of the alarm began to blink on the panel next to the door.

I let out the breath I had been holding.

Footsteps sounded in the hallway beyond the big arched door. I crouched behind one of the leather armchairs. The housekeeper paused at the arch. She said something in Spanish in a low voice. A man laughed. Christ, she had the pool man with her. She laughed. I peeked around the chair. He had his hands on her hips and was following her closely as they moved off toward the kitchen.

Move. Move. Find the gun. Make sure it's loaded. Get out.

My running shoes made no noise on the thick Oriental rugs in the living room or on the tiled floor of the hall. I went quickly down to the study, went in, and closed the door. The desk was against the back wall. The desk chair was a designer's dope dream of carbon fiber and leather and probably cost more than most people's cars.

I sat down and opened the top right-hand drawer where I had found the gun the first time I was in the house.

It wasn't there.

I searched all the drawers. There was a box of bullets in the bottom drawer, but the gun wasn't in any of them. All right, think. If it isn't here, where would it be if it's still in the house? If you own a gun for protection, you want it where you feel most vulnerable. People are scared of what might come for them in the dark.

I opened the door and checked the hall. It was empty. I heard the voices and laughter of the housekeeper and pool guy in the kitchen. I went up the stairs two at a time and down the hall to Groban's bedroom. The bed was a mess of sheets. He had left clothes in a pile on the floor near a closet and two towels near the bathroom door. From the way the bedclothes were tossed, he slept on the side near the window. I sat on the edge of the bed and opened the bedside table drawer.

The gun was there. I picked it up. It was an ugly thing of black metal with a black plastic handle. The barrel was only about two inches long. It was heavy in my hand. I didn't know guns. Girls who grew up in Pacific Palisades didn't know guns unless they had one of those wack fathers with hero fantasies, and we'd never had one of those in all the fathers we had. How would I know if it was loaded? I knew enough to keep my fingers well away from the trigger. I turned the gun around and pointed it at my face. I could see the blunt ends of bullets in the cylinder. The gun barrel was a black hole. I put the ugly thing back and shut the drawer. Time to go.

I stopped at the top of the stairs and listened. The housekeeper and the pool guy were still in the kitchen. I looked out the upstairs hall window. There was nobody on the street. I ran downstairs and out. The alarm began to wail the moment I opened the door.

I was two blocks away when I heard the siren of the security car. I bent down next to a tree and pretended to tie my shoe as it blew through the intersection a block away, lights flashing.

Chapter
Thirty-Five

❦

I beat myself up at the gym to work out my nerves. Sakchai had pointed out some flaws in my footwork, and I was trying to correct them. I did some time on the heavy bag trying to make sure to use my core to fire my kicks through. Then I spent an hour doing single-leg dead lifts, front squats, pistol squats, and Bulgarian split squats until my legs were rubber.

When I went home, there were lights on across the courtyard in Keira's unit.

I showered, put on blue jeans and a gray cashmere pullover, and went over and rang Keira's bell. A minute later the peephole in the door darkened as she put her eye to it. Then a chain rattled off and two locks clicked, and the door jumped open. Keira stood there with a smile on her face and a martini in her hand.

"Well, it's about goddamn time," she said, and pulled me in. She hugged me with her free arm. "Do you want a drink? It's a martini night for me, I am so goddamn glad to be home."

"Sure. Maybe two."

"Definitely two. Maybe three or four." She padded up the stairs on bare feet, and I followed her. She wore tailored dark-blue pants and a white shirt that emphasized her deep tan. Her silver hair had recently been cut. It clung to her skull like a curly cap. She sprawled on the big leather sofa and pointed a foot at the kitchen. "In the freezer, in the pitcher. A glass in the cabinet to the right of the sink."

I took in the room as I went. My mother liked good things, well-made things, and that's what I'd grown up with. Good things cost money. The furniture was expensive. There were Navajo rugs on the floor. Mom had Navajos in her bedroom that looked like these, and they had each cost over $20,000 fifteen years ago. Big abstracts hung on the white walls.

"Where have you been?" I got a martini glass from the cabinet and filled it from a glass pitcher in the freezer.

"Where haven't I been?"

"A lemon?"

"In the fridge, in one of the bottom drawers." Her cell phone rang. She looked at the screen and then picked it up. "Hi. I've been hoping you'd call." Her voice was throatier now, seductive. Definitely a man on the other end. "I'd love to, but I can't tonight. How about Wednesday? Oh, that's great. I can't wait. See you then."

I carried my martini to one of the big armchairs that faced the sofa over a smoked-glass coffee table. "Great tan." I saluted her with my glass.

"Dude, nothing is for free. I worked for this tan."

"Where'd you get it, Mexico?"

"No, the Caribbean, a bunch of people on a guy's yacht. Antigua, Martinique, Barbados, Trinidad."

"Nice to have friends who own yachts."

"Yeah, well, maybe, but you know, sometimes a prince turns back into a frog. What do I mean, sometimes? Most of the time."

"Still, the tan's great."

"Yeah, the tan's great, the food was great, the sailing was great, the skin diving was great. Only the people were lousy. People can really fuck up a good time." She looked at me over the rim of her glass. "It is spooky how much you look like her."

"I know."

"Of course you do. Did you ever do that twin thing to confuse people? You know, like at school or something?"

"Sometimes. I was usually the one who wanted Julie to be me so she could take a test or something I hadn't studied for."

"Would she do it?"

"She wouldn't if she thought I was just fucking off."

"Did you do it for her?"

"Not school. She didn't need me in school. I went on a date for her a couple of times when she got cold feet and didn't want to stand the guy up. And I covered for her at summer jobs a few times when she needed time off, that kind of thing."

"I could have used someone like that in my life a bunch of times." The phone rang again. She checked the screen and then sent the call to voice mail. She held up her empty glass. "You ready for another?"

"Sure."

She swung her legs off the sofa and stood up in one athletic movement and took my glass from my hand as she went by. I followed her to the kitchen and leaned against the counter while she made the drinks.

"Did she ever talk to you about what she was doing?" I asked.

"What do you mean, what she was doing?" She said it casually, but there was something underneath. "Like at the law firm? Not much. I guess there's a thing where lawyers don't talk about what they're doing. Client-attorney privilege—is that right?"

"I meant outside the office. Did she talk to you about that?"

She slid me my drink. "Like boyfriend?" Why was she deflecting me? "She was going out with a guy named Riordan, what? Tony, I think. I only met him once. He seemed like a nice guy. But he wasn't the guy for Julie, and she knew it."

"Why not?"

"He was smart, cute, but, you know, not enough edge. Your sister had edge. She needed someone who could go with that. That wasn't him."

Julie knew there was a dark side, but I hadn't thought she ever tapped into it. I was starting to learn how much there was I didn't know about her.

"Besides Riordan. She was doing something outside the office pro bono. Do you know the group called SWOP-L.A.?"

"I read something about it. Sex workers or something, right?"

"Yes. Julie was doing legal work for them helping streetwalkers picked up by the cops in Santa Monica. She quit after a couple of months. She told them she'd found something uglier that needed her attention."

"Really? Huh. She didn't talk about it."

In prison, if you can't read people, you can't stay safe. Keira's tone was too bland, her expression too mystified. Here was something she didn't want to talk about.

"I'll be right back. I'll show you."

I ran over to my place and was back in a couple of minutes carrying a manila envelope. Keira was on the phone again as I came up the stairs from the front hall. Her voice was warm and low, and she gave a throaty laugh. "God, honey, I have missed you too. I'd love to do it Friday. Can we do it Friday? Seven o'clock is perfect for me. See you then." Something about her tone hooked me, but I didn't get it right away.

My drink was on the table next to my chair. I took a slug and then upended the envelope over the coffee table. Photographs from Julie's computer spilled out. I found the one of the woman I had seen outside Groban's party in Malibu and pushed it to Keira. "Do you know this woman?"

She picked up the photo and studied it carefully. "No. Who is she?"

She was lying. "Come on, Keira."

"I don't know her."

"You forgot to ask what happened to her."

"I could tell what happened to her. Somebody beat her up."

"Do you know any of the others?" I spread the pictures out faceup so she could see them.

"No, I don't."

"Look at them."

"I did. I don't know what you're doing, but I don't like it."

I'd held the photo of Julie back, but now I put it down on the table in front of her. "How about her? Do you know her?" She didn't say anything. I put my phone on the table where she could see it. I had keyed it to the photo of Jimmy I had taken outside his place. "Do you know him?"

"Jimmy Lasker. I've seen him around."

"Do you know a woman named Randi Porter?"

She hesitated. "We were in an acting class together maybe five years ago."

"Jimmy Lasker paid her to leave town after she, quote unquote, fell down stairs."

She took a deep breath and blew it out. "Cody, you do not want to go there."

I held up a photo. "She was my sister."

She said nothing.

"You're in the business, aren't you? That's what paid for all this." I gestured at the expensively furnished room. "They're all in the business, aren't they? All these women. Was Julie?"

"Jesus, no." The idea genuinely shocked her. "Cody, you should let this go. This is dangerous stuff."

"Who is Jimmy Lasker? How does he fit in this? Is he a pimp?"

She barked something that was almost a laugh. "Not at these prices. When you charge enough, you become a facilitator. At least that's what he calls himself." She drained the rest of her martini. "There are men who like to hurt women."

"No shit."

She put up a hand to stop me. "They call it rough sex or thug fuck or something, but they're just being nice to themselves. It's rape, and any woman who's been there can tell you rape isn't about sex. A lot of women who used to think they had to take that shit aren't taking it anymore. Some of the men have figured it out and say, okay, things have changed. But there are a lot of men out there who don't like change. They want to do what they want to do. It's safer to pay for it than to beat on the old lady or the girlfriend, so they'll pay for it. You grew up here. You know what this town is like. Everything's for sale. Jimmy Lasker figured that out. He found the girls with the kinks, or ones who would go for it if the price was high enough. And he made sure everyone knew that if anyone really got hurt, the guy would pay and then he was off the list."

"Gee, a real humanitarian."

"Hey, everybody's got to have rules, right? Jimmy says guys play pro football, they box, they do that cage fighting shit. They get fucked up doing it, but the money's too good to pass up. Think of it like that and it's not so bad. Drink?" She got up with her glass and went toward the kitchen.

"What about Julie? What was she doing? She wasn't going out to make a few bucks on the side."

"No." Keira rattled ice into the pitcher and threw in gin and vermouth. "She thought some guy would go too far. A girl would get really hurt and the law would come into it. Then it's the girl against the guy, and the guy is rich and connected. And what are we? A bunch of whores. Guess who wins? She wanted to throw some weight to the girls' side if it came to that. She got to know some of the girls."

"Through you?"

"Yes. Through me. If you tell anybody . . ."

I stopped her. "I know."

Keira came back with her drink and flopped down on the sofa. The gin was working on her. "She started doing interviews, taking photos when the girls came home. But she didn't think it was enough. There was this guy she knew, someone on Lasker's list, some big deal in the movie business. She was going to take a run at him. She said she had to do it to know it." She drank half her martini and raised the glass in a toast. She saw something in my face. "What?"

"She went out on a date as a hooker?"

"No. She knew this guy. She knew from some of the girls that he was a hitter. She thought she knew how to play him. She figured if she got a date, she'd know for sure about the abuse. If it came to testimony, she was an upstanding citizen, a movie star's daughter, a lawyer with a big-time firm. Nobody was going to dismiss her as just another hooker with her hand out for a settlement."

"I don't believe you. I don't believe she'd do that."

"Don't move," Keira said in a slurred voice. She tried to get up from the sofa and fell back. She leaned forward until she could get both hands on the coffee table and levered herself up. She stumbled against the doorjamb when she went into her bedroom. I heard the closet door open and the rattle of hangers being banged aside as she looked for something. She came back out of the bedroom and threw something at me hard. I put up my hands in defense and caught it.

"That's what she wore. She borrowed it from me. If you're going out with one of those assholes, you've got to look the part."

Silver metallic cloth. The dress Tony Riordan said Julie had worn to Groban's house.

Keira fell back on the sofa. She reached for her glass and knocked it over. "Shit. God's way of telling me I've had enough." She ran her finger through the spilled drink and licked it. "You should see your face. You didn't think she would do something like that?"

"No."

"Maybe you didn't know her as well as you thought."

"I knew her."

"Yeah, yeah, yeah. I thought I knew my brother till he went off and became a priest. You know what she admired about you? She said you'd jump in and do whatever the fuck and the hell with the consequences. You never pulled back. You know what else? You know why she decided to help a bunch of hookers?"

"Why?"

"Because nobody else would."

Keira passed out on the sofa, and I navigated home without falling in the pool and drowning. I lay in bed staring at the ceiling. Julie didn't do the things Julie had done. I stuck my hand in the fire to see if it was hot. She didn't. Or did she, and I just didn't know it? I had a cellmate my first year who told me, "It ain't what you don't know that gets you in trouble. It's what you know for sure that just ain't so."

I woke up the next morning in my clothes with a brutal hangover. Four Advil, two glasses of ice water, three cups of coffee, and an egg. It tried to come back but I held it down, and a while later I felt strong enough to cross the courtyard and ring Keira's doorbell. No answer. I leaned on the doorbell until I heard the shuffle of footsteps inside. The door opened a crack, and one of Keira's bloodshot eyes looked out at me. "Fuck off," she said in a tired voice. She shut the door.

I leaned on the doorbell again. The noise must have been like a drill to her brain, but she lasted a minute before she opened the door again. "Cody, go away."

"I need a list of the men who used Lasker's service."

She shook her head and tried to close the door, but I leaned on it hard and forced her back. I stepped in and shut the door behind me. Keira sat down on the stairs up to the living room and put her head in her hands.

"I need the list."

Keira blew her breath out hard and raised her head to look at me. Her face was slack and thick from sleep and drink, some of the beauty leached away. "You think one of those assholes killed Julie."

I didn't say anything.

"If one of them did, he'd kill you too if you get close to him."

"Let me worry about that."

"I don't have a list. I just know who some of them are. If I tell you and you start asking around, whoever did it will figure out that I live across from you and that's where you got the names. I don't want him to come looking for me."

"She was your friend."

"Yeah. Right. She was, and someone killed her. She's gone. I liked her. I liked her a lot, but what you're doing scares me, and I'm not going to help you."

"Okay." I didn't have to know who all the pigs in Lasker's little black book were. I knew who had killed Julie.

Chapter
Thirty-Six

I bought a good red wig and a pair of rhinestoned glasses shaped like big cat eyes with plain glass lenses at a costume shop in Hollywood. The red wig and the glasses would draw eyes from the details of my face and make a description hard to get right.

When I drove to the Valley, I was wearing the wig and glasses, baggy blue jeans, and a flannel shirt that was too big for me. The shooting range I chose was in Burbank. There were a couple closer to Julie's place, but I wanted to put distance between where I learned to shoot a gun and where I was going to use it. Everything I did was layered with caution and misdirection.

The range was in a concrete block building in an industrial park of light manufacturing businesses—a furniture store, an electronics repair shop, and a couple of computer effects studios. I had chosen Live Fire because it advertised a "Ladies Lunch Shoot" on Wednesdays. I wasn't going to go shoot with the ladies—women notice too many details about other women, especially someone new to the group—but I wanted to go someplace that catered to women, a place where I wouldn't stand out.

The range instructor's name was Jack. He was a pudgy man in his thirties with thinning blond hair. He wore a no-iron blue-striped shirt and pressed khakis. He looked like an accountant or an insurance sales-man. I guess I'd been expecting some ex-military hard-ass with a shaved head and a tattoo. I told him I knew nothing about guns, and he said I'd come to the right place to learn.

He showed me a display case full of pistols for rent and kept up an enthusiastic commentary on the differences and advantages of automatics and revolvers. I half listened while I searched the display for what I wanted. I found it near the far end, a black, short-barreled pistol that looked, to my eyes, like the gun in Groban's bedside table.

"How about that one." I tapped the glass above the pistol.

"Okay," he said. "Smith and Wesson thirty-eight Detective Special. A good gun for personal defense. Is that what we're looking at here, self-defense?"

"It kind of looks like the gun my boyfriend showed me."

He looked pained for a moment. Another woman without a clue. "Great," he said. He lifted the pistol out of the case and flipped open the cylinder. "First thing is to make sure the weapon is not loaded." He showed me the empty cylinder. "A lot of people get hurt by guns that 'weren't loaded,' if you get my meaning. Safety first. Never point the weapon, unloaded or not, at anyone. Downrange or at the floor. Cylinder out until you're ready to fire. Don't worry; we'll be going over that again and again. Safety first at all times. Okay, let's go." He took two pairs of earmuffs from hooks near a door marked RANGE, gave me one of them, and put the other on. He opened a heavy door, and even through the earmuffs I could hear the crack, crack, crack as someone fired three quick shots from the firing station at the far end. Jack led me to a walled booth with a waist-high counter top and an overhead track that carried the targets. The back wall was fifty feet away, and there were marks on the ceiling every ten feet for target distance. The paper rectangle with a bull's-eye in the middle hung just in front of the counter.

Jack put the open gun on the counter with the barrel facing the back wall. "Point the gun downrange even if it's not loaded. Safety first. You don't want to hurt anyone."

If you weren't ready to hurt someone, what was the point of a gun? Nobody carried a pistol with a two-inch barrel to shoot a rabbit in the backyard for dinner.

Jack put an open box of bullets on the counter. He ran through instructions and then handed me the pistol and showed me how to load it. He made sure I kept it pointed downrange with my finger off the trigger alongside the trigger guard. The cylinder closed with the satisfying click of machine-tooled parts intersecting. The gun was a solid weight in my hand. Jack pushed a button and moved the target back to fifteen feet.

"Okay, now. Both hands on the gun the way I showed you. Thumbs forward. Feet and shoulders square to the target." He spoke loud enough to be heard through the earmuffs. "Remember, don't pull on the trigger, squeeze it back. Get to the point where it resists and then keep up a steady pressure. You want to surprise yourself with the shot."

BANG.

I flinched back. The target paper flicked, and a hole appeared in the upper left-hand corner.

When I turned toward Jack, he put out a hand to keep my gun hand pointed away. "Okay. Good. Now I want you to do exactly what you did there, but I want you to keep firing till you empty the gun. Take your time between shots. Breathe, squeeze, breathe, squeeze."

By the time I had shot all the bullets in the box, the target was at the back wall and some of my shots were in the circles. My shoulders and arms were tired from holding the gun in position and from the jolt of the recoil.

Out in the front room Jack praised me for my shooting and promised me that my accuracy would get better with practice. He tried to sign me up for membership. "Maybe after the next session," I lied. I wasn't coming back. I had what I needed about how to use a pistol. And accuracy wasn't going to be a problem. When I next used one, my target was going to be close enough to touch.

I had learned things I hadn't expected: I liked the lethal, compact weight of the gun in my hand and the seductive power of pulling the trigger here and punching something way over there, the power to jump distance and cause destruction.

Chapter
Thirty-Seven

❧

I went to the Goodwill store down near the marina and bought the worst-looking clothes they sold—ragged jeans, worn-out shirts, down-at-heel running shoes, a crappy cotton jacket, faded head scarves. Then I went looking for runaways.

I drove around Ocean Park and Venice where I used to hang out when I was on the street. Street kids move around a lot. They get pushed out by economics, police pressure, citizen complaints. Their squats get knocked down and replaced by high-end condos. Their drug supplier gets busted and they move to where they can connect.

I saw kids on the street panhandling, dumpster diving, carrying their possessions in plastic bags or ragged backpacks, but they were singles or in twos and threes, and I was looking for the place where they went to ground when they needed to sleep or to get off pavement.

Back when I was on the street, a group of volunteers offered a vegan meal to the homeless on Thursdays at the north end of the Promenade. It was the last resort for us, the place we went when we couldn't steal, beg, or buy the burgers, hot dogs, or tacos, the salt and fat we craved. The volunteers had been driven off by merchants who learned that packs of street people on the sidewalks depressed commerce. The group had moved to the Salvation Army on Fourth Street. I went down there on feeding day in my Goodwill clothes.

There were about fifty people waiting for food. They were the hard-core homeless, older men and women in worn, dirty clothes. Life is hard on the streets, and it's almost impossible to stay clean. They sat on benches or on the strip of lawn with their possessions piled around them, close at hand. It was the habitual wariness of people so far down they can't afford to lose anything to carelessness or theft. Their faces were weather-beaten and seamed. A few of them slept on the grass. One old man sat rocking on a bench. His eyes were glassy and staring, and he was in deep conversation with himself, an incoherent mumble punctuated by shouts and slaps on his knee or chest. The other people on the bench ignored him. They had seen it all before. There was nobody under the age of forty at the Salvation Army, nobody who could point me where I needed to go.

In the next few days, I checked out the food banks and churches that fed the homeless. I had no luck, and I was beginning to think I would have to figure out another way to get what I needed. On Friday I stopped by the Church on Pearl at Pearl and Sixteenth. A line of people waited at the door. Most of the people in line were middle-aged or older. I didn't think I was going to have any luck. I took a quick look, but there was no one there to help me. I headed back toward where I'd parked the car near the Santa Monica College stadium.

Halfway down the block a young woman sat on the curb eating charity tacos off a paper plate. Her head moved to the music coming through her earbuds. Her hair was cut short and ragged and dyed a weird shade of red. She looked familiar. For a moment I couldn't place her, and then I realized I had seen her the day I flew back to LA. Her hair had been green then. She had been panhandling on the corner of the Pacific Coast Highway and Entrada.

Street kids have a feral wariness. She sensed that I was there and gave me a quick look. She dismissed me as no threat and bent back to her tacos and the music.

"Hey," I said. "Do you remember me?"

She looked up again. She chewed her food as she studied me. She held the plate with one hand and put the other on the curb to give leverage in case she had to get up fast. I knew what was going through her mind. Was I someone she had scammed or robbed? Was I a cop or a social worker, someone who was going to screw up her life with charity or the law? "No. Never seen you before." Denial is safest.

"You were panhandling on Entrada. I gave you sixty bucks."

She squinted up at me while she thought about it. Her face was drawn, and her skin had an unhealthy pallor. Her hand holding the plate was grubby and her fingernails were bitten down. She was too thin, and her clothes hung on her and made her look small and fragile. She couldn't have been more than eighteen, but life was beating her down fast. "You were in a cab," she said. "I remember the sixty bucks. No one ever gave me that much before. Thanks." She smiled briefly. "Well, one guy offered me seventy-five, but he wanted to fuck me."

"What's your name?"

"Why? What's it to you?"

"Mine's Amy. Mind if I sit down?"

She shrugged. "Free country."

I sat on the curb next to her.

She glanced over at me to reassess and decided I was okay. "They call me Scat. It's not my real name." She took the last bite of taco and chewed for a while until she thought I needed more explanation. "You know, Scat, 'cause I'm quick."

"Uh-huh. They called me Book when I was out here. I used to read. A lot of them thought that was kind of fucked up, carrying a book around."

"You were out here?" She didn't quite believe me. I was wearing the Goodwill clothes, but compared to her I looked rich and fat.

"It's been a few years."

"Uh-huh." She folded the paper plate over and over again until it was a wad and then flicked it down the storm drain at her feet. "You got any spare change today? I could really use some money, Amy." She wiped her hands on her jeans and slanted a look at me out of the corners of her eyes. From the set of her face, she was ready to be rejected.

"I need something. You could help me get it. I'd pay for that."

"Yeah? Like what?"

"I need to score."

Her face closed up. "Score? What do you mean, score?" I let the silence build. "What are you, a cop?"

"Do I look like a cop?"

"How the fuck do I know? Cops are tricky. You know, undercover and all that shit."

"I'm not a cop. I just need to score. I need some pills."

"I don't know what you're talking about."

I reached over and tapped her sleeve where I knew it covered needle marks. "Yes. You do. Look, all I want is to meet the guy. Every place I squatted had a guy who could hook you up. Are you telling me it's different now? I'll pay you a hundred bucks."

She weighed greed against caution. She shook her head. "No. I don't know. I can't help you." She pushed herself up and took off down the block. I caught up with her before the end of the block. "I'll do it any way you want. I'll meet the guy anywhere he wants, any time he wants. He can set it so he feels safe."

"Leave me alone." She lunged out into the street without looking, and a car had to swerve to miss her. The driver leaned on the horn, and she gave him the finger and kept going.

I went after her.

She was halfway down the next block and moving fast when a man stepped out from between two parked cars and body blocked her hard onto her back on the strip of lawn past the sidewalk. She cried out in shock, then rolled to a fetal position with her arms around her head as the man began to kick her. His face was red with rage. He yelled at her, "What are you doing here? I told you not to come here. I told you, you stupid bitch."

"I was hungry, Stevie," she pleaded. She tried to roll away from his kicks, but he followed her. He was wearing running shoes, but the blows still must have hurt.

"I told you, you go to your corner and you don't leave your corner till you've made your money."

"I was going to. I was going there. I was hungry," she wailed. "Stevie, don't. I'm sorry. I was going."

"Hey," I shouted. "Stop it."

He looked over at me. "Fuck off." He kicked at her head, missed, and almost fell, which just made him angrier. "Goddamn you, you stupid cunt." He raised one foot to stomp her, and I slammed into him. He landed hard on the grass, and it knocked the wind out of him. He lay there gasping for breath. I bent over Scat. "Are you all right?"

"I don't know. I think so." She was trying not to cry. She looked past me. "Stevie, don't."

I turned as Stevie pushed himself up. "Stay down," I said.

He shook his head. "Fuck you." He was a thin six-footer with long, scraggly dark hair and a narrow face sporting a week of stubble that looked like dirt. He wore a soiled Lakers T-shirt and cruddy cargo pants. As he got up, he took a folding knife from one of the deep pockets and opened it. It had a wicked-looking serrated blade that would make a terrible tearing wound. I backed up. He smiled when he saw me retreat and came after me. I wanted to get off the grass onto the sidewalk. Then I stopped. I was on solid ground now. He was still up on the grass. I slipped out of my jacket and let it dangle from my left hand. He stopped at the edge of the grass a few feet from me. His eyes were bright, and he was smiling. He didn't see me as a problem.

He jabbed the knife at me. I didn't back up. "I'm going to cut the shit out of you." I didn't say anything. I just watched him. He faked a lunge at me, but I didn't move. He didn't know what to make of it. He took another step toward me and crouched with the knife out in front. He held the point up. His other arm was out for balance. I didn't know if he knew what he was doing or whether he was copying something he had seen in a movie. It didn't matter. He didn't have to be good. The knife could cut me by accident or bad luck. Ginger used to try to check my impatience. She said that sometimes you want to start it and sometimes you want to wait for the other guy to make a move. I didn't know how to get past the knife without getting hurt. I waited for him.

He made little feinting moves with the knife, but that was just busy-work. When he shifted his feet, I knew he was coming. He led by flapping his left hand at my face to distract me and then took a fast step forward with the knife aimed low to gut me. His running shoes slipped on the grass, and it threw him off a little. I swung my jacket at the knife. It caught the point. He jerked back and ripped the jacket out of my hand. For a moment he was off-balance. I threw a left hand at him, a weak jab that he avoided. It was a fake that allowed me to keep turning to hit him with a right-hand spinning backfist. If I'd caught him on the jaw, it would have been over, but he ducked, and my fist hit him high on the side of his head. It knocked him sideways and he stumbled away. I went after him to finish it. He got his feet under him and turned toward me. I'd hurt him. He hadn't expected that. It made him more cautious. And it made him angry.

"Give it up. Go away before I really hurt you," I said.

He stepped off the grass onto the pavement. He'd figured that out. He followed the knife toward me. When he thought he was close enough, he stabbed out with the point. I banged his arm to the side, and the blade slipped by me as I stepped in and punched him hard in the mouth. I felt teeth break. It knocked him back. He swiped at me with the knife. I sucked back, and when the blade went by me, he was off-balance. It gave me time for a roundhouse kick. It caught him on the neck and jaw. He slammed into a parked car and bounced to the pavement. He wasn't out, but he was done. I stamped on his right wrist, and his hand flexed open and the knife fell out.

Blood flowed from his nose and his broken mouth, and his breath came in gasps. I crouched down next to him and put the knifepoint against his throat. He closed his eyes. "Don't ever touch her again. If you come near her, I'll find you. Do you understand?" He nodded. "Open your eyes. Tell me you understand."

He opened his eyes. "I understand," he mumbled. When I stood up, he closed his eyes again and lay still. I dumped the knife down a storm drain and picked up my jacket. The blade had ripped a three-foot hole in the fabric. Scat was watching me with wide eyes.

"Are you still hungry?" I asked.

Chapter
Thirty-Eight

The squat was off Culver Boulevard, not far from the 405 Freeway. It was an old four-story building in the middle of a block of two-story apartment houses that were no longer occupied. Most of the windows of the smaller buildings had been broken, but someone had gone to the trouble of boarding up the windows of the big building. A chain-link fence surrounded the entire block. The NO TRESPASSING signs that hung from it had been sprayed with graffiti. A construction company permit hung on the fence. It was dated two years back.

I watched Scat slip through a hole in the fence. She picked her way through broken furniture, smashed bathroom fixtures, and discarded doors that littered the ground near the building and disappeared around a corner. "I don't know if he'll go for it," she had said. "I mean, Gator's kind of weird. Like he'll deal somebody one day and then not a couple of days later. And he doesn't say why."

"Talk to him. I'll wait," I told her.

We had walked a few blocks from where Stevie and I had sorted out the proper behavior of men toward women, and then I'd called an Uber that drove us to Rae's restaurant on Pico. I didn't want Scat to see my car. The less she knew about me, the better. At Rae's I watched her put away as much food as I eat in a week. "Where did you learn to fight like that?" she said around the last bite of pancake.

"In prison."

"No shit?"

"No shit."

"I'd like to be able to fight like that. No one would screw with me then."

"It's not worth going to prison to learn."

"What'd you do? I mean, like to get busted?"

"You know those tags on mattresses that say do not remove under penalty of law? I tore one off."

She laughed, and for a moment her face was as young as she was. "No, come on. What did you do?"

"I was high. I ripped off a place. I got caught. I went to prison for five years."

She looked stricken. "Shit."

"Yeah. That's what happens." She looked suddenly small, and vulnerable as a sparrow. "How long have you been on the street?"

"I don't know. A year and something."

"A bad situation at home?"

"Yeah," she said in a small voice.

"You ever think of getting out?"

She looked up at me. "Where would I go? What would I do?"

"There are places, people who want to help."

"Oh yeah? You ever been in one of those places? You ever talked to those people? Sure, they want to help, but only if you do everything their way. You live in a shelter, and maybe they get you a job at Burger King or something, and you still have to live in the shelter, 'cause flipping hamburgers you don't make enough to get a place of your own, deposit and rent and all that."

"And you'd have to kick."

"Yeah." She shrugged at that impossible weight. "How'd you do it?"

"I went to prison."

The hopelessness of it hit her. I knew how that felt. She wiped a few tears away with the back of her hand.

"Come on," I said. I left money on the table, and we went.

I walked her up to a big drugstore on Pico and bought two burner phones. I gave one to her and kept the other. We exchanged numbers.

"If you ever want to kick, if you ever want to get off the street, call me."

"Okay." She watched me wide-eyed.

"I don't mean when you're feeling shitty and you think I'll buy you a meal. I'm not your charity dip. I'm your lifeline. When you know you're ready, call me. It's a one-time offer. If you fuck it up, we're done."

She read my face, closed her eyes for a moment, and then said, "Okay." She put the phone away carefully, as if it were fragile.

I had been on the bench across from the abandoned building for more than half an hour, and I was beginning to think I'd been scammed. I hadn't given Scat any money, but maybe she thought the burner phone was enough. She might get twenty bucks for it. On the street twenty bucks can feed you for a few days, more if you eat ramen.

I stood up and stretched.

A man came around the corner of the block to my left. He stopped and watched me. I stayed where I was. After a minute he looked past me. I turned to see what drew him. Scat was down the block to my right. She looked past me and nodded. When I looked back, the man was walking toward me. They had been scoping the neighborhood to see if someone had me staked out.

Gator, if that's who it was, walked with a herky-jerky motion, and every once in a while one hand would fly out from his side. He carried a brown canvas shoulder bag and wore a down parka way too big for him, blue jeans, boots, and a dark wool watch cap. It was over seventy degrees out and the sun was shining, but every meth freak I knew was cold all the time. Meth raises the body's core temperature but constricts the blood vessels, so you're burning up and shivering at the same time. When he got closer, I saw that he had a big, protruding jaw and buckteeth that didn't quite allow his lips to close. Maybe that's where he got the name Gator. His walk and jerking hand weren't the only meth twitches. The flesh around his left eye spasmed. Like a lot of meth heads, he was rail thin. When you're on the drug, eating seems like a waste of time.

He looked me over, nodded, and then slumped onto the bench. I sat down next to him. He smelled of all the bad body smells. "What kind of pills you into?" His voice was high and breathy as if it was hard to push from his throat.

I told him what I needed.

"That's kind of old stuff. There's better now."

"Better how?"

"Works faster."

"And if you give it to someone, he'll do what you want?"

"Oh yeah. Do whatever you want. Like a robot."

"You're sure?"

"Oh yeah, I'm sure," he said with a knowing grin.

"Do they remember?"

"No." The grin again. I wanted to slap it off his face.

"How many have you got?"

He dug around in his shoulder bag and came up with a pharmaceutical blister pack holding four green pills. "What's the dose?"

"One. Unless she weighs like a ton. Then one and a half, something like that."

I paid him what he asked.

"First time I ever sold this stuff to a girl."

"Uh-huh. We're in a time of equal opportunity."

"Whatever." He got up and went across the street, slid through the hole in the fence, and disappeared around the building.

Scat came and sat beside me. I gave her the hundred dollars I'd promised her. She looked in the direction where Gator had gone.

"How old is he?" I asked.

"I don't know. Twenty?"

"He's never going to make twenty-five."

"Maybe he doesn't want to. You ever think of that?"

She stood up, eager to go fix now that she had the money. "If it ever gets to be the right time, call me," I said.

"Yeah. Sure."

I watched her go, knowing she would never call. She would drown out here. It surprised me that I cared.

Chapter
Thirty-Nine

I took one of the green pills out of the blister pack and put it on the glass shelf under my bathroom mirror. For three days, morning and night, I looked at the pill, and the pill looked at me. It's one thing to make a plan. It's another to face the steps you have to take to make the plan work. I had not taken any drug stronger than an aspirin since I went to prison, except when Julie was killed and they gave me sedatives. They forced me to take them. I wanted to feel the pain. After that there would be only absence and memories.

Taking this pill could be the first step on that slippery slope back to who I had been. It scared me and I kept putting it off. Then one evening I carried the pill into the kitchen. I set up my phone to record video. I dropped the pill into a glass, added ice and bourbon, and stirred. The pill dissolved almost immediately. I carried the glass into the living room and sat on the sofa where the phone video could record me. I held the glass on my knee. The cold condensation soaked through my jeans. Do it, or don't. My heart raced. How many bad decisions are you allowed in life?

I picked up the glass and took a sip. I couldn't taste anything but bourbon. I took another sip. Nothing. I finished the drink. Ah, there, now something was happening. It hit fast. For a moment it was like the buzz you get from cocaine, but it was a full-body buzz. Then a warm wave took me over. My eyelids weighed pounds. I wanted to get up from the sofa, but it was too much trouble to move. And then . . .

I woke up sprawled with my neck bent awkwardly by a sofa arm. My head ached. What was I doing asleep on a sofa? Where was I? I rolled over and looked around. Okay. My apartment. When I sat up, I thought my head would fall off. It was dark outside. There was a glass with a half inch of ice melt on the coffee table. My phone was propped up near it. When I reached for it, I had to steady myself with the other hand or I would've fallen on the floor. The phone was set on record. Why had I done that? I turned it off. It was almost midnight. My head felt like a balloon full of hot dust. My body was slack and tired. I dragged to the kitchen and doused my face with cold water.

What had happened? Why had I set the phone up to record? The recording should tell me something. I drank a glass of cold water and went back into the living room to flop on the sofa again. I propped the phone on my thigh and started the recording from the beginning.

I watched as I got a glass from the cabinet. I dropped a green pill into the glass and added ice and then bourbon. I stirred it with my finger and then held it up to the light to see if the pill had dissolved. I had no memory of this. I watched myself sit in the chair and take a sip of the drink, then another and another until the drink was finished. Within a minute my eyes went wide. I stared down at my hand on the arm of the chair. I looked up at the wall opposite me. My face was washed of all expression. After a while I tried to get up, but the drug made the effort too hard. I sank back. My eyes closed. I slumped to the side and did not move again.

I jumped to the end and watched myself wake up. Four hours had passed since I took the pill. What about the rest of the day? I remembered going to the gym. I'd had lunch at the HiHo burger joint in Santa Monica, the training meal of champions. I had walked to where I'd parked the car. Then blank until I woke up on the sofa.

I looked for a place to hide the rest of the pills. I could have left them in the medicine cabinet in the bathroom, but my imagination was working overtime. What if someone mistook them for a painkiller? What if Curtis or my mother or the cleaning lady was feeling experimental? "The guilty flee where no man pursues." Our creepy stepfather used to say that. We didn't figure out till later that he was talking about himself.

I finally put the blister pack of pills in the toe of one of Julie's old running shoes and pushed it to the back of the closet. If someone found it there, what I was planning was not meant to be.

Chapter Forty

It was a warm day, a promise of spring.

"Be careful," Curtis said. "You're going to burn." He reached over from where he lay and poked my belly. The skin went white under the pressure and then turned pink. "See."

"Okay, okay."

He got up and moved the blue umbrella so it shaded us. We were at the Jonathan Beach Club off the Pacific Coast Highway in Santa Monica. Julie and I had spent a lot of our childhood beach time here. My grandparents had joined in the 1960s, and my mother had kept up the membership. The club was a fortress against change. It had dress codes and behavior codes. The main dining room was formal. There were staff members who had worked there for years who knew us by name—Julie or Cody, with a fifty-fifty chance of getting it right. The membership was mostly lawyers and businessmen. My mother was one of the few movie star members. There were a few producers and executives, but it was too conservative for the glitterati. I had suggested to Curtis that we go there for lunch. I thought he would laugh at the idea—too old-fashioned, too uncool—but he had jumped at it.

"I used to sneak in here when I was a kid," Curtis said. "I'd come on a Saturday or Sunday when there were a lot of people here. I figured the staff couldn't know everybody. I'd walk up the beach and hang near the water until some people were heading back up to the club, and I'd stay close until we got to the umbrellas. Then I'd just sort of become a member. I'd use the pool. I'd charge snacks to people from school." He smiled at the memory.

"What the hell for?" I asked.

"Says the girl who had everything."

"Hey." He heard my annoyance.

"Didn't you?" He meant it.

"Maybe . . . the things you mean."

"Then what?" He rose up on one elbow so he could see me better.

"I don't know. Sometimes I felt like I had no place, that everyone else knew who they were and what they were and I didn't have a clue."

"It must have been hell, an existential crisis while sitting in the lap of luxury."

"It was hell. You were lucky. You had the simplicity of poverty."

"You're right. Nothing cuts through the confusion better than a lack of choice. No worries about whether to wear this or that. Just put on the blue jeans and the clean shirt if there is one and go. Spring vacation in Paris, or the Bahamas, or maybe skiing in Aspen? Too much to think about. Don't go anywhere. It's simpler."

"Ow," I said, and leaned across and kissed him.

"When I was, I don't know, fourteen, I guess, Terry and Mark invited me here on a Saturday. They told me to bring my bathing suit and we'd have lunch, spend the afternoon. I didn't have much to do with them at school, but I thought, great, the Jonathan Club. I even went out and bought a new bathing suit. I stole the money from my mother's purse. Bilabong board shorts, gray, blue, and red. I wasn't going to show up looking like the poor cousin."

"Did you have fun?"

Something twisted his face. "Fifteen minutes after I got here, they told one of the security people that they had seen me sneak in. I tried to laugh it off. They swore they'd never seen me before. The guy threw me out. Big joke."

"That is really shitty."

"Yeah."

"But all is forgiven?"

"Nothing's forgiven."

"You work for them," I pointed out. "They're your bosses."

"Are they? They're the money, but they don't know how to make deals and they don't know how to make movies. I know how to make deals. Brandon knows how to make movies."

"How'd you persuade them to let you in?"

"I made them an offer they couldn't refuse," he said in a Godfather voice. He grinned his Wile E. Coyote grin. He got up. "I'm going for a swim. Want to come?"

"No, thanks. Maybe later."

He took his towel and headed for the water, which saved me from making up an excuse for leaving where we were sitting. It was one o'clock, and I had something to do.

I walked to where I could see the outdoor bar. Harry Groban was leaning against it while he talked with the bartender. He wore tan shorts and an untucked dark-blue short-sleeved cotton shirt. His feet were in leather sandals. His legs and arms were tan and powerful. He looked like a bear in expensive beachwear. A bloody mary was on the bar in front of him. When I shadowed him, I'd learned that his routine wasn't rigid, but there were certain things he tried to do on a regular basis. Saturday lunch at the Jonathan Club was one of them.

I was wearing a bikini that wasn't much more substantial than dental floss. I also wore a knee-length cover-up that closed in front with a couple of buttons. I unbuttoned it and let it hang open. What's the point of going fishing if you hide the bait?

"Hi, Harry. I didn't know you came here. I would've thought Soho House's place up in Malibu."

"Cody. Hi. I think that was meant as an insult."

"No, no. I just thought agents were always on duty, and I understand that's where the faces and names hang out."

"Which is why I'm here. Sometimes you have to stop schmoozing and selling." It sounded like the truth. He had an easy way about him. Many agents and producers had a practiced charm. You could see it in their eyes, which were always calculating. Groban's charm seemed innate. Or maybe he was just better at hiding the calculations. "How about a drink?" he asked.

"One of those. Thanks."

"Hank," he said to the bartender. "A bloody mary for Miss Bonner." He looked me over. "You look great." He smiled. "I know I'm not supposed to say that these days." He said it in a way that made it clear he didn't give a damn what he was supposed to say these days.

I smiled back. "That's okay. I'm kind of behind the curve on what I'm supposed to or not supposed to do or say these days."

"Oh yeah, your, uh, sabbatical." He raised his glass in a toast. "Do you talk about that? Are you over it?"

"I'm working my way through it still." Hank slid me my drink, and I took a sip.

"I'm sure it'll take time, but if you ever want to talk about it, I'd love to hear."

"Why?"

Some people back off when you challenge one of those polite offers. Not Harry Groban.

"Prurient interest, pure and simple. What's it really like in prison? All I know is what the movies and TV tell me, and that's probably bullshit. I want all the real dirt."

I laughed. He touched his glass to mine.

"The sex, the violence, the food."

"The food was lousy."

"Well, that leaves two out of three."

"The violence was terrifying."

"Damn, still, one out of three's not bad. Tell me about the sex."

So there we were, right on the path I wanted to lead him down. I said nothing. I gave him a smile that I hoped was enigmatic.

"Come on. I'm an agent. I've heard it all."

"I don't know you well enough."

"We'll have to do something about that."

I laughed and deflected. We talked. We kept it quick and light. What we talked about didn't matter. We were flirting, and the talk was part of the delivery system. He would touch my hand to emphasize a point. My knee would brush his. I stood facing him, arms uncrossed, the body language of availability. It was hard to do. It made me feel

vulnerable, and I didn't want to feel that with him. We were both aware of what was going on. He finished his drink, hesitated for a moment, and then said, "I'm having lunch with a couple of people. Not movie people. Why don't you join us? I think you'd like them, and they'd like you."

I smiled with regret. "I can't, Harry. I came with someone."

"Another time, then." He leaned in and kissed me chastely on the cheek, touched my shoulder, and went off toward the clubhouse.

Curtis was toweling off by our chairs when I got there. "I saw that," he said.

"What?"

"You know what. Just be careful."

*　*　*

I teased Harry Groban. I "ran into him" at Whole Foods in Brentwood. Five minutes of talking about nothing, but it gave him a chance to kiss me on the cheek again. It gave me the chance to laugh at his wit, to touch him on the arm, to lean in close. I saw him at a screening of a new Ben Affleck movie—a bank robbery, fast cars, and fast talk, betrayal by a woman, gunfire. When Curtis and I walked out to the lobby, Groban saw us and waved. He was surrounded by people involved with the film, and there was no way for him to break away. He waved us over, but I blew him a kiss, and we kept going.

"Are you going to tell me?" Curtis asked while we waited for the valet to bring the car.

"Tell you what?"

"What you're doing?"

"What do you mean?"

"Groban."

"Nothing. I'm not doing anything."

"Okay."

Groban called me the next day and asked if wanted to have dinner on Friday. With regret I told him I was busy that night. I hoped he'd try again. I suspected that Harry Groban, the most powerful agent in Hollywood, wasn't used to women playing hard to get.

We were working two sides of the same street. He was being the charming, attractive older man, no threat, interested only in my career and me as a person. I was playing the unsure young woman, attracted to the flame but made skittish by the heat. He thought we were headed to bed.

I had a different idea of how it was going to end.

I managed to run into him again on the Twenty-First lot. He was with Will Smith and a scruffy, long-haired younger guy who was dressed so downscale he had to be a writer or a director. Groban pointed a finger at me and held up his hand, asking me to wait. He said something to the two men, shook hands, and then crossed the street to join me.

"Cody, how are you? Hey, how come I keep running into you but we never find a way to talk?"

"You're always doing that movie-business heavy lifting surrounded by people."

"We should find some time."

"We could talk about my acting career." I threw it away like a joke, but he picked it up.

"We should definitely do that. This afternoon at four? I've had a cancellation."

"I don't know. The office seems too businesslike for something as goofy as my acting career."

"Okay. How about my house this evening? We can talk for a while, and then I'll take you out for dinner."

I pretended to think about it. "I'd like that."

"Seven o'clock?"

"Sure."

"I'll send a car for you."

That wasn't going to work. "Thanks, I'll drive."

"Do you know where I live?"

I almost said yes, but I caught myself. "The house in Malibu? I was there for that party."

"No. That belongs to the Agency. I'm up in Brentwood. Here, I'll give you the address." He took a business card from his pocket and wrote the address.

I took it. "I'll find it."

"Seven."

"Seven," I agreed.

"I'm looking forward to it."

"So am I." I smiled, but fear rose in me like heat.

Hours before I was due at Groban's house, I laid out clothes on the bed and tried different combinations. Hair up, hair down, this much makeup, no, too much, try again, these earrings. These buttons open? No. Too many. I was like a girl going out on her first date.

No necklace. I didn't want anything around my throat that he could get his hands on.

The dress I finally chose was a scarlet-and-silver halter-top with a midthigh skirt. The skirt was loose enough to have some swing to it when I moved. The material was a light cotton-silk blend that molded to my thighs when I walked. The halter-top showed that I did have boobs without being too obvious about it, and it had just enough structure to keep them from falling out when I reached for a drink. Spike heels that matched the dress. A touch of eye shadow, a light gloss of lipstick, just enough musky perfume to make him wonder whether it was really there.

I took the three green pills from where I had hidden them. Two went in the outside pocket of my purse. I put the last one in a small hidden pocket of the dress's belt so it would always be close to hand. I got the last things I needed from my desk and put them in my purse.

One last look in the mirror.

Dressed to kill, and with a wild look in my eyes. Men see what they want to see in women. Maybe he'd think it was passion.

Chapter Forty-One

❧

"You look wonderful." Groban closed the door behind me and kissed me on the cheek.

"Thank you. You don't look too bad yourself." He wore charcoal pants, a cream-colored shirt open at the collar to reveal a thatch of dark chest hair, glove-leather loafers with no socks, and a look of amused certainty, as if I had confirmed something for him by showing up. He turned to tap in the alarm code, and I moved to where I could see and memorized the sequence.

He put a hand on my elbow, a gesture of control, and guided me to the living room. I glanced at a mirror in the hall as we went by it. I looked calm, but my heart was churning.

"Wow," I said, when we went down the two steps into the living room. "A beautiful house."

"It was in *Architectural Digest* last year. They did a four-page spread. They were going to do Spielberg's, but they decided this was more interesting." He tried to throw it away is if it meant nothing, but pride burned through.

"They made the right choice, didn't they?" Flatter him, appreciate him, disarm him.

"They did. And it gave me a chance to stick it to Steven."

The lights were on in the backyard, and the swimming pool gleamed green blue. I had a mind shot of the redheaded woman being hammer fucked in the shallow end.

"How about a drink?" he asked.

"Tequila?" It was what she had been drinking that night. Anger pushed down my fear.

"Very good." He took a bottle from a shelf behind the bar and poured heavy jolts into two squat crystal tumblers. He handed one to me.

"Ice?" I suggested.

"You don't want to dilute it. It's too good for that."

"I'd like ice."

He didn't like being contradicted, but he opened the silver ice bucket on the bar, and I took two lumps and stirred them in my drink with my finger. I took a sip. It was smooth and had a subtle vegetal taste. "Do I get to see the rest of the house?"

"Sure. Come on."

I had been in every room before when I crept the place, but I complimented the art on the walls, the collection of ivory elephants in the hall, and the jade in the study. We went upstairs for a quick look at the guest rooms and a longer one in the master bedroom. "Nice room," I said with a smile as I passed him and went out into the hall. "You could spend a lot of time in there."

He laughed. If he had any doubts about why I was there, they were gone. As we went down the stairs together, he held my arm in a way that made me feel like I was on a leash. Tonight he gave off something dangerous and careless that he kept under wraps when he was out and about in his daily life. It was as if your friendly German shepherd turned to look at you and you suddenly saw the wolf blood blaze in his eyes.

Back in the living room we talked about my mother's movie, which would wrap soon, and about what she might want to do next. "Has she said anything to you about the Warners script?" he asked. I don't think he cared. It was small talk while we sniffed each other.

"No."

He stood close to me, just enough inside my space to make me uncomfortable. He was testing, but I didn't give him the satisfaction of taking a step back.

"I think she should do it," he said.

"She'll do what she wants."

"Yes. That seems to run in the family. What do you want, Cody?"

"I haven't decided yet."

"Yes, you have."

I punched him in the chest just hard enough. "Don't push me."

"Okay. Okay." He smiled. Maybe he was looking for a fight, not surrender. Maybe he got off on that.

"I'm going to get a drink." I showed him my empty glass. "Do you want one?"

"Sure."

I took our glasses around to the back of the bar and put them on a shelf out of sight. I poured tequila into both and added ice cubes to mine so I wouldn't mistake which drink was his. I felt in the hidden pocket of my belt for the pill and pulled it out between two fingers.

Groban started toward me. "No ice in mine."

"I remember," I said, hoping to stop him. He kept coming. I fumbled the pill to the floor by my foot. He was almost there. No way to pick it up in time. I pushed it under the refrigerator with my shoe.

Groban leaned over the bar and picked up his drink and went back to the sofa to wait for me.

When I sat down next to him, he put a hand on my knee. "Okay, Cody, what's up? The last couple of weeks you ran into me half a dozen times. You always made sure I saw you, but you never said more than half a dozen words."

"I've been running around to movie things with Curtis or my mother. It's a not a big surprise to see you at the same events."

"Sure," he said, but he didn't believe me. "Why did you come this evening?"

"We were going to talk about me getting back into acting."

"Bullshit. Come on." He was angry. "Maybe I had you figured wrong. You know what the hardest thing to find is in Hollywood? Someone who tells the truth. I spend my life lying to liars. I thought you'd be straight with me." He dug his fingers into my knee.

I slapped his hand away. "Tell me about my sister."

"Your sister? What do you want to know?"

"She was in this house. What was she doing here?"

Something flared in his eyes. "What is it with twins? You look alike. You think alike. You do the same shit." He tasted his drink and put it back on the table. "She did what you did. She showed up like you did in the corner of my eye for a couple of weeks. The restaurants, screenings. Whenever I came into Mitchell, Collier, she'd come into Collier's office to bring a file or something. So I thought, what the hell, let's see what happens if I push. So I pushed." He took another sip of his drink.

I reached for my drink and knocked my purse off the end table. "Shit." When I picked it up, I fingered the pills from the outside pocket and palmed them. "What happened when you pushed?"

"She came over here dressed like a hooker." He watched me for a reaction.

I didn't give him anything. I just said, "And?"

"She was playing a role. So I picked up my cues and went where she led me."

"And where was that?" I leaned closer. I put my hand on his leg.

Excitement made his breathing quick and shallow. "Rough sex. She wanted rough sex."

"What makes you think she was playing a role? Maybe that's who she was and she was making it clear. Why do men find it so hard to understand what women want?" I swung up onto his lap, facing him, my knees trapping his thighs. The movement hiked my skirt up. I gripped the back of his head with one hand and pulled him into a kiss. I reached back with the other hand, found his glass, and dropped the pills in.

Groban pushed his tongue into my mouth, and I almost gagged. He mauled my breasts with both hands and then pushed one hand into my crotch. I broke the kiss. "Hey, easy, easy." His eyes sparked and his breath pumped. He tried to pull me back down to him, but I punched him hard in the chest. "We've got all night." I twisted around and picked up his glass. Residue of the pills coated the bottom. I quickly stirred it up with my finger while my body blocked his view. I turned back to him and pretended to take a sip. "Here," I pushed the glass at him. "Take a breath."

He drained the glass and tossed it away without looking. It shattered on the floor. He pulled me sideways onto the sofa and flipped me on my back. "Harry, no. Come on. Go easy."

"Shut up."

He had my panties half off. He forced a knee between my legs and rose up to tear at his belt buckle.

"Not like this. Harry, slow down."

"The hell with that."

He wasn't going to stop. From where I lay, there were three places I could hit him. I didn't have much leverage, but they might drive him off me. And then what? They would leave strike marks. The autopsy would recognize them for what they were. There would be questions. The whole point of the plan was that there would be no questions.

He got his belt undone. He ripped the zipper open and pushed his pants down. His erection tentpoled his boxers. He struggled with the cloth. I tried to buck him off, but he was too heavy. I was about to be raped.

"Harry, no. Goddamn it."

He slapped me like someone curbing a dog. I hit him, but I had no leverage. All it did was make him smile. He leaned down for a kiss, but I snapped my teeth at him, and he hesitated. He raised his hand to slap me again.

"Don't. Just slow down. You don't have to do it this way."

Something changed in his eyes.

"Let me go, Harry. Let me up."

His grip on my arm loosened. The drug was kicking in.

"Harry, get off me." He looked down at me as if trying to remember who I was. "Harry, get off me now." He obeyed.

He swung his butt over to the coffee table and sat there slumped, head down, with a puzzled look on his face. I took a deep breath. My heart slowed. I pulled my clothes back together and sat facing him. "Harry?"

"What?"

"What's the password for your computer? Tell me the password."

He mumbled something.

"Tell me again. Tell me the computer password." He said it again, and this time I got it. "Okay, Harry, stand up. Come on. Stand up. Pull your pants up." He did what I asked, docile as a lamb. "Harry, we're going to go take a walk. Okay? Come on." He went with me. His walk was loose and disjointed. The liquor he had drunk accelerated the drug, and two pills was a big dose. He stopped in the hall. "Come on, Harry." I had to get him to the study. It was only twenty feet away. "Come on. Just a little further." He put his hand against the wall and then slowly slid down to the floor. I crouched down next to him and shook his shoulder. "Get up, Harry." He didn't move. His breathing was shallow but steady. I lifted an eyelid. His eye rolled up. I shook him again, but I knew it was no good.

What if someone came to the door? What if a neighbor wanted to borrow a bottle of wine? What if his office sent him an urgent contract to look over? What if? What if? When you're planning it, it looks like nothing can go wrong. When you're in it, everything can go wrong. I had to get this done and get out of there.

I put on the surgical gloves I had brought with me. I grabbed him under his armpits and pulled. Groban weighed over two hundred pounds, and I didn't know if I could move him. Fear can make you strong. I leaned back and heaved, and he slid toward me. The floor of the front hall was polished tile, and once I got him moving, he came along. When I pulled him into the study, it got harder. The carpet dragged against him, and his heels left grooves in the nap. I stopped. To my overheated brain, the marks made it clear that someone had dragged a body into the room.

I needed him across the room at the desk. I pulled the wheeled desk chair over to where he lay. I got in front of him, chest to chest, and lifted him as high as I could, but every time I pushed him at the chair, it rolled away. I sat him up on the floor. He slumped forward. I pulled him back and found I could hold him there with one hand. I pulled the chair around until it was pressed against his back. Then I got behind it and pushed against it with my thighs. I reached around and got my hands under Groban's armpits and pulled and lifted and dragged him up into the chair. He tipped against one of the arms. I held him with one hand while I wheeled him to the desk. I turned on the computer. While it booted, I went back and rubbed my shoe along the scuff marks. When I finished, they were almost invisible.

No one would notice, would they?

I typed in the password. When the desktop came up, I went to the living room and washed my glass, dried it, and put it back on the shelf. I did nothing about Groban's broken glass. Whoever found the scene would think he had thrown it in rage or despair. I dug the pill out from under the refrigerator. I poured most of what was left of the tequila down the sink and wiped my prints from the bottle. I carried the bottle in to Groban and pressed his fingers against it in a few places, carried it back to the living room, and left it on the coffee table, a sign of a man's solitary drinking.

Chapter Forty-Two

～

Groban slumped unmoving in the desk chair. His mouth was slack. His eyes were closed. He was helpless. While I was gone, three emails had come in on the computer. They were all from his office, copies of appointments for the next few days.

When I opened the bottom drawer of the desk, my heart stopped. The gun wasn't there. For a moment I couldn't breathe. Easy, Cody. It's upstairs. Remember? He had it in the bedside table.

I went up to the bedroom. It wasn't in the drawer.

I scrambled around the bed and jerked open the drawer of the other bedside table. It held a box of tissues, an inhaler, and a pair of leather restraints. No gun. I pawed through the drawers in the dresser, but I didn't find it. I sat down on the side of the bed to think. No gun. No gun. What, then? A knife from the kitchen. Could I do that? Could I slit a man's wrists?

You don't know what you're capable of until you're faced with the moment on which it pivots. First kiss, yes or no, now or later? Do you go into the bank, or do you walk away? Do you kill a man, or do you let him live? I could leave. If I did go, it would be over. I could never come back to it.

I stood up. I kneed the drawer to the bedside table closed. I turned away from the bed. I stopped and turned back. Where else would a man put a gun?

I reached under the pillows. It was there. I opened the cylinder. It was loaded. I carried it downstairs.

Groban hadn't moved. I picked up his right arm and put it on the armrest. I put the gun in his open hand and closed his fingers around the butt. I bent his forefinger and pushed it through the trigger guard to rest on the trigger. I kept my hand over the hammer so it couldn't fire by accident. I lifted his hand and turned it so the barrel of the gun pressed against his temple.

I took the gun from his hand and let his arm drop. Not yet. Practice everything before you do it so when you go through with it, everything works according to plan.

There was almost nothing in the computer. The last email he had sent from it was three days ago, and most of the incoming messages were spam or from his office. I searched for mention of Julie, for photographs of the women I had found on Julie's computer. I found Jimmy Lasker's name and phone number, I found nothing else that would connect Groban to the women. He was too smart to keep those kinds of trophies in his home computer. But I had thought of that.

I took a flash drive from my purse and plugged it into the computer's USB port. I downloaded Julie's photographs of battered women to a folder on Groban's desktop. Julie's photo was not one of them. I didn't include her. She didn't deserve to be there. I labeled the folder TROPHIES and saved it. I printed out three of the photos, dropped one on the floor, put one in Groban's lap, and left the other on the desk. I called up his word program and wrote his suicide note in block letters.

DISGUSTED WITH WHAT I HAVE DONE. DISGUSTED WITH WHAT I HAVE BECOME. DON'T KNOW OF ANY OTHER WAY TO STOP.

I printed it out and pressed his right thumb and fingers to the paper. I dropped it and let it lie where it landed.

I looked around the room one last time. Everything was in place. It was time.

I picked up the gun. I put it in Groban's hand and closed his fingers around it again. I had trouble getting his forefinger into the trigger guard.

Cock the gun and then raise his hand? No. Raise his hand first. Safer that way. Weird to think of safety with what I was doing, but that's what went through my mind.

The computer pinged. I glanced at it. A message from his office. It read, *CANNES FILM FESTIVAL RESERVATIONS: You are confirmed for your flight on the Warners plane as usual on May 11. You are booked into your usual room at the Hotel du Cap. Return flight on Warners plane May 20.* His flight was a week away.

I turned back to Groban. I lifted his gun hand to his head. I pulled back the hammer. Something tugged at the back of my mind. Whatever it was could wait till later. I touched the gun barrel to Groban's head.

Something about the Cannes Film Festival. The Hotel du Cap was where my mother stayed if she went. She had had a film in competition when we were fifteen, and she had taken Julie and me with her. I remembered the three of us standing in the sun on the terrace with our arms around each other, looking out at the blue-green water.

Usual flight. Usual hotel room. Next week in the middle of May. Julie had been killed in the middle of May two years ago.

I looked back at Groban slumped in the chair, the gun pressed to his head, his finger on the trigger. A little tug with my finger and he was gone. I wanted to do it. *He didn't go that year. He stayed here for some reason. He didn't go. He stayed here and killed Julie. Do it.* My finger touched his trigger finger. All I had to do was press.

I took the gun out of his hand and let the hammer down gently. I put the gun on the desk. I sat down in front of the computer. I was breathing as if I had run a mile. I pulled up the site for the Cannes Film Festival two years ago. I started at the first day of the festival. Almost immediately I found a photo of Harry Groban outside the Théâtre Lumière with Nicole Kidman and Bradley Cooper. On the day Julie disappeared, Harry Groban was on the terrace at the Hotel du Cap with Steven Spielberg and Jennifer Lawrence. The next day, the day Julie washed up on the beach in Malibu, he was at a dinner party at the Carlton Hotel with his arm around a French starlet who was falling out of her dress.

Harry Groban was definitely in France during the days when my sister went missing and when she washed up on the Malibu beach. He didn't kill her.

Chapter
Forty-Three

❧

I tried to run away from all of it. I grabbed Julie's wetsuit, board, and sleeping bag and drove down to San Clemente. I found a secluded campsite in the San Mateo campground and carried the board the mile down to the beach at Trestles. The weather was gray and cold, like me. There was a southwest swell at Lowers with up to double overheads, and I surfed every day until I was so exhausted I carried the board back up to camp on rubber legs.

You can't run away from yourself. In the darkest hours of the night, the acid worms of our blackest thoughts drill into us. They pull us up out of troubled sleep and make us face them. I would lie in bed reliving the feel of Groban's gun-weighted hand as I lifted it to his head, the touch of my finger on his trigger finger, the need to pull it, to step over that line to live for the rest of my life on the other side. It was like the impulse I'd given in to when I first went out on the street, and again when I first robbed a bank. I'd thought what I had learned in prison had gotten me beyond that. I'd thought it was behind me, but apparently it wasn't so far back that it couldn't reach out and put a hand on my shoulder.

* * *

I drove home. I had left my phone in the desk at Julie's so the outside world could not reach me. When I turned it back on, there were messages from Curtis and my mother wondering where I was. By the third day, they had taken on an anxious tone. I called them both. Neither picked up. I left them messages saying I was home and I would see them soon. There were two calls from Keira, who left her name but no message. Harry Groban had not called. I turned on the computer and checked the news feeds. There was nothing about him. Google brought up the standard information, nothing new.

If the drug had worked the way it was supposed to, he would have no memory of what happened. I had rolled him back to the living room on the desk chair and left him sprawled on the couch with the nearly empty tequila bottle on the table near him. I removed all signs that I had been there. I took the chair back to the computer and moved the Trophies folder off the desktop so he wouldn't see it if he turned the computer on, but if anyone searched, it would be there. I put the gun back upstairs under his pillow. When I checked Groban one more time, he was snoring. I disarmed the alarm and went out into the night.

*   *   *

"Harry Groban didn't kill Julie."

"Where've you been? Why didn't you call?" Curtis asked. "I didn't hear from you for three days. I was worried about you."

"Did you hear what I said?"

Curtis turned away from his computer and put his feet up on his desk. We were in his Black Light office on the Twenty-First lot. "Yes, I heard you. I think I told you that a couple of times. What made you decide?"

I stopped pacing. "I found some things out."

"Like what?"

"He was in Cannes when she was killed."

"Ah. So it's done with. By the way, Groban checked into Cedars for a couple of days. Exhaustion, apparently."

"How do you know?"

"The rumor mill. When guys like Groban check out unannounced, the little sharks smell blood in the water and the word flies around town. People begin to jockey for position. Groban shows up at his office a few days later looking healthier than Gwyneth Paltrow, and everybody goes back to what they were doing."

Had the drug worked? Did he remember anything about that night? I guessed I would find out.

"Whoever killed her is still out there," I said.

"You were absolutely sure Groban did it. Now you say he didn't. It could be anybody." My stubbornness bothered him. "Let it go."

He started to say something more, but I jumped him. "I can't."

Chapter
Forty-Four

❧

"Cody, is that you?" Mom's voice came through the open French doors in the living room.

I went out into the backyard. She was on a big exercise pad on the grass by the swimming pool working with her personal trainer, Danika, a trim woman from Bombay dressed in a black T-shirt, black shorts, and black cross trainers who nodded and smiled at me. Mom was in pale-blue yoga pants and a ratty T-shirt from our high school. Her blonde hair was pulled back in a ponytail and tied with a blue ribbon that matched her pants. She wore no makeup, and while she would never be mistaken for a young woman, she was beautiful in a way that mocked age.

She lay on her back with one foot up on the shoulder of the kneeling Danika, who stretched her hamstring. "Are you all right, darling? You look awful."

"Thanks, Mom." I sat on the grass near her.

"Oh, for god's sake, I just meant you look exhausted. You're too young to be exhausted."

"I'm not sleeping well." An understatement. Sometimes I dozed fitfully. The nights seemed endless.

"Why not?"

"I don't know," I lied.

Danika lowered her leg, shifted a bit, and raised the other to her shoulder. Mom groaned. "I have some sleeping pills if you want. I only use them when I get on a plane. Do you want them?"

"No, thanks. I'll be all right."

"I think you should talk to Dr. Salavsky."

It wasn't the first time since I'd come home that she'd pushed her shrink at me. "The last thing I want to do."

She stiffened. "He's done me a world of good."

"You tried him on me once before, remember?"

"Yes, I remember." Her voice took on a familiar edge. "You weren't a bit open to what he was trying to do. He was trying to help, and you fought him every inch of the way. You did it to get back at me."

"I was fifteen. I didn't know what the hell I was doing. It wasn't his fault, and it wasn't yours." She'd had Dr. Salavsky take a run at me after one of my adolescent fuckups. He had a bland, calm manner and a soft, calm voice that made me want to scream. His heavy red mouth was surrounded tightly by a thick, dark, closely cropped beard. He had a habit of pursing his lips and twisting them while he thought. When he did that, his mouth looked like the red ass of some small animal trying to back out of a bush. Once that thought crossed my mind, I was done for.

"If you don't want my help, there's nothing I can do." She slapped Danika on the shoulder. "Not so hard. You're hurting me." Danika eased off. My mother hit her again. "I said you're hurting me."

"Mom, don't."

"Mind your own business."

Danika eased her leg to the ground and stood aside.

I walked closer. "If you want to hit someone, hit me." She stared at me, her face hard as wood. Then the anger leaked out of her. She closed her eyes and shook her head side to side. "I'm sorry, Danika. I'm sorry. Please forgive me."

"It's all right, Ms. Bonner. No problem." She offered her hand. My mother took it and got up. She put an arm around Danika's shoulders and hugged her. "Thank you."

"I'm going to go look for something upstairs," I said.

"Don't take anything else out of Julie's room. I want it the way it is." Just enough edge to let me know I wasn't forgiven.

It took me ten minutes to find what I was looking for. It was stuck down low in a bookshelf near the window between a well-thumbed copy of *The Hobbit* and a philosophy textbook from Stanford. It was a small notebook with lined pages. The red cardboard cover had faded to pink. On it were two badly drawn entwined hearts. One said *Julie* in my crude writing. The other said *Cody* in Julie's neater hand. We were six when we did it. I slipped it into the back pocket of my jeans and went downstairs.

Mom was standing in a sentinel's pose by the pool, legs spread, back straight, shoulders square as she stared across the yard toward the neighboring house. She was drinking a dark-green smoothie from a tall glass. Danika and the exercise mat were gone. She turned when she heard me and watched me with a mother's eye that instantly cataloged my many faults and few merits. "Did you find what you were looking for?"

"Yes."

"What was it?" She put the empty glass on a table and sank into one of the poolside chairs.

"Do you remember the invented language Julie and I used to speak? We called it *shabway*. I don't know how we came up with that name." I sat down in a chair near her and put my feet up on the one opposite.

"Oh god, yes. I used to hate hearing you speak it. Hated it."

Her fierceness surprised me. "Why?"

"It shut me out. You deliberately made it up so I wouldn't know what you were talking about."

"No."

"Yes. You did. How many times did I ask you to stop and you wouldn't?"

"I don't remember that."

"Well, I do. You just kept right on going with it."

"Mom, we were little kids. We weren't trying to keep anyone out. We were having fun. It made us feel closer to each other. That's all we were doing."

She looked at me for a long time with a face like stone, and then she took a deep breath in and let it out with a sigh. She nodded. "I was having a bad time with your father. We both knew it was falling apart, but we weren't talking about it. You two seemed to be having so much fun." She shook her head. "God, what kind of mother is jealous of her six-year-old daughters?"

"Oh, Mom, you were great," I got up and went to her and knelt down so I could hug her. She was stiff for a moment and then relaxed and put an arm around me.

"You two had your own little world. When I was alone with one of you, you were quite nice to me, but when you were together, god, hell on wheels. Sometimes Julie would obey. You just looked at me."

"Did you do what your mother told you to do?"

"Not if I could get away with it." She laughed. "Okay. Enough. We are not going to go back over the past and dig up all the bangs and bruises. There's nothing we can do about them now, anyway."

"Okay by me." I kissed her on the cheek and stood up.

She shaded her eyes from the sun with one hand and looked up at me. "We're wrapping on Friday. I want you to come to the party."

"Mom, wrap parties are for people who're involved with the movie."

"It would make me happy. I wouldn't have taken the part if Julie hadn't persuaded me. I couldn't see it, but she kept telling me how good it was. She was right. Please."

"Friday."

"Yes."

"Okay."

"Thank you." I started to go, but she reached for my hand to stop me. "What made you think of your old language?"

"Julie used it to write something on her computer, and I can't remember enough to figure it out. I remembered that we'd started to put together a little dictionary thing, and I thought she might still have it."

"Did you find it?"

I showed her the faded notebook. She took it and turned it over in her hand and then opened it and flipped through a few pages. She closed it and handed it back to me. "Wow, if I'd known about that, I could have learned all your secrets."

"Yeah. Wow. You'd have learned who we thought was cute in second grade."

"Do you think she left you a message on her computer?"

"Maybe."

"About what happened?" She waved a hand at the dark thing out there she could not talk about.

"I don't know."

"When you know, will you tell me?"

"Yes, I will."

Chapter
Forty-Five

⌒

The photos of the abused women on Julie's computer had no identifica-tion. There were dates on each of them, and then a short sentence in *shabway* closed out the file. I opened our old dictionary and thumbed through it. We wrote in pencil. Words were erased or crossed out. We had tried to do it alphabetically, but that was beyond our six- and seven-year-olds' grasp. We'd remember another word, and there would be no room for it, so we'd put it in wherever it would fit and draw an arrow to where it should have gone. We had worked on it seriously for a week, then off and on for months, and then I got bored. Julie had gone on, so the last few pages were easier to read. She had even done a couple of pages of sentences to show how the language worked.

It didn't take me long to get nowhere. The best translation I could come up with read, *All (everybody) (everything) is in the hide box. Box* could also have been *place* or *drawer* or *closet* or anything that could hold something. Our language was a little loose about specifics.

Two hours later I had nothing to show for my search of the house but four broken fingernails, barked knuckles, and frustration. I had opened every drawer, cupboard, and closet in the place. I had tapped and probed every panel that might come loose. I had even checked the stove broiler, the freezer, and a box of broken pottery planters in the garage. I had gone through the car. I had stood on the table on the terrace to see if she had hidden the "hide box" in the gutter. Nothing.

I went back to the desk and read through everything again in case I had stupidly missed something. My stupidity was still intact, because I couldn't see anything. I punted the wastebasket across the room. I closed the faded notebook with a slap, opened the desk drawer, and flipped the notebook in. I slammed the drawer.

What had I just seen? I opened the drawer again. The notebook lay across an envelope from my bank.

Idiot.

I found my phone and called the bank vice president who had helped me transfer Julie's accounts to my name.

"Bob Mitchell here."

"Bob, this is Cody Bonner. I don't know if you remember me . . ."

"Very well. You and your sister are hard to forget. What can I do for you, Cody?"

"Did Julie have a safe deposit box?"

"Hold on. Let me look." He was back in a minute. "Yes, she did. One of our smaller boxes. It's in your name now."

"Do you have a key?"

"Well, the bank, of course, has the master key. It takes two keys to open it, the master and the individual box key. You have that."

"I do? I've never seen it."

"Oh. Well, it must be in your sister's effects someplace."

"If I can't find it, how do I get into the box?"

"We'd have to drill it. It would be expensive. Better to find the key."

"But if I can't find it, how long would it take to drill it?"

"By the time we do the paperwork and everything, about a week."

"What does the key look like?"

"Hold on. I'm getting one from my desk. Okay. It's about two inches long. It's flat. It doesn't have that groove on the side the way door keys do. And there's a metal tag with the box number attached at the round end. It's probably in a small red plastic envelope with a snap closing."

"Okay. Thank you." I hung up.

I hadn't seen anything like that in the places I had already searched. I didn't have much time. The bank closed at five. It was after four now. Where would Julie hide a key? Where would I?

When we were kids, I used to take things I wanted from her dresser— earrings, perfume, hair clips. She began to hide them from me. It took me weeks before I caught her retrieving a bracelet I liked. She had hidden it on top of one of the exposed beams in my bedroom. She'd probably figured out I was too lazy to look up high and I would never look in my room for something of hers.

Half an hour later, I found it high up in the broom closet in the kitchen. A small red plastic envelope with a snap closing. She had taped it to the part of the light fixture that came out of the ceiling and had loosened the bulb so it couldn't turn on and scorch the plastic. It held the key to box 1156.

I had twenty minutes before the bank closed. I could just make it if the traffic wasn't gridlocked.

I bolted out the back door.

Jimmy Lasker was walking Keira down the garage alley. He carried a small suitcase. His other hand gripped her tightly by the upper arm and forced her to a quick pace.

"Keira." They looked over and saw me by the car. Keira tried to stop, but Lasker jerked her by the arm, and she almost fell. "What's going on? Where's he taking you?"

"None of your fucking business." He jerked at Keira's arm again.

"It's all right, Cody," she said. But she was scared.

"No, it's not." I came out of the garage and got between them and the street end of the alley.

"You are really getting to be a pain in the ass," Lasker said.

I took a stance.

He smiled and shook his head. "What the fuck? You some sort of kung fu queen?" He put the suitcase down, let go of Keira's arm, reached back, and pulled a small black automatic from under his shirttail.

I took a step back.

"Pick up the bag," Lasker said to Keira. He watched to make sure she obeyed.

I pulled my phone from my pocket and turned on the video.

Lasker pointed the gun at my head. "Fuck off."

"The man with the gun is Jimmy Lasker," I said into the mike. "He lives at 10776 Wilshire Boulevard. He is one of the principals of the Asgard House in Hollywood. The woman's name is Keira Barnes. He is forcing her to go with him."

"Shut up. Give me the phone."

"Are you going to shoot me, Jimmy? How many people know you came here today?"

"Give me the fucking phone." His anger was crowding him toward the edge.

I stepped farther away from the building. The terrace to my apartment was two stories up. I turned and threw the phone as high as I could. It just cleared the terrace wall and clattered on the tiles. "How long do you think it will take the cops to find it after you shoot me? Or are you going to spend time breaking into my apartment to get the phone back and hope that nobody sees you?" My voice was steady, but my heart was pounding.

He was breathing hard. The gun was steady on my face. He took a step toward me.

"Don't, Jimmy. Don't," Keira said.

"Hey," a voice called from down the alley. "What's going on there?" An older couple who lived in the end unit stood outside their garage. The man had his phone in his hand. He held it up. "I'm calling 911. I'm dialing."

Lasker slipped the gun into his pocket. "Let's go," he said to Keira.

"No. She's not going with you. Keira, do you have a place you can go?"

"Yes."

"Call me when you get there and tell me you're safe. If I don't hear from you, or if I don't like the way you sound, I'll show the cops the video."

She looked from Lasker to me while she made her decision. She kissed me on the cheek and hugged me. "Be careful." She picked up her suitcase and headed toward her garage.

"Don't do it, Keira," Lasker said.

She kept going, and a few moments later she backed her car out and headed down the alley. Lasker had to step back or she would have run him over. She went out to Olympic, turned right, and disappeared.

Lasker stepped toward me. I braced. "I'll see you again."

I watched him walk away down the alley.

It was almost five o'clock. The bank would be closed long before I got there. Whatever was in Julie's safe deposit box would have to wait.

Chapter
Forty-Six

‿

I was at the bank when it opened in the morning. The only thing in Julie's safe deposit box was a thumb drive. I took it home, put it in my laptop, and read the contents. It didn't take long.

* * *

"For Christ's sake, Cody, give it a rest," Curtis said.

I smashed the big bag with a leg strike, and when it swung back toward me, I hit it with a straight punch and a backfist strike.

"Hey, Cody, come on."

Curtis was standing in the open door from the living room. He was dressed in a bathing suit and held an iPad in one hand. The bag hung from the branch of a tree that grew up through the deck. When it swung toward me, I kicked it away.

"Cody, Jesus."

"What?"

"Stop. Take a break. You've been at it for an hour."

"I don't need a break." I went back to pounding the bag. I was wearing gloves, but my hands were sore. My legs and forearms were red from the pounding. My body was wet with sweat, and it streamed down my face, but I kept at it. I needed something the smack of flesh against the bag offered, something exhaustion would release in me, pain that would cover pain.

Curtis stepped between the bag and me.

"Get out of the way."

"No."

"Okay. Your choice."

He didn't move.

I slammed a right at him and stopped it an inch before his face. He flinched, but he didn't step back.

"Cody, come on."

I turned away from him, stripped off the gloves, went into the pool in a flat dive, and swam as hard as I could to the end and back. When I stopped, Curtis crouched at the side of the pool and offered me his hand.

"I don't need your help."

"Take it anyway."

"Why?"

"Because it's offered."

I took his hand, but when he pulled, I pulled back, and we held that position. "What are you so pissed off about?" he asked. "You've been like this since you got here?"

"Like what?"

"Like pissed off. Do you want to tell me about it?"

"No."

He pulled harder. I set my feet against the pool wall and pulled back. Stalemate. He quit and used the strength of my pull to go over my head into the water. I turned to see. He came up and took two strokes and pinned me to the side of the pool with his body. He tried to kiss me, but I moved my head. He tried again, and I moved again. His body pressed hard against me. He looked at me for a long moment and then slowly inclined his head toward me. I let him kiss me, but I did not kiss him back.

"You think a fuck's going to help?" I asked.

"We can always hope."

Goddamn that smile and that look in his eyes. I put my arms around his neck and my legs around his waist, and he walked us up out of the pool like some two-headed beast. We made love on the sun pads on the lawn. It was closer to a fight than to love—urgent, rough, grabbing, demanding, me not him. When I was done, I got off him and went into the house.

*   *   *

Curtis found me in the living room. I heard his bare feet on the tile floor when he came in. I was eating a peach and watching the sun set. There was a haze over the ocean, and the sun going down through it was bright orange. He had showered and changed. He wore loose cotton drawstring pants and a white T-shirt. He took the peach from my hand, bit off a chunk, and gave it back to me. He sat in the chair opposite and put his bare feet on the coffee table. "What was all that about?" he asked mildly. There was a red mark on his neck where I had bitten him.

"I'm sorry."

"There's nothing to be sorry for. Just tell me what's going on."

"Julie had a safe deposit box I didn't know about. I found the key on Thursday, but it was too late to go to the bank. I went there yesterday morning. I was hoping it would tell me who she was scared of, who might have wanted to kill her."

"Did it?"

"I don't know. After all that, I thought I'd have an answer. I just have more questions. I need to know. I need to finish this." I finished the peach and threw the pit out the open door. It bounced a couple of times on the deck and disappeared over the edge. Maybe it would take root and become a tree. Would I be here to see it? "Do you know Jimmy Lasker?"

"I know him to say hello to. He runs Asgard House. He's one of those guys who knows a lot of people in the business. He can do you favors. He can get you stuff that's hard to get. He puts people together."

"He's a pimp. He specializes in providing women who don't mind if some asshole beats them up as long as the price is right. Julie figured that out. She had photographs on her computer of different women who had been abused. Just the photos and dates of when they were taken. No clients. I guess she thought it was safer to keep things separated, because there's a flash drive in her safe deposit with a list of the men who used Lasker's service, dates, and notarized testimony from the women about what the men did to them, what they paid for the privilege."

"Who's on the list?"

"You're not."

"I would have remembered."

"Jimmy Lasker, of course. Terry, but not Matt. I thought they did everything together. Brandon—that surprised me. He started going out with Laurie Franks in high school. They've been married for, what? Ten years."

"Maybe that's the reason for hookers."

I jabbed a finger at him. "You don't joke about this. Harry Groban's on the list, of course. Not Martin Collier, but one of his partners at the law firm, a studio head, a couple of stars, a TV late-night host, an NBA player, an NFL quarterback, that guy who owns all the car dealerships, a state senator. Someone on that list killed Julie."

"Jimmy Lasker's my bet. He's a thug. He has a record. Lasker must have been making a lot of money out of this. She was threatening that."

"He was in the hospital when Julie was killed. A car accident. I checked."

Curtis got up and came and sat on the arm of my chair and put his arm around me. "What are you going to do?"

"I'm going to do what Julie was going to do. I'm going to blow the whistle on them."

"When? How?"

"I know someone at the *L.A. Times.*"

"Okay, but we've got to think this out. You're talking about some of the most powerful men in town. They're not going to go easily. They're going to fight, and they have the resources. You're a convicted felon. You just got out of prison. They'll use that against you. You can't just dump it on the *Times* and hope for the best. You have to make a plan. You have to be bulletproof before you go out with it."

"I know. I know."

We talked about it for hours, but nothing seemed to get us anywhere near bulletproof.

At the end of it, the only thing I really knew was that the man who killed Julie was on that list, but I still didn't know which one he was.

* * *

I woke up in the middle of the night. The doors to the bedroom terrace were open. A breeze fluttered the curtains and brought the sounds of the ocean. The moon was bright. It turned the leaves of the big eucalyptus near the terrace silver. They rustled and scraped in the breeze. Curtis was awake.

"What are you thinking about?" I asked.

"What you told me. What you're going to do."

"Curtis." He turned toward me. "Do you love me?"

The moonlight was on him. He raised himself on his elbow and looked at me. His eyes were wide, and his face was still. I held my breath. I had never asked that question of anyone before. My mother told me she loved me, and I thought she did, but I didn't think she liked me much. Julie didn't have to tell me. There had never been anyone else I cared about until now.

"Yes. I do." He touched my face lightly and lay down next to me. He pulled me close, and I went to sleep in his arms.

Chapter
Forty-Seven

❧

Assistant district attorney Hy Finley was a man of iron habit. He owned five sober suits he rotated daily. His shirts were button-downs from Brooks Brothers, the kind of shirt his father would have worn. All his ties were muted in color and pattern. His shoes were wing tips, either black or dark brown. He was a thin, chinless man with pale-blue eyes and thinning hair that he plumped up with product. He was ambitious, but in seven years with the DA's office, his ambition had gotten him only a couple of rungs up the ladder. He knew it was because he had no talent for easy friendship. His mother had once called him a cold fish. He clung to the idea that his worth would become obvious when he got the chance to prosecute a case important enough to bring its own heat. Its heat would warm him up.

Every working day Finley had lunch delivered at twelve thirty from a small Greek restaurant a few minutes' walk from the DA's Temple Street offices. He always started with spanakopita. Then he ate one of three meals: souvlaki, lamb kabob, or pastitsio. He drank two glasses of nonfat milk from a carton he kept in his office refrigerator and finished with a cup of coffee from a thermos he brought from home. He always ate alone. He finished by one o'clock, disposed of the takeout containers in a plastic bag that he tied off tight to contain the smell of food, and washed his milk glass in the sink in the small bathroom off his office.

Steckley knew of Finley's ambition and his frustration at being passed over for men who were not the lawyer he was. He made an appointment with Finley's secretary for one fifteen and arrived five minutes early. At exactly one fifteen, he was allowed into the inner office.

Finley nodded to him and gestured toward a chair. They knew each other from the courtroom but had never spent any time together. "What can I do for you, Detective?" Finley's voice was a deep baritone that sounded strange coming from his thin body.

"About five years ago a woman bank robber knocked over two banks in LA, one out on the west side, one downtown not far from here."

"I remember," Finley said. "The robberies stopped. She disappeared."

"She left town, got caught sticking up a bank in the Midwest, and went to jail for five years. She got out a few months ago. She's back in LA."

"And you know who she is."

"Yes. Hold on. I'll show you." He took his laptop from his briefcase and opened it on the desk. He turned it so Finley could see. "Do you mind?" He went around to stand by Finley's chair and pulled the laptop close enough to work the keyboard and track pad while they both could see the screen. "I started out with the tapes from the bank robberies here and Department face recognition software, which pretty much didn't give me crap. As you can see, she was heavily disguised, and she had a good idea of where all the cameras were. Then I heard about this robbery back east." He worked the keyboard and track pad. "There. You see? She went in bare-assed. No disguise. The cameras nailed her."

"You're saying the woman who did all the planning and disguising out here is the same one who did it back there with no planning, no disguise?"

"Yes."

"Go back."

Steckley ran the tapes of the LA bank robberies.

"No way to tell if that's the same woman," Finley said.

"Hold on," Steckley said. "I started buying my own recognition software. I ran the LA tapes against the one back east through the new programs. Take a look." He ran the tapes.

Finley leaned closer to the screen. After a while he said, "Okay. Could be the same woman. Could be a hundred others. The town's full of blondes." He was disappointed.

"Right," Steckley said, undisturbed. He knew how to build the sale—start with a little. Add a little more. Then hit with the clincher. "I just got the latest software in last week. I've spent around four grand of my own money on this." He worked the computer. "Now take a look."

Finley leaned forward as the program ran. After a couple of minutes, he pushed back and sat up straight. "Okay. It's her. Who is she?"

Steckley turned off the computer. "Her name's Cody Bonner." Finley didn't recognize the name. "Her twin sister was murdered two years ago, found on the beach in Malibu. Their mother's the actress, Karen Bonner. Academy Award winner."

"Holy shit."

"Yeah."

"Who knows about this?"

"You. Me."

Steckley watched Finley lean back in his chair to think. He was hooked.

"You want a warrant. You want me to sign off on probable cause."

"Yes."

"Let me give some thought to the judge. We want someone who isn't going to examine all the evidence. Karen Bonner's kid for robbery. That's a secret you don't want to share until the time is ripe."

"Homer Bandol," Steckley suggested.

"Yeah, yeah. Good choice. Right after lunch when he's in a good mood with most of a bottle of wine in him." Finley smiled. "Let me find out what his schedule is for the next few days."

Chapter
Forty-Eight

❧

In the morning, the day was bright, hot, and still. The sky was cloudless. The leaves on the trees hung motionless. There was a smell of smoke in the air. At breakfast the TV in the kitchen told us that a small brush fire was burning north and west of us in Calabasas. Fire crews were on the scene. They expected to have it under control in the next few hours.

I drove Curtis to the lot. The movie was finished. "A couple more setups. One more scene from back on page fifteen," Curtis said. "We should wrap a couple of hours after lunch unless something fucks up. Always a possibility on a movie set. Then I've got some work to do in the office and a meeting about post."

"I'll see you at the party."

"Great."

I stopped in front of his office building. He started to get out and then stopped. "What are you going to do?"

"I might go shopping. I need some shoes for this evening."

"Uh-uh. I mean what are you going to do? You've hardly talked the last couple of days. Half the time when I speak to you, you don't hear me. What have you been thinking about?"

"Nothing." He started to say something. I kissed the tip of my finger and pressed it to his lips. "I'll see you at the party." He wanted more, but he could see he wasn't going to get it.

"Cody, be careful. Don't do anything stupid." I smiled at him. For a moment he looked angry. Then he shrugged. "Okay." He got out of the car and went into the building without looking back.

I didn't know if what I was planning was stupid or smart. It didn't matter. I was going to do it, because I had nothing else. Maybe killing Julie was an accident. Maybe it was deliberate. But whoever had done it had gone to a lot of effort to make her disappear. It must have come as a shock when she washed up on the beach. Julie's mystery changed from a disappearance to murder. Interest in a disappearance dies. Murder has no statute of limitations. Her body on the beach had to have shaken the killer. Twelve of the people on Julie's list were going to be at the wrap party. The odds were good that her killer would be one of them. I had something in mind for him.

I parked under the townhouse and went up through the back entrance. I hadn't been there since the pissing match with Jimmy Lasker. The air in the apartment was stale. I opened windows and the door to the terrace, but the air outside was still and heavy. Nothing moved. It was as if the day was storing energy for something big.

The clothes Julie had worn the day she left the office for the last time were still bundled in plastic on the floor of the closet in the bedroom. I hung them on hangers in the bathroom, turned the shower on hot, and closed the door. When the wrinkles had steamed out, I carried them out onto the terrace and hung them in the sun. The dress was pale green, and the panties were light blue. The dried blood was almost black against the pale fabrics.

Whoever had kept the dress as a trophy hadn't kept the shoes Julie had been wearing. I drove to Century City and found a pair of stiletto heels in the same color at Kate Spade. I had time on my hands. I wanted to go to the gym, but there was a good chance that whoever I sparred with would hit back, and what I had planned for the evening couldn't work with a black eye or a busted lip. Instead, I drove out to Santa Monica and ran four miles on the Palisades to sweat out my anxiety.

It didn't work. Whenever I thought of what I was doing, my heart would surge and fear would flip my stomach.

I drove home in the sluggish traffic stream leaving the west side at the end of the day. The radio said that the Calabasas fire had moved south and west toward Malibu, but authorities were confident they had it in hand. At home I stood in a shower as hot as I could bear for ten minutes and finished with a blast of cold water.

I found the photo Curtis had taken of Julie on the Warners lot to celebrate the deal closing. Her hair was in a chignon, a tidy, businesslike look for a young lawyer on the way up. My hair was nearly as long. I needed a Google search and fifteen minutes of trial and error until I figured out how a chignon worked. I found the same shade of lipstick and eye shadow in Julie's cosmetics drawer. I pulled the heavy gold braid earring I had found at the Agency house from where I had put it in the bottom of her jewelry case and left it on the bureau top. I brought the dress and panties in from the terrace and put them on and unpacked the shoes I'd bought. Finally, I put on the earring.

When I looked in the full-length mirror on the back of the bathroom door, I couldn't see myself at all. My dead sister looked back at me, dressed as she was when she went out to die.

Chapter Forty-Nine

～

Detective Aaron Steckley was in his car when assistant district attorney Hy Finley called to say that he had the warrant for Cody Bonner's arrest. "I caught Judge Bandol right after lunch. He had most of a bottle of Pinot Noir in him. I could have gotten a warrant for the entire Chargers team for impersonating professionals. Stop by my office and pick it up."

"I'm on the road," Steckley said. "I've been in court all day down in San Clemente. An asshole I busted a couple of years ago went into a poker room waving a gun and took off with money that wasn't his. They caught him a couple of blocks away when he couldn't get his car started. He called me as a character witness."

"Good luck with that."

"Yeah. He's gone. But the Five's a parking lot. I'll be lucky to get back to the city before I grow old. You'll be home. Can you leave the warrant for me someplace?"

"Pick it up in the morning at my office. Bonner's not going any-where, and I want to talk to you about how we proceed on this."

"Proceed? What do you mean, proceed? I'm going to bust her, and you're going to send her to Chowchilla. See you in the morning." He hung up and found he was grinning like a maniac. Got her, goddamn it. Got her. He banged on the steering wheel and blew his horn until the guy in the creeping car in front of him stuck his hand out the window and gave him the finger.

Chapter Fifty

People making a movie feel like they're at the edge of disaster every day. When it's over, everyone has survivor's euphoria, and the wrap party is the blowout of all that tension. By the time I got to Asgard House, the party was on fire.

A young woman with green hair and multiple face piercings was throwing up in the front flower bed. I recognized her as one of the lighting techs. Movie companies are divided into two classes: above the line and below the line. Above the line are the producer, director, screenwriter, the actors, the casting director, and sometimes the director of photography, the creative elements of the movie. Below the line are the lighting techs, grips, wranglers, stagehands, prop masters, and other wage slaves. At every wrap party I've ever gone to, the below-the-line people have been the hard partiers and the wrap a spasm of democracy with the half-life of Cinderella's coach.

The upstairs bar was packed. The music was loud. My mother was dancing with one of the camera operators. I waved to her and kept going through the room, looking for the people on my list. Brandon was doing some cosmic funk with a chunky brunette and didn't notice me go by. I pushed through the crowd to the bar and ordered a martini. As I turned away with the glass, Harry Groban touched me on the shoulder. My heart jumped.

"So, what happened last week?" he asked. He used his bulk to move me away from the bar.

"What do you mean, what happened?" What did he know? What did he remember?

"Our date."

"I rang the doorbell. No answer. I figured you'd been called away. I was a little more than pissed off you didn't bother to let me know."

"You didn't hear?"

"What?"

"I had some sort of blackout. The housekeeper found me the next morning. I didn't know what the hell was going on, couldn't remember a thing. I ended up in Cedars for a couple of days. They gave me a clean bill. No explanation." He looked tan, fit, recovered from what I had put him through. He massaged my shoulder. "So let's try again. How about Tuesday?"

"I don't know, Harry. I think that boat's sailed."

"I'm serious."

"No, Harry. I'm done."

He didn't like it. "What the hell?"

"I changed my mind. It's done."

His face hardened. "Okay." Very cold. He turned and walked away. He had had no reaction to how I was dressed. I hadn't expected any. Julie wasn't one of his crimes.

I carried my martini back into the crowd looking for men on my list.

Two heavily tattooed grips were arm-wrestling at a table near the dance floor while a crowd cheered them on.

An olive flew past my ear and bounced off a man on the dance floor. He turned and gave the finger to a group of friends at a table, who hit him with a blast of olives and pigs in blankets.

A Hollywood stud with a proud mane of blond-streaked hair leaned across the table toward a striking black-haired woman with a face like a hawk to offer her the excitement of his close-up. He passed too close to the table candle, and whatever he had sprayed on his hair caught fire. His head was suddenly haloed in blue flame. The woman, thinking fast, poured her drink on him while he shrieked and batted at his head. The flames went out, and what had been his pride was now a scraggly, wet char. The man sat stunned. The woman reached across and patted him on the cheek. Then she got up and walked away.

There was a corridor in the wall opposite the bar. I noticed people disappearing down it in ones and twos. The people who came back out were often pinching their noses and walking taller.

The dope room.

A laughing blonde dragged a director on my list down toward the unseen door. I followed them.

The corridor was dark. As I approached the door at the end, it opened, and a couple came out sniffling and laughing. I stepped aside to let them pass. The door was still open. The room beyond was well lighted. There were comfortable sofas and chairs near the walls. Two women were making out on one of the sofas. The secondary male lead of *Injunctions* was passed out in a wingback armchair. There were about ten other people in the room. Some of them were doing lines off a mirror on a pool table. Mark Siegel was doing a line off the forearm of a young woman in a long sequined skirt and see-through blouse. Terry Gwinn was feeding booze from his glass to a blonde.

The wall at the far side of the room was mirrored. I could see myself, a pale, ghostly presence a few feet back from the door in the darkness of the corridor. If I took a step forward toward the light, I would be framed against the darkness behind me.

Make an entrance, my mother always advised.

Here we go. I took a step forward and stopped in just inside the door.

Terry Gwinn saw me first. He was raising his glass to his mouth. He froze and stared at me wide-eyed. He tried to put the glass down and missed the table, and it fell to the floor. Mark looked up and staggered. He reached out to the pool table for balance. He was still holding the woman's arm, and he must have tightened his grip, because she said, "Hey," in alarm, and tried to wrench away. I saw Terry's eyes fall to the bloodstains on my dress's hem. His face twisted ugly. Mark said, "No," in a strangled voice.

I pointed a finger at Terry and then at Mark. I nodded. Then I stepped back into the darkness.

My heart raced. Mark and Terry killed Julie.

I walked through the party without seeing or hearing anyone. I left Asgard House and drove home in a state of shock and rage. They had known her since kindergarten, and they had raped her and killed her.

What was I going to do now? Could I prove it? Could I kill them?

I didn't have to worry about it, because they came for me in the night.

Chapter
Fifty-One

Something woke me, a creaking stair, the brush of a sleeve against the wall, the click of a latch, some vagrant noise the inner animal sensed. I opened my eyes. It was still dark out. I started to sit up. The door crashed open, and they were on me before I could get my arms out from under the covers. I head-butted one of them. He grunted in pain and slapped me hard. Their weight pinned me down on the bed. The covers held me like a straitjacket.

"Get it in her. Get it in." Terry's voice.

"Hold her, goddamn it. I'm trying," Mark said.

I bucked and thrashed, but I couldn't get free. I felt a pinch as something stabbed my neck. I heaved against them. A knee dug into my side.

"Got her."

My grip began to go loose. Then I went away into the black.

* * *

I woke up in daylight. I was on my back on a bed. I was still wearing the long cotton shift I'd slept in. My hands were pulled back over my head and duct-taped to the bedposts. When I looked around, I saw I was in one of the upstairs bedrooms in Curtis's house. Why had they brought me here? My head was thick with whatever drug they had used on me. I yanked against the restraining tape, but there was no give. I pushed up against the headboard to see if I had enough slack to reach the tape with my teeth. No.

The door was open, and I could hear a murmur of voices from the living room. Past the open windows, the tops of the big eucalyptus trees beyond the pool deck swayed in a strong wind. The leaves sawed against each other with a dry rattle. I smelled smoke. The fire in the hills was still burning.

Footsteps on the stairs and then along the hall. The door pushed wider, and Curtis came into the room. He looked wary and stiff. Curtis was usually in charge of the situation, no matter what it was. Not today.

"Undo me."

He stopped just inside the door. "I can't right now."

"Let me go." I was trying to be calm, but my voice cracked.

"Cody, just take it easy. Everything's going to work out."

"Let me go. Then it will work out."

"I can't."

"You mean you won't." He said nothing. "They killed Julie."

"I know."

"And they're going to kill me, aren't they?"

"No. Nobody's going to get hurt."

I didn't believe that. "Why did they bring me here?"

"They didn't know where else to go."

"Why here, Curtis? Why to your place?" He didn't answer. "Did you help with Julie?"

"I was in New York. You know that."

"You were in New York when they killed her. You were back here the next day." I jerked at the tape holding my hands. "Tell me. Those two wouldn't know how to make a sandwich without someone showing them how to put the bread together. They wouldn't have a clue how to dispose of a dead body. She didn't go in the water until two days after she was killed. You were back by then."

He watched me without expression and said nothing. Then he closed his eyes for a moment and nodded.

"Oh god, that's how you made the jump from junior partner at Mitchell, Collier to CEO of Black Light Films. You knew what they'd done. You blackmailed them to take you on. You finally got there, didn't you? Head of a film company with a million-dollar salary and all the perks. Wow. Fast, even for the Coyote. All you had to do was help them cover up the murder of my sister, your friend." My sadness almost outweighed my anger.

"She was dead. Nothing I did changed that. Nothing I could do would bring her back."

"Wile E. saw his chance and took it. What did you do, make them sign a confession?"

"I used my phone to record everything they said to me. I filmed some of it. Moving her body, the paddleboard." He walked over and stared out the window. "They were in such a panic, they didn't know I was doing it. They were so grateful afterwards. Of course, a couple of days later they decided they didn't need me anymore. What could I prove? Why would I talk? I was an accessory after the fact. What could I say? I showed them a copy of the recording. It changed their minds."

"Wow. Lucky you."

"You start down a road like that, you never know where it's going to lead." It was almost an apology.

"Why did they kill her?"

"They didn't mean to. They knew she was poking around about the women that Jimmy Lasker was running. They thought they'd teach her a lesson or something. The sex got rough. It went too far."

"You knew I thought Harry Groban killed her. You pointed me at him. You moved the dress to Groban's beach house. It wasn't his trophy. It was the Gwingels'. How did you know I was going to find it?"

"I was going to find it for you if you didn't."

"What if I'd killed him?"

"I don't know. I guess I thought you were too smart to get caught. You thought he did it. You'd never look for anyone else again. It would've all been over."

"Oh god, Curtis, can't you see what you've done?" I jerked hard at the tape holding me, and the headboard banged against the wall. "You shit. You fucking shit. You helped them throw my sister away like a piece of trash. You tried to get me to kill someone who didn't do it. Just to protect your fucking career. You said you loved me, and you did this to me? You're a monster." I had never before been so scared. My stomach churned with anger at his betrayal.

"I'm sorry," he said.

"You're sorry? Oh, that's great. That makes all the difference."

"I'm just playing the cards I was dealt. All I could see was what was in front of me. She was dead. It was an accident. They were in a panic. It was my chance. I wasn't thinking of whether or why. I was thinking of how and what. You were in jail. I had no idea I would ever see you again. This was my chance. Finally. What was I supposed to do? What?"

He couldn't see it. It was just angles of the game. "You've lost control now, haven't you? Would they believe me if I promise I won't say anything? Cross my heart and hope to die? No. They're going to kill me, and you're part of it. Curtis, I'm not some angle. I'm me. Look at me. This is on you. What are you going to do? You said you loved me."

He was saved from answering.

"Hey, hey, hey. Look who's awake."

Mark and Terry crowded through the doorway. I hadn't heard them coming down the hall. They had the bad, jangled energy of guys who had stayed up all night, fighting off sleep with drugs. They walked to the bed with the jerky, twitchy walk that speed gives you. Terry lifted the hem of my shift and pulled it up above my waist. I was naked underneath it. "Hey," Mark said. "Look at that. It looks like déjà vu all over again."

"Twins double your fun," Terry said.

"Cut it out." Curtis bumped Terry aside and pulled the shift down. Terry tried to get back to me, but Curtis blocked him.

"Hey, fuck you, Whyle. We're going to have some fun with her, and there's nothing you can do about it, 'cause you are no longer in charge here. You're in this one all the way."

"No."

"Yeah. All the way. Right, Mark?"

"All the way," Mark said. "Hey, it freaked me out when I looked up and saw you in that dress," he said. "I thought it was a ghost." He reached over and squeezed my breast. "Yum." His breathing was ragged, and the wildness in his face scared me. I tried to kick him away, but I couldn't get the angle, and I only hit him a glancing shot that knocked him back a couple of steps. He came back with his fist raised to hit me. Curtis grabbed him by the throat with one hand. Mark clawed at Curtis's wrist to break free, but he couldn't. His face turned red. He slapped at Curtis. Terry watched without moving as if he couldn't figure out what to do. Mark's knees sagged. His eyes bulged, and his hands pawed weakly at Curtis's hand.

Brandon Tower came through the door with a gun in his hand. Relief flooded me. It was going to be all right.

Brandon pointed the gun at Curtis. "Let him go, Curtis. Let him go now."

Mark's legs gave out. Curtis held him up by the throat.

"I swear to God I'll shoot you."

Curtis let go, and Mark fell to the floor, gasping. Terry touched him with a toe. "You okay, man?"

"He'll be all right. Let him get his breath back," Brandon said. "We've got to get this done. The fire's getting closer. The guy on TV said it just moved this direction two miles in three minutes against the wind. They're evacuating this area. Terry, you do it. You did it before."

"Fuck you," Terry said, suddenly angry. "It was sex. She liked it. She was asking for it. It was an accident. I didn't mean to. You know that. You were there. You were doing what you were doing."

Mark was on his feet again. He rubbed his throat while he looked down at me. "I'll do it. I want to."

"No," Brandon said. "Curtis is going to do it."

"No," Curtis said.

"Yeah, you are," Brandon said. "You're going to do it. I'm going to record it. Then we're all equal partners again. You've got yours with us doing it. We've got ours with you doing it. Everybody's the same. It's fair." Brandon thinking the problems through quickly and finding the way to go, the talent of a good director.

"Do it now," Mark said. The excitement lit up his face. "Do it like Terry did."

Curtis's voice was calm. "Do you want to get caught? I've got a sprinkler system inside and on the roof. What if the house doesn't burn?

Firemen and cops will be coming through to check that no one's stayed behind. What if they find the body?"

"We'll carry her out and put her up in the trees," Brandon said.

"We can walk her out while she's alive. Don't you think that would be easier?"

The twins looked to Brandon for guidance. "Yeah," he said. "Of course. Get her up."

I did not want to die today.

Chapter
Fifty-Two

❦

Steckley was in Finley's office at nine when the DA arrived for work. Finley gave him the arrest warrant and said, "You call me when you have her. I'll want to get some press on this. I need to give them enough time to get the cameras down here."

"Okay."

"Do you know where she is?"

"Yeah."

"Then go get her."

Steckley got his car and headed west. When he hit the Pacific Coast Highway toward Malibu, he could see the plumes of smoke rising over the distant hills. The radio announcer could barely conceal his glee as he reported in dramatic tones reserved for disasters that the fire was now out of control. Neighborhoods were being evacuated. There were few cars on Steckley's side of the highway, but the lanes headed south away from the fire were clogged.

The tracker on Bonner's car told Steckley that she'd left her townhouse in Century City at five in the morning. She had driven to Curtis Whyle's house and was still there. If she drove out with the first evacuations, he would know it. If she waited, he'd take her at Whyle's house. Either way, he had her. The thought made him grin. Almost six fucking years, but he had her now.

There was a roadblock where Sunset Boulevard came down out of Pacific Palisades and joined the Coast Highway. Steckley rolled down his window and showed his badge and explained that he was headed to Malibu to make an arrest. "Better step on it," the CHP officer said. "If they don't get a stop, they think the fire'll be down to the highway in an hour or so."

The smoke was heavy on the hills ahead. Firehawk helicopters swung up through the smoke to drop their thousand-gallon loads of water and red fire retardant. A half mile offshore a CL-215/Bombardier 415 Super-scooper slid along the surface of the bay, filling its belly with water. It rose, dipped a wing, and turned inland to drop its load.

The traffic headed south was thick and slow moving. The only vehicles moving north with Steckley were the occasional firefighting units that blew past him, wailing sirens and flashing lights. When he checked the tracker, Bonner's car was still at Whyle's house. Four miles farther on, he turned off the highway and started up into the hills. As he came around a corner, he looked up in time to see a line of fire crawl over a distant ridge. It chewed its way downhill until it reached a stand of eucalyptus trees, where it seemed to hesitate for a moment. Then the trees exploded in flames that towered fifty feet in the air. He turned another corner, and the fire was lost from view, but the air was full of ash that fell on his windshield like dirty snow.

* * *

When they brought me out of the house, the air was filled with ash that fell on us like dirty snow. I could hear sirens below on the Pacific Coast Highway. A helicopter hovered over a hill not far away and dumped a load of red fire retardant. It banked toward us on its flight to reload, and Brandon jerked me back into the doorway out of sight until it racketed by overhead.

A new noise intruded, a low growl from the other side of the hill above the house. The fire was eating its way toward us. Curtis heard it too and knew what it was. "Brandon, turn a car around and leave it running. We've got to do this fast and get out of here. Terry and Mark, come with me."

They were used to obeying him. Brandon tucked the gun in his belt and headed for his car. Terry and Mark started up the hill ahead of us.

Curtis grabbed me and pulled me away from the house, across the drive, and up onto the slope. The hill was covered with chaparral scrub and eucalyptus trees, but there was a path up through the bushes. Smoke rose high above the crest. I couldn't see flames yet, but fires burn fast uphill. It would top the hill soon. If I was going to do something, I would have to do it soon.

Curtis felt me tense. He looked at me and mouthed *Not yet*.

What? Was he going to help me? For a moment my heart rose. He was going to help me. Then I realized, no, it's a Wile E. Coyote ploy to get me to go along quietly.

A ragged line of fire came over the top of the hill. A tall eucalyptus burst into flames. Tentacles of flame reached out, and the fire jumped to the tops of two more trees. The brush on the slope caught, and the fire crept downhill. I was running out of time.

I jerked back against Curtis's pull. It yanked him off balance. I sledged at him with clasped hands. I was trying for his throat, but he ducked, and I hit his forehead, and he fell over backward. He yelled, "No!" as he went down.

Terry shouted in surprise. He and Mark were uphill from us. They turned and charged. I stopped Terry with a foot strike. I caught him on the chest, and he went down with a grunt. Then Mark hit me, and I slammed to the ground with him on top of me. I heard a shout from Brandon. I clawed at Mark's eyes, but he turned his head away and clubbed me with a fist on the side of the head. I kneed him, caught his thigh, and jabbed his neck with an elbow. He head-butted me. I felt my nose break.

Then Curtis was on him. He barred an arm around his neck and yanked him back off me. Mark threw his head back, trying to skull-butt Curtis in the face, but Curtis was taller, and he turned and took the blow on his shoulder. I scrambled to my feet and kicked Mark in the balls. He shrieked. I stopped that with an elbow strike to the mouth. He sagged, and Curtis let him fall.

Terry hit Curtis from behind and rammed him away. Terry was screaming in rage as he came for me. I tried to hold him off with a leg strike, but his downhill momentum blew him through it, and he slammed into me and knocked me down. He got his hands around my throat and began to choke me. I jabbed at his eyes, but he turned enough to make me miss. My nails opened his cheek. I tried to buck him off, but he was too heavy. He squeezed. I clawed at his hands. I tried to pry a finger loose to break it. My world began to go dim. This was how Julie died.

Curtis crashed into Terry and drove him off me. He tried to kick Terry, but he rolled away. Curtis went after him.

Mark staggered downhill past me. His face was twisted with fear and effort. I looked up the hill. The fire was halfway to us, a wall of flame chewing its way down through the chaparral. A heat blast ran in front of it.

I turned to warn Curtis just in time to see Brandon aiming the gun from the edge of the driveway below us. His first shot blew a chunk of dirt near me. The second buzzed by my head like a steel hornet. Brandon steadied the gun for another shot. Curtis shouldered me aside just as Brandon fired. The bullet hit Curtis and staggered him.

* * *

Steckley drove around the curve in the drive, and the house came into view just as he heard the first shot. The Bonner girl was on the hillside fifty yards below a wall of fire. A man ran past her toward the driveway. Curtis Whyle was standing over another man. Another man was standing at the edge of the slope, firing uphill at the girl. Whyle knocked her aside, and the shot hit Whyle and spun him away from her. Steckley stabbed the brake and was out of the car before it stopped rolling. He cleared his gun from under his jacket and yelled, "Drop it!" The man with the gun turned toward him. They both fired. Steckley's shot blew a hole in the windshield of the car next to the gunman. The gunman's bullet punched Steckley backward. He thumped back against his car fender and slumped to the ground. His gun fell from his lax hand. He toppled over on his side. Shit, he thought, why now?

* * *

When the bullet hit Curtis, he clasped his arms around his middle, looked at me wide-eyed, and fell to his knees. I heard two more gunshots. Brandon was in a crouch facing down the driveway. The cop,

Steckley, fell back against his car, sat down, and toppled over. What the hell was he doing here?

Mark blew past Brandon and jumped through the open door to the driver's seat of Brandon's car. I heard him yell, "Come on. The fire. The fire."

"Terry," Brandon yelled. "Come on." He fired two more shots at us. I don't know where they went, because I was going for Terry. He was trying to stand up. He had all his weight on one leg. I drove my foot hard against the side of his knee, and something snapped. He screamed and fell back to the ground. His leg was at a weird angle. He rolled over and began to crawl down the hill. He cried out every time his broken leg snagged something.

Brandon saw what had happened. He fired one more shot at me and then got in the car. I could see Mark pointing at Terry and protesting. Brandon yelled at him and jabbed the gun at him. Mark put the car in gear, and they bolted down the drive.

I knelt beside Curtis. He was alive. He tried to give me one of those crooked smiles, but it didn't really work. "How the fuck did I get here? This was definitely not in the plan."

"We have to move." The fire was thirty yards away. The heat was searing us. I helped Curtis up. His shirt was covered with blood. He put an arm around my shoulders. When I put my arm around his waist, he groaned in pain. I lowered it to his hips and took what weight I could. We staggered down toward the driveway. Maybe it would act like a fire-break. Curtis said the house had sprinklers. Maybe we'd be safe there.

The fire roared behind us. It was so hot that it burned my back through my shift. We passed Terry doing his broken crawl. "Help me," he said. "Please help me. Don't leave me here."

We left him there.

A eucalyptus tree at the far end of the house exploded in flame. Three tall cedars that shaded the bedroom wing caught and went up like Roman candles. The roof sprinklers went on, but the fire was so hot it turned the water to steam. I heard glass break as the fire invaded the house. The roof sprinklers stopped working. We weren't going to find shelter there. Our only hope was the dead cop's car. What was he doing here?

We stumbled down the driveway. The air was so hot I could barely breathe. "Leave me," Curtis said. "Get out of here."

"Shut up."

The driver's door was open. The car was in park. The engine was still running. I opened the back door and got Curtis onto the seat and buckled him in sitting up in the corner. "I'm all right," he said. His voice was weak, and his face was white. He kept his arms clamped over the wound in his belly. I started to close the door. "Hey."

"What?"

"I'm sorry."

"Yeah."

"I love you, Cody Bonner."

"Oh boy. God. Stay with me, Curtis."

I shut the door. When I stepped back, I almost put my foot on the cop. He groaned. He wasn't dead. His shirt, like Curtis's, was soaked with blood. A crash made me look up in time to see the far end of the roof collapse into the house.

On the hillside Terry began to scream as the brush around him went up in flames. By the time I dragged Steckley around to the passenger side, the screaming had stopped. I got Steckley up into the car and strapped him in on the back seat opposite Curtis. I ran around to the driver's side. The fire reached the edge of the driveway. It stopped there looking for something to eat. The air was full of smoke and ash. The fire howled, and trees exploded like bombs. Cinders rained down on me, and I had to beat them out of my hair.

I turned the car around fast and headed down the drive. When I rounded the first curve, I slammed on the brakes. The fire raged down both sides of the road, making a tunnel of flame. There was no way out. I turned around and drove back up toward the house, where the driveway and the grounds around the house would give us some open space.

It wasn't enough. The fire was so hot that the air in the car became unbearable to breathe, even with the air conditioning on full blast. We were going to roast to death. A low hedge that separated an expanse of lawn from the drive burned fiercely. A gust of wind from the fire on the hill blew through and carried the smoke away for a moment, and I could see the swimming pool on the terrace down from the house.

Last chance and nothing to lose.

I swung the car around and plowed through the burning hedge. As we went out onto the lawn, two of the tires went flat, and the car tried to slew around. It took all my strength to hold it toward the pool. I rammed it out onto the terrace, blowing aside a glass table and its chairs. The tires melted, and the rims ground along on the slate. I hit the gas, afraid that we were traveling too slowly and would hang up on the pool rim. We went in at the shallow end. Car metal hissed when it hit the water. The engine coughed and died. The momentum of the plunge pushed us down the slope to the deep end, and we came to rest with the nose of the car against the pool wall with the back wheels still on the slope. The car wallowed and then slowly settled, and water began to seep in under the dash.

I got out of my seat belt and climbed into the back seat between Steckley and Curtis. Neither man was conscious, but they were still breathing. When I looked through the back window, the flames from the burning trees and house were a wall of red and orange. Even in the pool I could hear the firestorm's howl.

I remembered reading about people driving into rivers who survived by waiting until the water was high enough inside the car that the pressure on the door was equal inside and out and they could open the doors and swim out. They could breathe the air bubble trapped under the roof until it was time to open the doors. With the car tilted nose down in the pool, the air bubble was right above our heads.

The car slowly filled with water. It rose to my chest and then higher. Both men tended to slump in their shoulder belts, and as the water grew higher, I had to hold their heads up. My arms ached from holding them. The water around us turned pink from their blood.

The water stopped rising.

Curtis woke up. "Are we dead?" he asked.

"No," I said. I explained that I had driven the car into the pool as our last chance.

"Cody Bonner. Cody Bonner, you're a miracle." He tried to laugh, but the pain turned it into a gasp. "What about them?"

"Terry's dead. I don't know about Brandon and Mark. They had a car."

"Who's this guy?" He gestured at the unconscious Steckley.

"He's a cop. He thinks I robbed two banks in LA five years ago before I took off."

"Did you?"

"Yes." Why shouldn't he know? We were going to die here.

"Wonderful." He smiled and closed his eyes.

"How did they get a hold of Julie?" I asked. I needed to know before I died.

"Mark found her waiting outside the office. Her Uber hadn't shown up. He offered to drive her home." He talked with his eyes closed. Maybe he was trying to conserve energy. Maybe he just didn't want to look at me while he told the story. "She said okay. Then he wanted to show her the new house he and Terry bought in Malibu. He was really proud of it. You know Julie. If she thought it would make someone happy to do something, she'd do it even if she didn't really want to. She said okay." His voice ran out. He took a couple of shallow breaths and went on. "Julie had Mark and Terry turned upside down since eighth grade. They didn't know what to say to her, how to behave with her. She was always nice to them, but she was always out of reach. It drove them nuts." Silence for a moment. "She had a drink. She looked at the house. She liked it. She wanted to call an Uber to go home. Mark persuaded her to have another drink and then he'd drive her back. He slipped her a roofie." Pain twisted his face for a moment. "Terry and Brandon arrived. She was kind of out of it. Things got out of hand."

"Things got out of hand?"

"Yeah." He opened his eyes to look at me. "That's what they said. Things got out of hand, and then she was dead." He closed his eyes again and slumped against the seat back.

"Curtis, please." He didn't move. I touched his neck. His pulse was weak but steady. He had slipped back into unconsciousness. He'd told me all he was going to tell me. I didn't need the details. I couldn't stand to hear them.

I have no idea how long I sat there holding their heads up. After a while I realized I didn't hear the fire anymore. When I craned around to look out the back window, the flames were gone. The water and sky were a uniform gray. Time to go.

*   *   *

I left them lying on the pool apron. The only thing I could do was get help as fast as I could. I put on Curtis's running shoes and tied them as tight as I could to keep them on. The heat from the driveway came through the soles.

I walked in an alien world. The air was full of ash and smoke. Everything that could burn had burned. The house was gone except for the chimney, which stood alone in the rubble. The landscape was black and gray except for pockets where coals glowed red and orange like jewels.

I found Brandon and Mark half a mile down the driveway. The car was barely recognizable, a shell of metal with two blackened, twisted things on the black springs of the burned-out front seat. I kept walking. I came around a bend and found a fire crew putting out hot spots.

What did they see when they looked at me—a young woman wearing only a cotton shift made nearly transparent from the water, walking out of that blackened landscape? A ghost? Of what? Of my sister Julie? Of who I had been?

Chapter Fifty-Three

～

Curtis died on the pool apron of his burned-out house.

Steckley lived.

The first news reports ran with the feel-good story of Steckley's and my miracle escape from the fire. They skewed sharply when the news came out about the bullet taken from Steckley's gut, and the one found in Curtis, about the charred corpses in the burned car, the partially melted gun. Not much of Terry was found, just a few fragments of bone and enough of his jaw and teeth to confirm who he was.

The hospital held me for two days while they dealt with the burns that dotted my head and body and packed my broken nose. Then they released me into my mother's care. Hugs and tears, and then cameras and lights when we left the hospital. Karen Bonner, movie star, and her heroic, mysterious daughter, former felon. Did she fire the gun that killed Curtis Whyle, CEO of Black Light Films? They had fun with that one for a while.

Thanks to Mom, there were security guards and a lawyer at the house in the Palisades. They ran interference and got us in through the crush of reporters, TV crews, and onlookers.

The first evening back in the house, I told her what Terry, Mark, and Brandon had done to Julie, and what Curtis had done to cover it up.

She started out in tears. By the time I finished, her face was a terrible mask of pain and fury. "I'm glad they're dead. I'm glad you made that happen."

The next morning, I found her sitting on one of the cedar benches out by the swimming pool. When I bent to kiss her, I realized she was wearing her clothes from last night and that she hadn't slept. She patted the seat next to her and put her hand on mine when I sat down. Her face was drawn with sadness. "I never knew you, did I? I never really knew who you and Julie were. I think I made you up to fit who I wanted you to be. Julie was the good one, and you were the wild one. I got that wrong, didn't I?"

Did she? I don't know.

I put my arms around her. She was stiff and resistant at first. "It's okay, Mom. It's okay. Really. Nobody's fault. Nobody to blame. We're going to be fine." Then the tears came, first hers, and then mine.

* * *

I went to visit Steckley in the hospital. He had tubes running in and out of him. He was pale and drawn, but his eyes were bright. He saw me hesitate in the doorway and raised a hand to weakly wave me in.

"Sit down," he said. His voice was a rasp.

I pulled a chair next to the bed.

"I've got to thank you," he said. "I don't like owing you. You're a felon. You robbed those banks. You and I know it. You should pay for that."

"What are you going to do?"

"I don't know. I just don't know. You saved my life. I've got to think about that. It's got to count for something. Jesus, I don't know."

I patted his arm. "When you figure it out, let me know."

He said I had to pay for what I had done. He meant I had to pay for breaking the law. I didn't give a shit about that. What I cared about was the pain I had given my sister and my mother. And the bank tellers who had stood looking at me, wondering if I was going to shoot them. The chaos, anger, and hurt I had left in my wake. Can you pay that back? Can you find redemption for that?

Curtis had put himself in the way of a bullet to save me. Wile E. Coyote would never have done that. Wile E. Coyote would have kept playing the angles. Curtis Whyle stepped up and saved my life. Did it redeem him for what he had done to Julie, for aiming me at Groban knowing I might kill him? I don't know, but he loved me. He sacrificed himself for me. And Julie sacrificed herself for a bunch of women no one cared about. I would have to find a way to live my life that would pay those sacrifices forward.

*　*　*

The story began to die. Then a package arrived at LAPD headquarters. It was from Marty Collier, Curtis's lawyer. Curtis had left it with him with instructions to pass it to the police if he should die in suspicious circumstances. It contained the recording Curtis had made of Terry, Mark, and Brandon disposing of Julie's body and an accompanying letter from Curtis explaining his role. The story burned hot again. TV trucks clogged the streets near our house. The security guards caught four different men trying to climb the walls into the backyard. Three of them had cameras. One had a knife.

Someone bootlegged clips from Curtis's video and sold it on the internet. The world got to see and hear the Gwingel twins and Brandon trying to bury my sister at sea.

I did not watch.

*　*　*

Mom's lawyer huddled with the cops. Everyone was satisfied that Mark, Terry, and Brandon had killed Julie, had tried to kill me, and had died in the attempt.

A DA named Finley called. He wanted to talk to me about the old bank robberies. He made an appointment for me to come down to his office. Steckley called and told me not to bother. The next day Finley called and canceled the appointment. I guessed that Steckley and I were clear.

I called Lara Jannicky, the *L.A. Times* reporter who'd covered the Groban rape trial. The *L.A. Times* headquarters had moved to El Segundo, near the LA airport, while I was in prison. We met at a bar in one of the airport terminals. There is nothing more anonymous than an airport bar. Nobody gave us a second look. I gave her the recordings and photos Julie had made and told her some of what she would find on them. I told her about the pictures she would find of Julie.

"Are you sure you want to . . ." She stopped. "Okay. Thanks. I might have to call you for some follow-up."

"You have my number."

I warned Mom about what was to come.

"Did you have to?" she asked.

"Yes. People need to see what they did. People need to know."

She closed her eyes for a moment while she thought, a familiar gesture. "Okay." Then she hugged me. "I know you're right."

When the stories ran, some of the women Julie recorded came forward. Some did not. Other young women, actresses, production assistants, a makeup artist, a set designer stepped up. Harry Groban and the rest of the men spoke through lawyers. All of them denied that they had participated in anything the women spoke of. The lawyers made oblique references to how some of the women made their livings to throw shade on all the others who came forward. The Agency put Groban on paid suspension while the case was pending. He went to Europe on an extended vacation.

Jimmy Lasker disappeared. The cops wanted him on various charges of prostitution and assault. The word was that men who were on Julie's list made generous donations to his well-being and travel plans. Another LA story.

Asgard House closed its doors.

The studio took over the postproduction of *Injunction* and turned it over to another director to help cut the film.

The big agencies wooed my mother, and she went to ICM. A couple of weeks later she signed to do a picture with Brad Pitt that would shoot in Paris.

I got a postcard from Keira. It showed a large yacht on a bright tropical sea. *Well done. Fuck 'em. Love, Keira.*

Chapter
Fifty-Four

⁓

Do good deeds wipe out what you owe for the bad you've done? Steckley was struggling with it. So was I. Did what I had done to expose Jimmy Lasker and the men who used his service make up for my crimes? Maybe you only know if the slate is clean at the end of life.

I had come out of prison with the honed purpose of finding the people who killed my sister. What was I going to do now?

* * *

A phone rang in the apartment late one afternoon. It took me a while to figure out it was in my desk drawer, the burner I'd bought months ago and forgotten.

"Hello."

"Amy?"

"Yes. Who's this?" But I knew. I remembered her voice. I remembered making up the name Amy because I didn't want her to know who I was.

"Scat?" She said it as a question, unsure that I would remember. "You gave me a phone. You said if I really wanted help, I should call."

"I remember." The street kid. I'd promised her I'd give her one chance if she wanted to get right. I'd never thought I'd hear from her again.

"I want help. Will you help me?"

I wanted to say no. I didn't need more trouble in my life, and how could she be anything but trouble? Hang up the phone. Throw it away. Make a choice.

"Where are you? I'll come pick you up." Maybe this was how it would work. Maybe this was a beginning.

Acknowledgments

For my supporters at Crooked Lane: Terri Bischoff, Rebecca Nelson, Melissa Rechter, Madeline Rathie, many thanks for your generous and skilled guidance through the arcane process of bringing the book publication. Thank you, Rachel Keith, for your precise and creative copy editing. And once again, thank you Lisa Gallagher, agent, reader, counselor, and friend.